"I won't stay here,"
Drake managed to say.

"Oh, yes," she challenged. "You will."

He raised his chin, arched an imperious brow, but Cypress did not back down.

"You may think you're the best damn magician to come along since Merlin, but I've got a news flash for you, Benedict. You're hurt. You're tired. On top of all that, you just told me that I've got some kind of human-eating dragon living in the woods behind my house. No way am I letting you out of here until you at least help me figure out what to do about it. In the meantime, I've got a guest room where your honor will be perfectly safe. You may not want to spend the night with *me,* but you *are* spending the night."

Oh, he thought, but he *did* want to spend the night with her—he just didn't dare....

Dear Reader,

This is both a happy and a sad month, marking conclusions of two different kinds. The happy conclusion comes in the form of the book you're holding in your hands, Evelyn Vaughn's *Forest of the Night*. This is the final volume of her four-book miniseries, THE CIRCLE, and it provides a stunning finale for a series readers have rightly grown to love. I know you'll want to put it on your keeper shelf once you're done.

But there's sadness this month, too, because this wonderful book marks the final publication of our Silhouette Shadows line. I've enjoyed working on these darkly thrilling books more than I can say, and I'm going to miss them just as much as you will. So let me take this opportunity to thank you for all your kind words and your enthusiasm. They have meant so much to all our authors and editors over the course of the last several years. And even though there won't be a new Shadows novel for you every month, don't forget to check our other lines for the authors and the sorts of spooky, paranormal books you've grown to love, many of which will carry the Spellbound flash. You'll find that we're still doing books with a touch of the Shadows flavor, and I hope you'll enjoy each and every one of them.

Again, thank you for coming along for the ride.

Leslie Wainger
Senior Editor and Editorial Coordinator

Please address questions and book requests to:
Silhouette Reader Service
U.S.: 3010 Walden Ave., P.O. Box 1325, Buffalo, NY 14269
Canadian: P.O. Box 609, Fort Erie, Ont. L2A 5X3

EVELYN VAUGHN

FOREST OF THE NIGHT

SILHOUETTE® Shadows™

Published by Silhouette Books
America's Publisher of Contemporary Romance

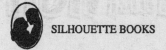

SILHOUETTE BOOKS

ISBN 0-373-27066-6

FOREST OF THE NIGHT

Copyright © 1996 by Yvonne Jocks

This edition published by arrangement with Harlequin Books S.A.

® and TM are trademarks of Harlequin Books S.A., used under license.
Trademarks indicated with ® are registered in the United States Patent
and Trademark Office, the Canadian Trade Marks Office and in other
countries.

Printed in U.S.A.

Books by Evelyn Vaughn

Silhouette Shadows

Waiting for the Wolf Moon #8
Burning Times #39
Beneath the Surface #52
Forest of the Night #66

*The Circle

EVELYN VAUGHN

has been a secret agent, a ghostbuster, a starship captain, an elf, a prince and a princess. When not involved in role-playing games, she teaches junior-college English and is an unapologetic television addict. She lived in five states before settling in central Texas, and has traveled most of the United States and Europe. She has been writing stories since the first grade. Although she has not yet found Mr. Right, she is enjoying Mr. Write with every book!

This book and I owe a lot to some incredible critiquing
(Cheryl, Sarah, Pam, Erin and Jodi);
some helpful brainstorming (Matt and Kayli);
some terrific editing (Melissa); and lots of random
information (especially from Toni on the spot).
Thank you all. Maybe I *could* have done it
without you, but not as well and it would
have been a lot less fun.

Dedicated to the readers, authors, and editors of
Silhouette Shadows.

PROLOGUE

The evil called to him.

Like an inaudible whisper, it had taunted him every night, interminable and increasing, like a conquered but never-forgotten addiction. From somewhere beyond the city, it called to him still.

A lesser man would have gone mad, but Drake Benedict did not have that kind of luck. Damnably sane, he stalked across his shadowy living room and turned his stereo up. Way up. He had been listening to Vivaldi's *Four Seasons*. Now the "Allegro" of "Winter" blasted like the Rolling Stones out of state-of-the-art speakers.

But noise did not help, any more than would closing his eyes. This call was not sensory but *extra*sensory, like a psychic beacon. Whatever originated the call, sentient or inanimate, it transmitted on a particularly dark frequency. Whatever the source, it was unmistakably evil.

Deep within Drake, something stirred in response to it: Curiosity, anticipation . . . longing. His *own* evil?

Unsettled, he pushed past louvered doors out onto his balcony and into the mild January night. He scowled past the still French Quarter courtyard below him. Perhaps some fool *should* investigate whatever miscreation hatched across Lake Pontchartrain, in the swampy woods north of New Orleans. The ring he wore—a dark-gold dragon with emerald eyes—implied this to be the wearer's job. But he knew better than to set his own unique abilities against something so unknown, so dangerously enticing. Should he fail, should this evil convert *him,* there could be literal hell to pay.

He'd seen better magic users than himself—the best he'd ever known, in fact—destroyed because they pitted themselves against evils that should not have concerned them. It had helped no one.

But to give up and go abroad, that *would* be cowardice.

From Bourbon Street, too few blocks away, the strains of jazz music and drunken laughter mingled with the frenzied scream of violins from Drake's stereo . . . and with his constant, unwavering awareness of the evil. Its call throbbed through him, dark and nauseating and full of promise, battering a headache out of his resistance. Should it continue much longer, he might be forced to attempt silencing it—or to answer it. Or truly go insane.

Insanity might prove preferable to failure.

But no, insanity did not run in Drake's family. Only magic ran in Drake's family: white magic, black magic, and power. And the proven ability to abuse that power. Children of alcoholics oughtn't take a single drink, and the only offspring of the most notorious British magic user in recent decades oughtn't to trifle with evil, no matter how tempting the challenge.

Across the miles and through the night, as it had every night for months now, the entity beckoned to him, with its offers of strength, of immortality—of a dark and overpowering silence.

Drake straightened from the black wrought ironwork of his balcony. No. He would answer the beast's dark bidding no sooner than he would protect innocents, benefit mankind, or—Fates forfend!—spread a little joy in the world. He would remain his own master and serve no other, black *or* white. He knew the consequences of joining either camp in that particular struggle.

As he had for months, Drake turned his back on the summons. As it had for over a year, the spine-crawling awareness of it followed him back into his home.

Expectant. Incessant.

Eternal.

Evil.

CHAPTER ONE

Shadows guarded the corners of the so-called voodoo shop. The ceiling, shaggy with drying herbs, cast an exotic pot-pourri of fragrances into the murky air. Bowls of semiprecious stones covered one table; another display offered a rainbow of candles, mostly black. And a wall of shelves held big jars, like in an old candy store, naming ingredients like cat bones and graveyard dirt.

Cypress Bernard, slowly turning to take in her eerie surroundings, caught the heel of a dress shoe on the rough plank floor. *What,* she asked herself, *is a down-to-earth woman like me doing in a hocus-pocus joint like this?*

Goddess jewelry. Goat skulls. Runes. Books on finding your soul mate. *Voodoo?*

Anyone who knew anything about magic could see that this place, mixing its traditions with the subtlety of a Cuisinart, favored *voudun* in decor only. Not that Cy held anything against eclecticism, let alone magic—with *her* diverse heritage.

The pot calling the kettle black, for sure.

Cypress knew magic. Nothing fancy, just good, solid folk magic. She'd had what Granny called "the gift" for longer than her memory reached. And she sure knew the difference between machine-sewn, cotton-stuffed "voodoo dolls" and the real thing.

But that was the French Quarter for you—all flash, and little substance. What on earth could Granny have been thinking in sending her here?

She glanced at her watch. Despite being up for a promotion at work, she'd used half a vacation day to run errands in New Orleans. She felt a heap more foolish here than she had at the costume rental shop, probably because she didn't like asking folks for help—but here she stood.

A young couple bought his-and-her voodoo dolls before strolling, hand in hand, out of the shadows and into the gray January rain. The proprietress, an ebony-skinned woman wearing vivid Caribbean colors, eyed Cy's tailored suit. "And what might you be needing today, miss?"

Her Jamaican accent sounded real enough, as far as Cypress could tell. "Can you tell me where to find the, uh, magistra?"

Bracelets jangled when the woman planted her fists on her hips. She cocked her head as if Cy were eccentric. "Come again?"

Cy's heart sank. She'd hoped her dear old witch of a grandmother had come through this latest illness as clearheaded as ever. "I was told," she said firmly, just to be sure, "to find your shop and ask for the magistra, whoever that is."

And she dug into the Daytimer she carried in lieu of a purse and produced the seal Granny had given her. The paper—not even parchment—held a dollop of hardened black wax with a Chinese dragon stamped into it. "I'm supposed to show you this."

The clerk had reached to accept whatever Cy offered, but now she hesitated. Then her fingers—long, dark fingers that made Cy's look pale in comparison—gently closed around the seal. "Mmm-hmm."

The shop seemed suddenly very hushed, very expectant.

Granny wasn't senile, after all. This woman knew something, which put her one up on Cy.

The magistra, was all Granny'd say. Since her pneumonia, she hadn't had breath for much more. *Someone that can help us.*

Cy had always been the one to help Granny, until now.

The proprietress beckoned her through the curtained doorway, into the back rooms. As soon as Cy left the shop's

commercial front, she realized that she'd jumped to conclusions. Back here, in far-less-flashy shoe boxes and re-
used food jars, lay legitimate signs of *voudun*—unnamed
spices, to be recognized by their smell, and sure-enough tufts
of Spanish moss for real, handmade dolls. A hefty boa
constrictor, kept in its terrarium only by a screen weighted
down with a brick, coiled patiently.

And the lady who led her here, back straight and head
high, was a far sight more than a clerk. More likely a
priestess.

The pot had *definitely* called the kettle black.

The priestess whirled on Cy. "What could you be wanting
with the magistra? If it's who I'm thinking it is, that man,
he means to be left alone. And what he wants, he gets, girl.
All of us 'round here know it."

But Granny didn't live 'round here. Usually she lived
north of the lake, like Cy. Had Granny been left out of some
kind of pagan loop?

Or did she think the town needed help too badly to care?

"I'll have to hear that from him," Cy decided, using her
best business voice. "I'm here about something very important."

"Mmm-hmm." The woman had likely heard that one
before, about everything from love spells to curses. Cy met
her gaze steadily, letting the priestess feel her own power.
The blood of Hispanic *brujas*, of Indian shamans—and,
yes, of *voudun* priestesses—ran thick through her own
veins, designer suit notwithstanding.

The woman narrowed her amber eyes, eyes that looked
eerily at and beyond Cypress. "Who sent you?"

"My granny, Deeny Vega."

"Deeny Vega from Stagwater? You're lying."

Cy continued to hold the woman's gaze, unfazed. She
knew she didn't look like her black granny, any more than
she looked like her white father. Her features were always
too ethnic or too Caucasian, her skin too dark or too light,
depending on who did the looking.

The priestess finally nodded, mage to mage, and handed back the seal. Whatever the test, Cy had passed. "Listen, girl. Don't you be telling the magistra it was me what pointed you to him, you understand? I don't want no trouble."

As opposed to all of us who do, right? But Cy got the strong impression that, by seeking out this "magistra," she was looking up trouble for sure.

"You be watching your back," insisted her reluctant source. "He can be dangerous, that one. You hear me?"

Cy nodded, shaken. Who—what—*was* this man?

After that warning, receiving directions to the magistra's front door—a second-story entrance off a cobblestoned private courtyard—seemed like a mixed blessing. Misty rain fell, shadowing the Quarter and the courtyard with a wintry half-light. Not for the first time, Cy felt suddenly, bleakly alone.

The irony of it, she decided, climbing the brick stairway, was that a few months ago she *wouldn't* have been here alone. She had friends, friends with certain...abilities. But the strange goings-on in her hometown had worsened over the past half year; all of their abilities were near exhausted. Besides, her friends—fellow witches, circlemates—had their own jobs, their own families, their own lives.

Cy saw no cause to inconvenience them with Granny's goose chase. Besides, she'd rather just risk herself.

She reached the top of the stairs and shivered, stepped back. This outwardly charming apartment, with its French doors, plantation shutters and wrought-iron railings, did *not* invite casual drop-ins. Anyone with the faintest instincts would sense Do Not Disturb and No Trespassing warnings as surely as if they were posted in neon. Obviously a magic user himself, the magistra had heaped quite the security whammy on his home to keep out unwanted forces—including, apparently, the likes of her.

She knocked anyway, then waited in the damp quiet. New Orleans's French Quarter deserved its party reputation for areas like Bourbon Street and the touristy Jackson Square. But this oldest section of the city also contained quieter back streets, like this one. Balconies overhung the sidewalks, and the buildings were flush together, except when separated by private courtyards like this, lush despite the season, complete with a gurgling fountain. She imagined that, if she held her breath, she could turn and see women in hoopskirts, or men in waistcoats and sweeping capes.

Being a witch didn't make her a fanciful person. But suddenly, without hearing a thing, Cy knew she wasn't alone. She released a breath—had she been holding it?—and turned to see the man watching her from the courtyard.

His black leather trench coat was caped. Did that count?

In the shadows of the high, ivy-veined walls, he stood tall and elegant. Broad-shouldered, not so much like a construction worker as maybe a…prince? She could only guess at his age; he wore composure too well for a youth, but his darkness denied too many years. Dark—that fit him, despite his fair skin. Dark, soft-looking hair flowed back from a squared face. Dark eyes set the misting air between them to crackling. He raised his chin in royal disdain; that her place on the steps required that he look up to meet her gaze seemed irrelevant.

The magistra, of course. This place belonged to a man who wanted to be left alone, who could intimidate a *voudun* priestess.

A man Granny had sent her to find and ask for help. *Best get through this.* Reaching into her Daytimer, she descended the timeworn steps. "Hi! Just the man I was looking for."

And that was no lie. Closer, she could see just what a good-looking man he was, with a firm mouth and dark lashes and a nicely broad patrician's nose. Good-looking, and stone-cold.

"Hi." The casual greeting sounded clipped and formal in his mouth, a bad pretense of being something he was not.

Something like nonthreatening.

"I'm sorry to disturb you," Cy assured him quickly.

He quirked a bemused eyebrow. "Good."

Good? Annoyed, she stood straighter, set her shoulders. "I was sent to find the magistra."

Did something change in his aloof gaze? A flicker of the eyes, a pressing of that cold mouth? "Magister," he said. "But I am neither he nor she. The magistra is dead." And she finally figured out why his monosyllabic answers had sounded clipped. He had himself a fine English accent.

She also realized, with guilty relief, that her reluctant quest was over. Just as well. Surely she and her friends could help Stagwater on their own; the good guys could still win. "I apologize. I must have been misinformed." She turned to go.

His authoritative voice stopped her departure. "By whom?"

The question should have seemed casual, but she felt the chill of internal alarms going off at the root of her spine. She looked back at him. Big mistake. His depthless eyes caught and held hers, like a snake hypnotizing its prey.

She narrowed her own eyes. So the magister was dead, huh? Given the choice, she'd trust the *voudun* priestess. This man was bluffing. "Someone who thought you might want to see this."

When his disinterested gaze touched the seal she extended, he froze. "Where did you get this?" He took it from her, studying it with . . . respect? For a moment, his expression softened, which made him way too handsome for his own good—or hers. She felt safer when he copped an attitude.

"From my grandmother," she explained. "Does it mean something to you?"

Only after examining the seal did he deign to glance back to her. There went that attitude again. 'Bout time.

She folded her arms, tipped her head, and waited.

He relented. "This is a marker, an IOU. Your grand-mother must have provided assistance to the magistra at some point. I assume she now wishes the favor returned."

Cy considered herself even less psychic than fanciful, but gut feeling maintained *he* was the magistra—magister. Maybe she was dealing with some sort of alter ego here; maybe it was like talking to Clark Kent about Superman, or Bruce Wayne about Batman.

"So can you return the favor?" she persisted.

"I have no intention of doing so. Good day."

"You can, but you *won't?*" So much for hunky super-heroes!

He might as well *be* a statue, for all his apparent concern. "Good day," he repeated, overarticulating for annoyance value.

Fine. Ethics—and good sense—argued against her trying to influence him through magic. She reached for the seal, but he didn't release it fast enough. Their fingers brushed—

And something jolted through her, like an electric shock. It singed her blood, shuddered over her damp skin and deep into her chilled bones, unbalancing her. What on earth—?

But she knew instinctively what it was. And, staring up at him, she knew he felt it, too. Despite his composure, the man's hooded eyes flared in a millisecond of shared, bonding surprise.

Power. Power like none she'd ever felt in her life. She knew magic. She *was* magic. But she didn't know magic like this.

What was *he?*

In the backlash of power, sensations surrounded him: The damp weather, the half-light, the *clop-clop* of a cab horse. All suddenly clamoring, magnified from their usual trivial status.

What was *she?*

Drake let the tawny-skinned woman reclaim the seal and her hand, while he regained his composure. But he could not so easily let go of the energy that had surged through him when they touched, as if together they completed a circuit. She was a mage; he had sensed as much. But never before had another mage heightened his own abilities. This woman's energy somehow complemented, even strengthened, his own, which was considerable.

Suspicious, he narrowed his eyes at her. How? And *why?*

She took a step back from him, perhaps equally disoriented, but not yet frightened. He was unsure whether to admire her courage, or pity her foolishness.

"Tell me your name," he demanded, to keep her here at least until he understood more.

She arched a dark eyebrow back at him. "Yours first."

Perhaps not so foolish after all. "Drake Benedict."

"Cypress Bernard." To his immense relief, she did not say she was pleased to meet him. He hated liars. "Mr. Benedict, can you help my granny or not?"

A more polite man would have suggested that they get out of the wet. He ignored polite for prudent. An invitation could be an even greater weapon in the wrong magical hands than a name.

"Even if I can, it is unlikely I will." But her "granny" *had* apparently helped the real magistra, and such debts *were* vaguely hereditary. It would not put him out too much to talk to her. Briefly. "Exactly what does your grandmother require?"

Ms. Bernard hesitated—hardly a response to encourage his rare consideration of assistance.

"Granny," she admitted finally, "isn't the one in trouble."

"Isn't she?"

"She's feeling poorly, but that isn't why she sent me."

Apparently the truth. He waited for her to make her point...and noticed that she smelled of mint, and rosemary.

"I live in Stagwater, Mr. Benedict. For over a year now, my friends and I have noticed certain goings-on in town. Spooky stuff. Ghosts. Worse. My granny Vega figured maybe you could explain why we're suddenly a Club Med for monsters."

Just the sort of mystery the true magistra would have relished—had she not gotten herself killed on a prior errand of mercy. That thought brought a pain as unexpected as his sudden interest in scents, sounds... in how moisture glittered, gemlike, on Ms. Bernard's thick black hair and trim suitcoat.

The sooner he told her no, the sooner they could go their own ways and the more surely he could remain uninvolved—until tonight, when the summons would taunt his dark side yet again.

The summons... "Where is Stagwater?"

"North of the lake."

Suspicions confirmed—was she a messenger? But no, this dusky woman, with her tailored appearance and straightforward demeanor, was not evil. He, of all people, would be able to sense it on her. Was there *any* connection?

Against his better judgment, he considered the situation she described. "Do you belong to a coven, Ms. Bernard?"

Her eyes widened at his guess. She had the clear traits of an earth sign, *and* she smelled like herbs—a witch. What other kind of mage might she be? "I work with three others."

"How competent are you?"

She frowned at his assumptions. "By whose standard?"

Fair question. "Have you perhaps summoned something, and lost control of it? Performed ritual magic outside the boundaries of a circle?" He eyed her sternly. "Tried your hands raising a demon you then could not control?"

The frown darkened. "You think sloppy magic caused this?"

He did not answer the question. "Incompetence," he insisted, "could have unexpected repercussions."

"I guess it could at that, but it hasn't. We're competent. So what else could it be?" Which, he imagined, *was* her answer.

"Like attracts like."

She searched his face. He could feel her gaze, like a gentle warmth. "I thought opposites attract."

"That, Ms. Bernard, is said of love, not magic. If random evil is flocking to your town, evil already exists there to so attract it. If no mage is at fault—" he ignored her affronted huff "—you might consider what happened just before the problems began. Learn if anyone cleared land, or broke ground for new construction, or made other changes that could have disturbed or attracted something. Now, will that be all?"

She blinked, perhaps as surprised by his sudden dismissal as he was. But he had already said too much, offered too much—broken his own rule of noninterference by too great a margin.

Her very presence, her determination, disturbed him deeply.

"You tell me if that's all," she countered. "You seem to know a hell of a lot more than I do."

He did know enough not to risk his own well-being for a woman he had just met and a town he had never heard of. He knew enough not to confront an evil such as he had felt, night after night, from across the lake. Temptation might prove too great.

Although, as powerful as he had been when his fingers brushed Cypress Bernard's, perhaps...

No. Absolutely not. That would mean involving himself with her, indebting himself to her—trading one possible addiction for another. *Never.* "I have given you more than you had any right to expect," he told her.

After staring at him a moment longer, she had the grace to nod. Of all magic users, witches held the most foolish rules about nonmanipulation. "I guess you're right. Sorry for having wasted your precious time, Mr. Benedict. Good day." She started to offer her hand, then paused, perhaps at the memory.

He kept his own hand firmly at his side. But his fingers, his soul, itched to experience their odd magic again.

All the more reason not to.

"Goodbye, Ms. Bernard," he echoed, and told himself he was glad to see her turn away. Short of harnessing her energy as some sort of strength battery, he had no more use for her—even if he did decide to investigate, to dare take the offensive.

He had what he needed: her name, her grandmother's name. And he knew the name of the afflicted town: *Stagwater.*

"What if Mr. Congeniality was right?" demanded Cy, tying a wick onto a pencil to suspend it over a candle mold. "We were together before the spooky stuff started, but... what if the effects were cumulative, and it's somehow our doing?"

Her three friends, who had finally gotten past their disapproval of her solo visit with the magister yesterday, exchanged wary glances across Brigit's kitchen. Wary, but not shocked. They must have considered the possibility, as well.

"How could it be?" protested the youngest of their circle, newlywed Mary Poitiers. Mary took everything to heart. "We do nature magic, not some highfalutin ceremonial..."

"Sorcery?" suggested Sylvie Garner, the bookish brunette, when the younger woman faltered. Syl stood by the double boiler full of wax, one hand protectively spread on her slightly rounded tummy as she melted a blue crayon for its peaceful properties.

"Sorcery!" Mary nodded vehemently. "To create evil things, we'd have to do black magic, right? I mean, um, evil magic."

Cy raised a dusky hand to fend off any awkward apologies. What else should they call the stuff—the left-hand path? This was no time to be worrying about political correctness. "I hope you're right. We've been *helping* this town. We do positive magic. So how come we're suddenly up to our ears in spooks?"

"A third party? Some other magic user?" Flame-haired Brigit Peabody was the only member of the circle who'd had formal training in witchcraft. Cy's magical lineage could probably rival Brie's, but Cy's was as piecemeal as her bloodlines. Brigit, however, was an official Celtic *witch*—a witch nursing a flame-haired baby. "If anyone else *is* out there, they sure have covered their tracks."

Watching the baby, Cy actively felt like the oldest member of the circle. Normally, since their ages were fairly close, she didn't notice. But normally she didn't think about being the only *unmarried* witch of the group left, either.

The only one left? That made it sound like someone was trying to kill them off for it. Untrue. Brigit had already been married to Steve—Sylvie's brother—before they formed the circle, two years ago. Sylvie and Mary had just happened to find their own Mr. Rights in rapid succession; Syl was already carrying twins!

That someone—or, more likely, some*thing*—had tried to kill each of them off was completely unrelated.

Not even something—somethings. A whole passel of them.

"We've got one case of lycanthropy," stated Sylvie, leaving the stove to open her sack purse—damned if the woman hadn't made a list! "Alleged lycanthropy." She smiled the quirky smile she'd picked up since her marriage. It had been over a year since some kind of werewolf had threatened their little town. Sylvie had helped capture the offender, and gotten herself a real scamp of a mate out of the deal, as well. Now she glanced at Brigit. "At least one case of possession."

Brigit had found herself threatened by her own husband. Except that it hadn't been her husband, exactly. He'd managed to fight off the evil, and together they had banished it.

It would've been too coincidental for circlemates Cy or Mary to run into anything. But the thing that had emerged from the swamp, bent on destroying Mary and a lifelong friend—now *her* new husband—apparently hadn't grasped the law of averages.

Three witches down, one witch to go? Oh no. *No* way. If the others jumped off a bridge, would Cypress? No, ma'am! She'd just be the rebel in love *and* monsters, thank you very much. Though, over the months, her chances of running into a creature of the night had risen considerably—at least if she stayed in Stagwater.

"One will-o'-the-wisp," Sylvie continued.

"Couchemal," said Mary, going to check on the wax.

"Ghost," Cypress put in. "Bottom line, that thing was a ghost. You've also got that skeletal thing, right?"

"I even have it down as 'skeletal thing,'" admitted Sylvie. "And at least three reported sightings of, and one attack by, what could be a bear."

Except that there weren't any bears in the area anymore. Rumor held it to be the Honey Island Swamp Monster, their local version of a bigfoot. The boy who'd been mauled wasn't talking.

"A couple who swear they saw ghosts over by the railroad track, teenagers who swear *they* saw ghosts at the park, and poltergeist activity in the high school cafeteria. The teachers insist it was a food fight, but an awful lot of the students disagree. And..." Sylvie eyed Mary. "Some kind of demonic activity in the Fouchard house?"

"The church sent in some priests, hush-hush, to do an exorcism," agreed Mary. Her brother-in-law was a priest, as well as an ex-boyfriend of Cy's. Cy liked to think the two facts weren't related.

"Did it work?" asked Brigit.

Mary shrugged as she sorted through jars of essential oils. "You know, the Fouchards didn't hang around to find out."

"We've also got howling dogs, weird weather, and..."

Oh, no. Like that wasn't enough? Cy leaned over her arms, crossed on the tabletop. "And what?"

"I talked to some people at the hospital," Sylvie admitted. "After that double suicide last month. It seems depression's on a major rise around here. More people are getting sick more often, too. I was wondering if the incidents were connected."

"And things feel funny," added Mary, jar in hand. She shrugged at the other three witches' glances. "You know how the air pressure changes, before a storm? It feels like the pressure around here has changed, like it's never going back to normal."

"Well, whatever is going on and whoever is doing it, it needs to be stopped," decided Cy. "Two kids ended up at the hospital after that so-called food fight. The Fouchards won't be selling that house anytime soon. Who knows if they'll ever recover financially? We can do a binding, or a reading, or we can just do a heapload of protection spells, but we need—I need—to be doing something to help."

Sylvie looked worried. "Unless this magister of yours was right, and our magic really is the problem. Then anything we do to make things better would only make things worse. Catch-22."

They exchanged unhappy glances. This was *not* good.

"Assuming this Benedict guy knows what he's talking about," Sylvie added, looking to Cypress for confirmation.

Cy raised her hands, palms out, to fend off the question—and thoughts of the cold-eyed, darkly handsome wizard of the French Quarter. "I don't know anything about the man, except that my granny figured he could help, and that she was wrong."

Which, she thought, and not for the first time, *might be a shame, after all. He sure talked the talk, anyhow.*

And things would probably get worse before they got better.

* * *

Briars gouged at her arms and legs. Ferns slapped at her, vines tripped her, and a bush's branch tangled into her hair. Then Lucille Witt fell over a rotting log, dropping her flashlight when she sprawled into the pine straw and the mud.

Damn it! She groped for and reclaimed her flashlight, and double-checked. Oh, no. No!

She'd broken a nail. And her sexy new outfit was ruined.

Lucille Witt hated the woods. When she wrote Charlie that note—*meet me at* our *spot*—she guessed she hadn't been thinking of the swampy Louisiana woods at all. She'd imagined a romantic forest, like in the movies. She didn't remember having this much trouble when she used to come out here in high school with Charlie. Or Joe. Or Tucker.

Then again, the boys had always gone first and carried the blanket, which probably made it lots easier.

The ground felt like it was moving under her, which made her think of snakes and ants and stuff. That got Lucille back to her feet real fast. She made sure she still had the blanket, then aimed the flashlight's unexpectedly weak beam ahead of her. Banging the case against her hip didn't brighten it. She headed deeper into the woods anyway, alone. Growing up made everything worse, didn't it? First, her right-out-of-high-school marriage to Tucker had gone sour. Then Charlie had come back from college married himself! And he'd looked so good, too.

Well, that Baton Rouge slut he'd hooked up with couldn't possibly do a man like Lucille could. Charlie had pretended to be shocked when Lucille let out that she still wanted him. But he'd done that in high school, too. Him going steady with Kitty hadn't kept him from meeting Lucille in the woods all the same.

Married or not, he'd be there.

Funny that it was so quiet, though. No frogs. No bugs.

Maybe Charlie had already been through and scared them. Encouraged, Lucille picked up her pace. The underbrush seemed to clear, finally, but the trees swayed in the wind, branches reaching at her like claws, ruining her hairdo, tearing her new blouse. Like they didn't want her and Charlie together. Damn trees. Damn wind. Damn darkness, damn silence—

Lucille stopped, dead still. How could it be silent if there was a wind?

But... how could the trees be moving, if there wasn't?

Slowly, she looked up at the tangled boughs that barred the desperately distant sky from her. Even the pine branches were bare. The trees here weren't just leafless. They were dead.

Lucille was still looking up, chilled, when something snatched at her ankle and yanked. With a shriek, she fell to the muddy ground. Her thoughts full of rapists and escaped lunatics, she beat at whoever-it-was's arm with the flashlight.

Which was how, in swinging arcs, she saw that it wasn't an arm. It looked more like... roots? Snakes? Dark tendrils seemed to uncurl from the earth itself. One slithered forward and bound her thigh. Another caught her free ankle. Something struck at and bound her wrist, and she dropped the flashlight.

It went out, leaving her in full darkness.

She couldn't think. She could only scream. Whatever it was—whatever they were—dragged her through the rot and mud and debris of the forest floor, too fast. When she felt herself yanked forcibly downward, impossibly downward, into an impromptu grave, her screams rose in frenzy—

And then, muffled by dirt, they stopped.

Silence descended again over the dead stretch of the woods, because, of course, Charlie had never meant to meet Lucille. He was safe at home with his wife.

And, strengthened by the local woman's sacrifice, Stagwater's darkness spread.

CHAPTER TWO

Answer, willed Cy, cellular phone pressed to her ear. *C'mon, girlfriend, answer.*

Only her gray Accord, parked beside the roadside ditch, stood between her and the overgrown lot by her granny's home. Cy hadn't parked in front, because a black Lexus already waited there.

Not the kind of vehicle one generally found on dirt back roads. Especially not beside vacant witches' shacks.

Will you answer?

"Hello?"

"Sylvie, it's Cypress."

"What's wrong and where are you?" That woman could even be empathic over cellular connections!

"You know how I've been checking on Granny's house while she's at the recovery home? There's someone else here today."

Sylvie's voice dropped, as if whoever it was could hear her end. "Who?"

But her guess was as good as any; Cy hadn't actually *seen* anyone. And if she waited much longer, she *wouldn't* see anyone, either. Even coming by straight from work—she still wore her silk suit, her chunky gold earrings and her ID tag—she hadn't beaten the darkness by much. What little sky lingered over the tall pines on both sides of the road was darkening fast.

"That's what I'm fixing to find out. Could you swing out this direction, in case there's trouble?"

"Asking you to wait on us would be pretty futile, huh?"

"'Fraid so. If someone's messing with my granny's property, I mean to find out why." Besides, she had a feeling of urgency, and even anticipation, like the stillness before a storm. "But I'll try not to hurt anyone."

"We'll be there," agreed Sylvie, and the line disconnected.

Cy slipped the phone through her open passenger window—crime wasn't exactly a big problem around here, and she doubted the Honey Island Swamp Monster would have any use for her toys. Then she stepped out of her leather shoes and, glancing both ways, wriggled out of her hose. Chill air brushed against her oxygen-starved legs; the damp clay of the dirt road, sharp with corners of half-buried broken shells, felt good and natural under her callused feet. Leave the footwear. Bring the lug wrench.

Now or never, girl.

She jumped the ditch and edged her way to the relative clearing of Granny's yard, where she'd spent so much time as a child. Feeling like Little Red Riding Hood with inside information, she crept up to the sagging porch and peeked into the living room window. Empty.

But the feeling, the urgency, remained.

She edged around the side of the house, pressed close to the weather-grayed wood. The chirring of crickets and toads, calling to the night, helped hide her almost-silent footsteps in the brown grass.

That, and a low chanting.

Chanting? She peeked around the house's corner to the backyard, expecting—what? Something besides the dead herb garden and rusting clothesline poles. But she saw nothing else.

The chanting continued. It came from the woods past the backyard, from the clearing where Granny had taught her the rudiments of earth magic—how to connect with nature, how to sing with its rhythms and access its wealth.

But Granny was recuperating in New Orleans.

And this chanting was male. Clipped. Hard.

She hurried across the familiar backyard. Pausing to crouch by the remains of the garden, she scooped up a good handful of cold dirt. *Speaking of earth magic*... She crept down the dark, worn path, calling on the Indian blood in her mongrel heritage for stealth. Then she ducked behind a browning wisteria bush and leaned out enough to see the clearing.

Barely ten feet from her a man stood, tall and regal, head high. Her quickened pulse leaped in recognition. It *was* him!

"I summon thee," Drake Benedict commanded, his voice low and hard. "I summon thee to do my bidding. Come, come..."

Summon—as in a *summoning?* From her Granny's magic place?

Mouth falling open, she hunkered into a more comfortable position to watch until backup arrived—she might be curious, but she wasn't stupid. A fancy metal bowl sat on the wide, wax-splattered oak stump that Granny used as an altar. Clouds of dark, sharp incense smoke billowed upward from the bowl, and a glow—from charcoal?—reflected out of it. In that unsteady light, she saw white sparkles circling the ground around the wizard. He'd created a ring of salt for protection, obviously from whatever he summoned.

Cy remained outside the safety of his circle. She decided to risk it.

Power brushed against her face, like the chill air and the scent of the incense. Tantalizingly close, yet as separate from her as from the nature that surrounded him, Benedict controlled that power with elegant mastery. His posture, the angle of his chin, the taper of his outstretched hands, all reflected that, as did his voice. It set a cadence, musical, almost as hypnotic as the incense....

She resisted its pull, taking a deep breath and visualizing strong shields around herself. Protective, *invisible* shields.

"I summon thee, now come to me! I summon thee, now come to me! *Veni, veni, veni*..."

Now he was speaking...Latin? He wore all black again, what looked like street clothes except for a long, vestlike garment embroidered with gold symbols she didn't recognize. His magic couldn't have been more different from Granny's, or even her more eclectic circle's. What kind of sorcery was she watching?

And why did it seem to speak to something deep inside her?

"Come to me!"

His authoritative tone held the twilight in thrall—she fought the urge to go to him herself, and she wasn't even the one he called. Was she? She *had* come. Magic—the magic she'd known since childhood, anyhow—worked in subtle coincidences, not flashy special effects. She didn't watch for anything physical.

So she almost didn't realize that the creature Benedict *had* summoned obeyed.

"*Nooo...*" It sounded like the wind, but there was none. Instead, within the churning of incense smoke, an insubstantial thickness seemed to roil. She stared. Was she imagining the half-formed shape writhing slowly, bemoaning its enslavement?

But it looked vaguely human, and she wasn't a fanciful person. She was the most down-to-earth witch she knew.

"As I will it," commanded Benedict coldly, "So you shall answer."

The form—the ghost—seemed to move. Or maybe it vanished and reappeared. Its mouth, or at least the place where its mouth should be, moved, and she heard its answer.

"*Yesss...*"

Benedict never looked away from it, so she couldn't see his face. The rest of him, from his straining, black-clad shoulders, arms, butt and thighs to his soft, dark hair, fascinated her.

And horrified her, of course. Fascinated and horrified.

"As I will it, you shall speak only the truth." His voice didn't sound strained, it sounded melodic. She could have listened for hours, although—she readjusted her balance—not like this.

Answered the voice from the smoke, *"Yesss..."*

"As I will it, so you shall remain until I dismiss you."

The ghost seemed to move again. Through the falling night and from her position, low to the ground, Cy could barely see it, but she sensed it thrashing, like a bird against a cage or a slave, caught back by chains. It wore chains of power rather than of iron, but chains nonetheless.

She straightened a bit, her growing horror making her bolder. Now she could make out a triangle of salt on the altar, around the censer. So that was what held it.

The struggle annoyed the magister; his voice cut the dusk. "As I will it, so you shall remain until I dismiss you!"

The silence deepened—not even crickets, toads or birds broke the stillness. The smoke, oddly pale against the shadows, quieted. *"Yesss..."* Assent whispered through the woods, the latest despair of a lost soul.

Whose soul?

"What keeps you here?" demanded Benedict coolly. And she wondered—who are you? It *was* a who, right? Or it once had been. Maybe one of the lycanthrope's victims. Maybe one of the dead boys from Picayune. It was a human soul. And it didn't want to answer, but because it was dead, it apparently had no choice—because of magic.

Dark, manipulative magic, completely unlike hers.

Evil?

The spirit moaned. She could smell its fear in the night.

"What keeps you here?" Benedict might have been a machine or a stone sculpture, for all the compassion he showed.

"You." The phantom spoke the accusation in its not-quite-there voice.

"No!" The magister's voice, in contrast, was a weapon, a choke collar, a lash. She felt her hand—the one not holding the tire iron—become a fist, squeezing her dirt into an unintentional clump. "What force keeps you in Stagwater?"

"The evil. The darkness."

"Clarify. What force keeps you here in Stagwater?"

"The anger. The hatred. The darkness."

"Tell me its name!"

The apparition moaned, helpless. The noise hurt Cy's heart, lifted the hair on her arms.

"Tell me its name!"

Another moan. Frightened. Trapped.

"As I will it, so you shall—"

"Stop it!" She pushed free of her hiding place, stalked toward the dark magician, crumbling the dirt in her hand— *Mother Nature, protect me.* "Stop torturing it!"

Benedict spun to stare at her, the faint glow of the censer highlighting the planes of his handsome, surprised face.

Then several things happened at once.

One moment, Drake was interrogating the first spirit to answer his summons—was on the verge of learning what he needed. And none too soon. He had underestimated how strong the draw of evil would be, this close to its source, and as the sun set he had to struggle to control not only the ghost, but himself, as well.

Exhaustion weakened him, but he had enough strength to see this otherworldly interview to its proper closure.

The next moment, a barefoot witch in a business suit was charging out of the underbrush at him, some sort of metal pole in one hand, something fisted in the other.

And the next—

A chill of awareness stabbed at him, the sense of other beings in the gathering darkness. He could feel their lurking nearness, their desperation—their jealousy. Lost souls, lost and angry souls, on the loose.

Damn! There was a reason he bound ghosts!

He extended a hand toward his uninvited guest—odd, that his first reaction should be protective. "Get in the circle!"

The witch hesitated—didn't trust him, did she?—and from the woods behind and above her, one of the shadows struck.

He sliced a symbolic opening in the protective sphere around him, knew he could not reach the woman in time. Her eyes widened, instincts warning her where senses could not—and she spun and threw a handful of dirt with accuracy. "Begone!"

As soon as that shadow fell back, another swept toward her, the two like little minions of the greater evil. Stepping outside the circle himself, he clutched at and caught the woman's wrist, lug wrench and all. Something dark, cold, dangerous, darted past them—and, in contrast, hot power surged through him, from her. Exhaustion vanished. Hyperawareness blasted through his nerves.

And the evil no longer called.

Now he clearly saw the blurred humanoid shape of one of the ghosts, twisting in the air above them, preparing for another dive. Apparently Ms. Bernard did, too. When he yanked her across the barrier of salt, she came without protest, bumping against his chest as he stopped short.

More contact. More shared energy. They blinked at one another—then remembered their danger.

Both their free hands reached out, smoothed shut the envisioned tear in the circle's wall, as if they had choreographed the movement. And although magical circles were rarely visible, Drake thought he now glimpsed a shell of bright blue around them.

What *was* this woman? What did she do to him? How?

Not releasing her wrist, he spun to stare at his containment triangle, and swore. The ghost had escaped during his distraction. Likely it had joined the other cold shapes circling him and the witch, waiting for their strength—and their protections—to falter.

He spared a glance toward the witch, who looked as if she had seen a— Yes, well. No more help from that front.

"You!" When he pointed at one of the careering shapes, an arc of visible energy left his finger and wrapped tendrils around the closest phantom. Amazing! "Return whence thou came!"

The witch at his side muttered something as, slowly, the creature disintegrated, fading back into mundane shadows.

"You!" He caught and held the second—was there no end to the energy this woman lent him? "Return whence thou came!"

This time he heard Bernard's mutter: "For the good of all, and according to the free will of all." Witches!

"You!" But the third, and presumably final, phantom vanished before he could force it. Unreality slowly faded from the night, leaving behind the kind of normalcy that encourages people to dismiss such encounters as mere fancy. From the woods, a bird cried out, low and lonely. The charcoal in the censer had burned away—no more incense clouded the clearing beneath the tall pines. All would be dark, but for the stars that brightened as the night fell, and for the hint of a moonrise to the east.

And yet energy—power—continued to pulse through him, like a transfusion from the woman he held. His gaze dipped to where his hand still encircled her darker wrist, then to her warm face, which lifted toward his. Her eyes, barely visible, demanded answers he did not have. He remembered the rush of her stumbling against him, body to body, an overload of contact...

He opened his hand even as she snatched hers away, the falling lug wrench barely missing her bare brown toes. He had enough self-control issues to deal with, without letting himself linger on that sort of sense-laden memory!

He half expected exhaustion to reclaim him when they broke contact. It did not. His sense of renewed power did fade, but slowly, and not to the depth he would have expected.

A summoning. A binding. Two banishings. And yet here he stood, practically refreshed. This woman's nearness unsettled him, tempting and so very dangerous.

Bernard spoke first. "What the hell are you doing here?" And the temptation of her lessened.

"Exactly what part eludes you? The summons? Or perhaps my rescuing you?" He still could not place why he had done that, especially since it had exposed him to the danger, as well. Had her unusual abilities drawn him? Had he already lost to temptation?

"Perhaps," he continued, angry at that thought and thus angry at her, "you do not recognize that you ruined my spell?"

"That much I get." She didn't sound sorry, either. But she did sound shaken. "As if we don't have enough ghosts in town, you're sending out invitations?"

"They were already local." He took a deep breath as the last of their shared power drained from him. Into its place whispered uncertainty. She *had* ruined his spell. He still did not know his enemy. And from the woods, in the direction of Stagwater proper, the evil called to him yet again.

When he turned and kicked dirt and pine straw over part of his salt-drawn circle, Cypress Bernard grasped his arm, as if to stop him. He clenched his teeth at a second wave of power that surged through him, the blessed cessation of the evil's call—and increased temptation.

Whatever she saw in his eyes when he angled his face toward her made her let go fast. Smart woman. The rush faded, again. The old evil beckoned. And something dark inside him, the proverbial devil on his shoulder, whispered at him to grab her, hold her, soak up whatever power she exuded, whether she wanted to give it or not. He could perhaps drain her, harness her energies in a receptacle of stone or metal for future use....

He stoically ignored all whispers.

"Is it—?" Apparently she felt the need to explain her actions. "Is it safe to open the circle?"

The night fairly radiated normalcy. But then, he would recognize that, because he had dealt with the otherworld before. He doubted his paranormal résumé would comfort Bernard.

"Safer than when you arrived," he pointed out, and sank to one knee to resume his task. He did not want to leave any useless bits of magic floating around, getting into trouble. Especially not with the still-unnamed evil so close.

He wished he had at least learned its name.

She crouched easily beside him to help, apparently comfortable getting her hands dirty. "You really *aren't* the magister, are you? Wouldn't the magister be a really good magic user who helps people who need it?"

"*A* magister," he told her. "Or magistra, Latin being gender-specific. Not *the* magister. And I believe I clarified that when we first met."

"I didn't believe you."

"I never lie." When she snorted at that, he found himself explaining, as if she deserved to know. "Speaking untruths lessens the power of one's words."

Heaven forbid she should think he had altruistic motives.

"And I guess you consider yourself pretty powerful?"

Was she teasing him? "Dangerously so."

She stiffened at his half-whispered answer. Frightened? Good. He had just explained, had he not, that he never lied?

His father had been very powerful—and after experimenting with the darker side of magic, he'd become very dangerous, as well. His father's brother, Viktor, had recently been urging Drake to consider the same path. *We are stronger, my lad. We can control it better than he did. It is always a question of control.*

Oh, yes. Drake's abilities could prove dangerous indeed, even without Cypress Bernard's assistance. *With* it ...

"That still doesn't give you the right to use my granny's magic place." She did not call it a circle, a temple, or an altar. How could a mere earth witch offer so much strength?

"Her invitation, requesting my help, gave me that right."

Bernard stood. "She requested help from the magistra."

"The only way the magistra can help is if you are up to a séance. Otherwise, I'm it." He reclaimed his still-warm censer, shook it so that the charcoal tumbled into ashes, then poured them out in a protective rune on the ground. He noticed the forest's dead weeds, dying trees and looming darkness. Not the natural darkness that all but hid Cypress Bernard from him now, though she stood close enough to touch. The kind of darkness, instead, that called, that the phantom had refused to name. Why?

Perhaps because it was nameless? Perhaps because it was a natural phenomenon, and no entity at all?

"What's happening here?" Something about the honest anxiety that thickened Bernard's voice and furrowed her forehead touched him as a more careful request would not have. "Why are you doing unethical magic in my granny's woods? Why are ghosts attacking me? What on earth has gone wrong in Stagwater?"

What on earth? As suddenly as that, he understood what might have been calling to him all these months. It had been under his nose, and his feet, all along. The thought relaxed his shoulders and neck, almost made him smile in relief. He must be more tired, more worn from his nights, than he had thought.

"It would appear," he offered, "that your town has been set upon by a black dragon."

Even in the dark, it was amusing, even gratifying, to watch her double-take at that. Perhaps one smile, albeit a superior one, would not hurt after all.

"A dragon," she repeated, finally losing that embarrassing warble. Her stomach eased some, too. She'd been with Benedict up to then. In his presence, ghosts turned visible, magic circles glowed, the air crackled and the earth tingled. He did magic effortlessly, and wore an aura of power so strong his hand around her wrist—and, for a moment, his body against hers—unbalanced her. To his debit, he captured and interrogated ghosts. To his credit, he rescued damsels from them, too. He fascinated her just as surely as he disturbed her.

If the ghosts that had swooped down at her were any sign, Stagwater was in deep trouble. And if the way he'd dispatched them was further indication, Drake Benedict might be the town's only hope after all, magister or no magister.

But a dragon? In *Louisiana?*

"A black dragon," he said again. The smile faded, which was a shame; she'd liked it. The corners of his mouth had crinkled into—dimples? Smug dimples. "The term is metaphorical. Have you ever heard of ley lines?"

Those she *had* heard of, and she clung to the distraction. "Aren't they tracks on the ground, like magical roadways?"

"Tracks *in* the ground," he answered. "Channels of magnetic energy that run beneath the earth's surface. For eons, magicians have tapped into this energy, particularly at nexus points where two or more ley lines meet, such as Stonehenge."

She nodded. She understood Stonehenge. "So what does that have to do with dragons and Stagwater?"

Again he crouched, to pack what little he'd brought—the censer, the vestment—into a leather satchel. "The Chinese are renowned for their understanding of geomancy."

"Earth magic," she said, to show she wasn't ignorant.

"Practitioners of *feng shui* call the ley lines *lung mei,* which means 'paths of the dragon.' Occasionally something blocks or sours a path of energy, turning it into a black stream."

She got it. "Or a black dragon."

Benedict shouldered his pack and straightened to his full height, which was a good half head taller than hers. "Exactly."

"And you think that we've got a ley line running through Stagwater?" She could imagine it, like a river under her feet.

"And that it has gone bad, and now draws other evils."

She began back down the path to Granny's, which she could have walked blindfolded. She didn't want to stand still too long, with sour energy under her. "The energy itself is evil?"

Benedict followed. "As more dark forces arrive—like attracting like—their energies combine to strengthen its magnetism until together they feel like a single entity."

She hadn't thought it felt like a single entity; the werewolf and the swamp creature hadn't much favored each other. But Benedict was the expert. "So the more evil there is, the more evil it attracts."

Benedict said, "Yes." As they reached Granny's yard, and the increasing moonlight, he strode ahead of her.

She kept up. "So it'll get worse exponentially."

"So it would seem." They circled the shack.

"What do we do about it?"

"*We* do not do anything." He glanced back, en route to his car. "I live in New Orleans. This is hardly my problem."

She stopped, stunned. "Wait one damned minute here! You come here, you use my granny's magic place to do your ceremonial juju, and then you can't even offer advice?"

"Not can't." He opened his expensive car's passenger door, tossed in his satchel. The artificial light from the interior washed over them both. "Shan't."

Did people even *say* "shan't" anymore? She reminded herself that she could handle this man and his superiority complex. It wasn't like she didn't deal with unpleasant people at work.

"You don't know, either, do you?" she said challengingly. *So much for nonmanipulation.* At least it wasn't *magical* coercion.

He turned back to her, eyebrow arched. "You are joking."

"I'll just have to go back to the French Quarter and ask them for advice, since the person they think is the magister doesn't seem to know jack." The dreaded double-dog dare.

She almost said, *And you can't do a thing to stop me.* She didn't say that, though, because something about the set of his jaw, the flash of his eyes and her memory of his incredible control as he summoned the ghost told her that he *could* stop her. Summonings weren't as immoral as, say, curses—depending on what got summoned, anyhow. She'd rather he was a good guy at heart, considering how attractive she found him. But why take chances?

His gaze searched hers. She shrugged one shoulder.

As if he hated himself for it, he said, "Dowse the area to find the ley line." He shut his door, and the night surged back over them. "Do it over an area map first. Then walk the affected area in person, to locate where the energy has soured."

Headlights from the dirt road illuminated them again—probably Sylvie. Cypress had a good view of Drake Benedict as he circled the front of his Lexus.

"But what do we do once we find the spot?"

"Use metal spikes to bind it, and hopefully change its polarity." Sounded like acupuncture for Mother Nature. "Now, if that is all—?" He eyed the black hearse that pulled to the side of the road, behind Cy's sedan.

Definitely Sylvie. Her ponytailed husband, Rand, who climbed out the driver's seat as Syl scrambled from the passenger side, ran a haunted house. A make-believe one.

"That's not all," said Cy quickly, low, before her backup got close enough to hear. "Look, when I first went to find you, I wasn't sure we needed your help. But I was wrong. None of my friends has ever dowsed like you're talking, and we don't know squat about ley lines. Whether you're a magister or not, you've got what we need to beat this thing. Can't you at least show us how?"

She searched his eyes; they were deep-set and dark in his noble face. Was he actually considering it? Or was he merely stunned by her inability to take no for an answer?

He started to ask a question: "What makes it your—"

"Howdy," said Rand Garner, and Benedict clammed up. Rand approached casually, a friendly expression on his lean face, but she had no doubt he was sniffing out Benedict thoroughly. "You've got company, Cy?"

Sylvie, beside him, cocked her head. She probably sensed that Cy wasn't scared of Benedict, not at the moment, at least. She probably sensed the battle of wills, and Cy's frustration, too.

"Drake Benedict, this is Sylvie Garner and her husband, Rand. Folks, this is the man I met in New Orleans."

"Delighted," said Rand with a toothy smile. He didn't offer his hand.

Neither did Benedict. "Quite."

"You had a reason for coming out here in the first place," Cy pointed out to him, hoping her friends would forgive her for finishing this particular conversation. "It'd be sloppy of you to leave things unfinished, wouldn't it?"

He glanced from Sylvie to Rand, his eyes narrowing in concentration. Did he see something Cy missed? Something weird about Rand, or something extraintriguing about Syl? Cy would have resented this supercompetence of his, if they didn't need competence so desperately.

Benedict looked back at her, resignation tightening his mouth, hardening his eyes. "I suppose if you are to do it right, you'll need at least the basics. I will meet with your coven..."

"Circle."

"...and explain what you are to do. No more. Agreed?"

"The circle?" Sylvie began to protest, while Rand looked from one of them to the other, ears practically perked.

She ignored Syl and offered her hand. "Agreed."

Drake Benedict looked at her hand, then merely nodded—at her and the others, sort of a group nod—and climbed into his car. "I shall call for directions." For a moment, interior light illuminated the incongruous softness of his hair, the planes of his princely face, his dark elegance. Then, as the door shut, darkness and tinted windows swallowed him.

"You forgot to say, 'Shake,'" quipped Rand from behind her, while Sylvie asked, "Who does that guy think he is?"

But as Benedict's motor purred to life, and the sleek car eased away from its degrading parking space, she hesitated to answer either of them. She'd wanted to touch him again, not just as good manners but also to feel his magnetic power and his fascinating, horrifying darkness surge through her again.

That, she decided, digging her toes into the damp dirt of the road, could *not* be good.

CHAPTER THREE

"I think I've got the hang of it," said Mary Poitiers. The small blonde all but lay across Cy's oak table, her elbows splayed to either side, her nose nearly touching the button that dangled from a thread. "This dowsing isn't so tough. Ask me something."

Brigit put down the baby pictures she'd been showing them. "Can we trust the magister Cypress has invited over?"

"Can we afford not to trust him?" added Sylvie.

"He's not a magister," Cy reminded her from where she stood in the middle of her one-story house's dining room. "And maybe we're just getting paranoid in our old age." She hoped so. She hoped she hadn't made a terrible mistake, inviting Drake Benedict to her home—and not because anything still needed to be cleaned, straightened or put away before he arrived.

Because her friends were here.

Her three friends filled the house with as strong a sense of safety and belonging as did the oak floors, the rows of herbs and flowerpots lining the windowsills under wooden jalousies, the bold black-and-white art prints on her walls.

But the house was hers to risk. The friends...

Brigit slanted an amused glance toward Cy. "Remember, 'Just because you're paranoid...'"

"Doesn't mean you get a discount on firearms," finished Sylvie, with a quirky grin, from where she sat at the table beside Dowsing Mary. When Cy, Brigit and Mary all turned and stared at her, Sylvie just winked. The girl's husband, Cy decided, had definitely been rubbing off on her.

But their marital activities are their own business.

Mary held up her button, to bring them back on course.
"Whether or not we can trust this Benedict guy shouldn't be
the first question. We've got to test the pendulum first. Ask
me something less..."

"Ambiguous?" suggested Sylvie, poking out her lip and
blowing upward at her brown bangs.

Mary hesitated. "Okay. Less ambiguous"

Sylvie considered it. "How about—are our husbands
worried about us tonight?" Apparently those of them with
husbands to worry thought it was a decent question. Brigit
even snorted.

Mary stared fixedly at the dangling button. "Are the
menfolk worried about us tonight?"

Cy felt sure the girl's fingers hadn't moved, but the button slowly began to swing, closer to and then farther from
Mary's perky nose. It had been only three nights since Cy's
last encounter with Benedict, two days since a game of
phone tag had confirmed tonight's meeting. But as surely as
Sylvie had read everything she could get her paws on about
ley lines since then, so had Mary been trying to get the hang
of dowsing. If any of them could master it, it would be their
young psychic.

"That means yes, right?" asked Sylvie, her own brown
eyes tracking the makeshift pendulum.

"Uh-huh." Mary smiled as the button slowed. "Ask me
a 'no' question."

"Uh, Cy?" Brigit's banked tone drew Cy closer while the
two younger, less experienced witches continued the experiments. "We really *don't* know much about this man." Of
all the witches, this past year had left Brie the most ghost-
shy. She'd come close to losing her life, her husband, even
her unborn child.

Cy couldn't even imagine facing a threat like that, but at
least she could try to answer it. "We know that he's good."

Brigit waited, unconvinced.

Cy grinned. "Fine, we know that he's *competent*." What kind of path Benedict followed was another matter. The circle, sworn to harm none, would never hold a spirit against its will. Might Benedict feel as little compunction about the living?

Brigit warned, "That makes him all the more dangerous."

"The man *is* good—I mean, able." Cy hunkered down beside Brigit's chair. "But there's four of us, and only one of him. Sylvie's empathic enough to sense if he means evil. Mary would get one of her psychic flashes. And together, you and I could probably blast the boy back out the door."

She hoped. They didn't have much choice.

"You'll still have invited him in. Once we're home and safe, you'll be alone here. How would you keep him out?"

"I've warded the other rooms to keep him out. Besides..." But she couldn't say she trusted him; she didn't. Not wholly. He intrigued her, attracted her, and that had her questioning her sanity already. But trust was a luxury they couldn't afford.

"If we completely give in to fear, then fear wins, right? So far, he's made sense. And we don't have any better ideas."

"None that we haven't already tried," Brigit conceded.

"And if our ley line, his black dragon, really is big bad stuff, we may need a big bad magician to counter it, right?"

"Fighting fire with fire?" Brie shook her head.

Cy remembered the sense of heat, of power, that Benedict had exuded as he commanded the ghosts. "You've got *that* right."

Brigit hesitated, then sighed in unhappy defeat.

Mary laughed. Sylvie shared a grin with the younger woman before turning to include the others. "Can she ask about our guest mage now?"

At their nods, Mary fixed her gaze on the little white button. "Can the man Cy's got coming over help us?"

Cy watched the makeshift pendulum just as intensely, almost holding her breath. She felt a weight slide from her shoulders when it began to swing, to and fro, in a "yes" pattern.

"Is he dangerous?" asked Brigit. After the button stilled, Mary repeated the question. "Is he dangerous?"

Again, the pendulum signaled yes. So much for relief.

Mary asked, "Can we trust him?"

The button slowly began to move in small, lazy circles. Her gaze rose from it, disturbed. "Either the pendulum doesn't know, or our subconscious doesn't know, so it can't read the answer, *or* the man could go either way."

Or Mary Poitiers just didn't have the hang of dowsing.

Guilt bit at Cy for even thinking that—if they couldn't trust in each other's abilities, they really *were* in trouble.

A burst of thunder shook the house. Lightning flashed around the edges of the jalousies, and Mary turned toward the front door. "He's here."

A jarring two-rap knock echoed her words.

"Show-off." Sylvie's voice wavered. "Both of you."

Cy took a deep breath, grounded herself, and went to invite a mage of uncertain principles into her sanctuary. She felt more vulnerable than on a first date—and less than on a third.

He filled her doorway as he entered, then filled her dining room. Presence, thought Cy. The man had the kind of presence usually reserved for nobility or movie stars. Or bad guys.

The cape-shouldered trench coat didn't hurt. She extended a hungry hand toward the damp black leather. "May I?"

Drake Benedict, quietly surveying her home and her friends, finally turned his intense focus to her. Did his unhurried movements indicate reluctance, or disdain? He held her gaze for a moment— Oh, my. Maybe none-of-the-above. Maybe her attraction wasn't one-sided. That could make him even more dangerous.

He dipped his chin in assent and, with a single shrug, shed the coat. For a moment, as her hands closed around the cold leather and before his arms came free, she felt a tingling hint of the rush his touch—*their* touch—could trigger.

She hung the coat beside the door, and Benedict approached the table. He wore all black again; could he be in mourning? His sooty sweater—cashmere?—hugged the breadth of his chest and his regal shoulders. "I see you have started without me."

With his rich voice, his clipped words, Cy couldn't tell whether he was teasing or not. She doubted he was.

"I'm Mary Poitiers." The psychic stood and extended her hand, the soul of friendliness. Benedict eyed it, then took it.

"Charmed," he murmured, impressing Cy with how well he did good manners when he applied himself. She watched closely, but if Mary experienced an electric charge, as Cy had at his touch, the girl wore a better poker face than anyone had guessed.

Benedict also shook hands with the other two witches, nodding to Brie and acknowledging Sylvie with a curt "We met."

None of Cy's friends screamed, "Evil, begone!" That had to be a good sign, right? He might just be a surly good guy.

Cy wiped her tingling palm on her jeans, retrieved the map and joined the others at the table. "There are no maps of just Stagwater," she explained, almost defensive about their small town. "But I've got one of Slidell and the surrounding area."

"That should prove adequate." His gaze lingered on her as she spread the creased paper across the table, but his words belied any interest. Good or evil, he was no people person. But he'd come. That counted for something. She'd asked, and he'd come.

Sylvie lit a pillar candle in an iron stand, and moved it to the table, at the edge of the map. Brigit folded her arms. "So, Mr. Benedict, what are you hoping to do here?"

"As little as possible." As if battling some distraction, he shifted his attention to Mary and her button. "You are not using plastic, are you?"

"Mother-of-pearl. And the thread's cotton. All natural."

"Pass it over the area of Stagwater in slowly increasing circles. Feel for the evil. See where it leads you."

Mary blinked at him, surprised. "Me?"

He raised surprisingly expressive eyebrows. "I believe there is an appropriate adage regarding teaching a man to fish?"

"So he can feed himself for a lifetime," Cy put in, glad for the chance to smile. He *was* thinking of their good!

"I do not plan to be drafted again," he added pointedly.

Or maybe not.

Sylvie turned off the overhead light, so that only the golden pool of the candlelight battled the night's darkness. That, and the occasional flash of lightning through wooden slats.

The witches formed a circle around the oaken table, out of habit—but this time, a fifth magic user stood between Mary and Cypress. And Cy had invited him. Was the tingle at the back of her neck her usual magic feeling, or a warning? Or did it have more to do with other intriguing aspects of Benedict's nearness?

After taking a deep breath, like a diver, Mary extended her pendulum. The mother-of-pearl button seemed to move slightly. Did her hand twitch, or just follow its motion? Slowly. Slowly. Suddenly the button began to shudder at the end of its thread—and Mary dropped it. "There's something there!"

Then she winced and looked up. "Sorry. But that felt bad."

"Do it again." Benedict acknowledged Brigit's glare at that. "We are *looking* for something bad, are we not?"

Some of us more than others. But if Benedict really was bad news, wouldn't he be trying to hide it? Or had she taken a trip to Rationalization City?

Mary nudged the button toward clear ground with a finger. She glanced at her friends, then at the "expert," and tried again.

Candlelight danced with shadows, mingling and parting across the gridlines of the map. Cy tried to focus more on the map itself—and noticed that the area that had bothered Mary lay very close to Granny's house.

The button began to jerk on its string again, right there, like a hanged man. Mary bit her lower lip, but kept hold of it, kept moving it. In a moment, it stopped, so she drew it back until it started gyrating again. She continued, back and forth, until she found a direction that kept the button excited. It moved away from Granny's house, into the woods nearer town. When she reached the center of the wooded area, the button nearly leaped off its string. Her arm started to tremble.

Before anyone could stop him, Benedict's hand captured Mary's—and guided her pendulum away from its frenzied dance.

Mary's hazel eyes shone up at him with...gratitude? Brigit slid a supportive arm around the younger woman's waist.

Benedict, looking all the darker in the play of shadow and light, reached into his pocket and withdrew a fang-shaped bronze pendant on a silken string. He didn't take a deep breath to ready himself; composed as ever, he extended the pendulum over the map where Mary had been dowsing.

The bronze tooth began to sway, to undulate at the end of its tether. Now Benedict softly caught his breath. None of the other witches seemed to notice. But something was wrong.

His eyelids lowered to half-mast concentration. Mary had found something, sure enough. "You've got yourselves quite the dragon," he murmured coolly, "and it is very black. Very sour..."

He moved his hand in a circle over the map. His eyes narrowed further as the pendulum moved, stilled, moved.

Brigit's arm lowered from Mary's waist to take her hand instead, and she offered her other hand to Sylvie. Sylvie, in turn, found and held Cy's. Cy hardly noticed.

They were supposed to be looking for a line, right? As in the shortest distance between two points? But if she saw the pattern in the pendulum's movements that she thought she saw...

Something was *very* wrong.

The bronze tooth moved, stilled, moved, like metal over invisible lines of magnetism. Not just one line. *Lines.*

Suddenly she hoped Benedict *was* faking this, but she doubted it. As she leaned closer to him, to the map, her arm brushed his, and he stiffened. Power rushed through her shoulder, sent tremors of energy shivering through her.

She caught a breath, and saw Benedict's lips part, his eyes meet hers, at the same time. Then Mary whispered, "Oh, m'lady!"

Did she feel it, too? But then Cy saw how the others were staring at the map—and with good cause.

A blackness shadowed the paper beneath the pendulum, as if burning into the map. It even smelled like smoke, acrid and sour. At first only a splotch, the stain spread outward in three directions, browning and then blackening on its own, like some demonic Etch-a-Sketch.

"Someone mark it," hissed Benedict.

Sylvie released Cy's hand—and the stain on the map began fading to gray. The stench that burned her throat lingered.

Benedict's arm trembled slightly against Cy's shoulder. Control, she realized, noting how he'd set his raised jaw. He was trying to control whatever was happening—and he wasn't sure he could. That scared her far more than he ever had. She slid her hand into his, savoring the continued diz-

zying rush of contact. His fingers tightened almost painfully around hers.

"Now!" he commanded, his voice hushed and sharp.

"Here!" Carefully, as if the darkness might seep up the
Bic's barrel, Sylvie drew sweeping lines to trace the path of
the fading darkness. Then she stepped clear.

Benedict stepped back, as well, drawing Cypress with
him. Mary and Brigit followed their example.

Then Brigit slapped on the overhead light.

The map looked as mundane as ever—except for three
ballpoint lines that intersected in the woods near Granny's
place. But the sulfurous smell and the charge of magic lingered in the air.

"We didn't imagine that." Sylvie said it defensively, as if
someone would accuse otherwise.

Brigit agreed, "Uh-uh."

Cy understood—she'd felt the same way the other night.
Magic wasn't supposed to work like this! At least not the
magic *they* practiced. What kind of magic was Drake Benedict using?

Whatever it was, his belated withdrawal of his hand from
hers stopped Cy's infusion of it. She searched his aloof expression while Mary asked, "Does that always happen?"

Benedict returned Cy's questioning gaze when he said,
softly, "No. That does not always happen."

Brie's eyes flashed dangerously. "So why did it?"

"What does it mean?" asked Sylvie.

Drake Benedict just stood there, silent, looking mysterious and unfairly handsome and dark—yet pale at the same
time. Cy grabbed a chair from the edge of the room and
pulled it over to her guest before he could blow his macho
image by passing out. He quirked an eyebrow at her, as if
amused by her misplaced concern; okay, so he never passed
out. But he did sit.

Mary sank onto a chair, as well. Arcane power cost physical energy—apparently that was one rule of magic that
didn't change for Drake Benedict. So maybe he was enough

like one of them to be trusted, after all, no matter how reserved or remote.

Cy hoped it was true. Because whatever these ley lines
were doing, they didn't look like something the circle could
easily counter on their own.

Their little circle had no hope of countering three black
dragons on their own. Not that it was Drake's concern, of
course. But as he watched Cypress Bernard and Sylvie Garner fetch cider and muffins from the kitchen, he did feel a
twinge of…sympathy? They appeared to be capable enough
magic users, especially together. Each provided her own
cornerstone to the refreshingly pure force of their group
strength. Bernard seemed to anchor them with an earthy
practicality, just as her touch had anchored and strengthened him while he dowsed. He had never seen the results of
a dowsing manifest visually before. He could grow accustomed, addicted, to such power.

Exactly the reason he should not have come in the first
place. Exactly why he planned to leave, as soon as he told
them what they must know.

The muffin, however, was delicious. The company annoyed him very little. Even the call of the evil—or evils—felt
diffused within the comforting wards of Bernard's quaint
home.

"You are not dealing with a mere line," he told them,
some of his father's and uncle's teaching tone to his voice.

"We're dealing with three," guessed Bernard, drawing his
gaze yet again. She wore an ankh around her graceful neck.
With her jeans, oversize sweater and big, floppy socks, she
rather resembled a particularly casual priestess of Isis.

Finish the job and go. "All of which meet at a nexus."

"Which makes it worse." Mary, the little blond dowser,
pulled her legs up into full lotus, as if her feet were in danger.

They did insist on their value labels, didn't they? As did
most fanatics. "Which makes it more powerful, in any case.

It gives the negativity more routes by which to do damage.''

"What kind of damage?" Bernard sat nearest him.

"You already know that it is drawing other negative phenomena to it. That, however, is only a side effect of the energy's corruption. It also tends to taint the atmosphere around it, and the people exposed, not unlike radiation poisoning. It could cause depression, nightmares, chronic illness—"

"It runs through my granny's house. And she's got pneumonia." He wished Bernard would not look at him as if he would do something about that. He was tempted to say, *Then she should not have built atop a ley line, should she?*

Instead, he said, "You had best check your own homes, as well." That bought him some time to sip cider and wonder at his uncharacteristic tact, while the witches double-checked the map.

Sure enough, the second line cut through something the witches called the Fouchard house, on an eventual interception course with Brigit Peabody's home. The third lurked dangerously close to this house, Bernard's.

"Which is way too much of a coincidence," she decided.

"There's no such thing," murmured Mary Poitiers, glancing toward the window, as if she would see a dragon peering back through the blinds.

"Sensitives often choose power spots to live, without realizing they do so," he explained. "At the time you chose your homes, the energy was likely positive. Since then, something has happened to reverse the polarity."

Bernard prompted him: "Like?"

"Like a road being put in, or power lines—of the mundane type. Or construction."

"So what do we do?" Her rich, dark eyes searched his.

"Relocate."

She smiled an attractive smile. Then, when she saw that he was serious, she frowned. "Don't you joke about this."

"I am not joking. If I were you, I would likely move."

"And leave everyone else in town to fend for themselves? We're the only magic users around. Who else could help them?"

Some other fool—or they could relocate, as well. But he had seen this kind of determination before; Bernard and her friends flattered themselves that they could save the world, one piece at a time, no matter the cost. Their conceit and foolishness angered him—he had seen the cost before, too. All the more reason not to pursue his unusual attraction to Bernard. He could grow dependent on something good as easily as on something evil.

It was *definitely* time for him to finish and leave.

"Your only other option is to contain the negative energy—damage control—and then to look for the source on the off chance that you might fix whatever went wrong. To contain it, find some iron stakes, such as those used on railroads. Go to the areas on the map where the lines stop, and dowse to find exactly where the energy turns." He looked at Mary. "Whatever your pendulum is doing at one point, it will reverse at the other. Do you understand?"

Mary nodded earnestly.

"Drive the stake into the earth, as far as possible, exactly where the energy changes. If all goes well, that will reverse the polarity and keep your evil from spreading. It might even turn the energy back." *But do not hold your breath.*

Bernard cocked an eyebrow. "And if all doesn't go well?"

"Then you return and try again. Always during the day, so that you will have less trouble with anything attracted to the dragons—you have encountered some of the creatures it has drawn, but perhaps not the worst. The energy put out by the lines, positive or negative, is hardly sentient. Use that to your advantage." He stood, but he could tell they were not satisfied. Or confident. "If you are lucky, it will merely exhaust you, perhaps make you grumpy, give you a headache, temporarily weaken your immune system. A good cleansing when you get home should take care of that.

Again, think of it as a form of low-level radiation. Not recommended for heart patients, pregnant women or nursing mothers—" he had noticed baby pictures by a purse "—but otherwise safe in small doses. Now, if that is all?"

But the witches were not even looking at him anymore. They were exchanging stricken glances. Unexpected envy of their bond almost overrode his curiosity, but neither was his concern. He should snatch his coat and leave. But for some reason—perhaps the same curiosity that had damned his father—Drake hesitated.

"That means I can't go," said Brigit Peabody.

"Or me," said Sylvie, surprising him—her airy dress quite disguised her condition. Then she further surprised him. "Or Mary."

"Mary?" Cypress and Brigit stared at the blond witch.

She smiled a sickly smile. "Maybe. The pendulum said I am, and it feels right, because I dreamed . . . But I'll take a test, to be sure. Cy can't do it alone."

Two of the four pregnant, and another nursing? What amazing irony. And time to leave now. Past time.

"*Can* I do it alone?" asked Bernard, nailing him with those rich eyes of hers. She knew he never lied. And *she*, as far as he could tell, had never dowsed.

"Not likely." He strode over to the coatrack, reclaiming his trench coat. He could let himself out.

She was on her feet and after him in a heartbeat. "But you could, couldn't you?"

"I would not, even if I lived here. It is not my problem."

"Well, it's mine, and I'm asking. *Could* you?"

He shrugged into his coat before meeting her expectant stare. "Probably. Were it my business. Which it is not."

She leaned against the doorjamb so that he could not leave without pushing past her. "Could we do it together?"

He imagined she must work in sales. "Hypothetically?"

She nodded. Obviously she did not understand what happened between them as he did. She did not realize that together they had abilities he had only imagined. He hoped she never would.

"Absolutely," he snapped. "But ability does not imply responsibility. I told you in New Orleans that I prefer to remain neutral."

"Then why—?" Bernard stopped abruptly and glanced into the dining room, where the rest of her circle watched. "Would y'all excuse us for a minute?"

Mary Poitiers smiled apologetically, found some dishes and hurried them into the kitchen, followed by Sylvie Garner. Brigit Peabody went only as far as the doorway to the kitchen, then folded her arms, like a bodyguard. "I'm not listening."

Bernard sniffed annoyance, but turned back to him. "Then why did you help us before, Switzerland?"

This was growing wearisome. No, they had passed wearisome long ago, in the courtyard outside his flat. "Partly because you held the magistra's marker—" He raised a hand to silence her when she opened her mouth, and lowered his voice. "No, I am not the—not *a*—magister. My mother was. And, as debts can be hereditary, I felt it worthwhile to clear it."

Then he waited for her to ask what his mother would think of him right now. She did not. She frowned. She looked as if she wanted to. But she apparently had her own brand of ethics.

His mother truly *would* be disappointed. His father, however, would heartily approve—which suddenly presented a compelling excuse for Drake to give in. Damn! The point of remaining neutral was to avoid this Ping-Ponging from camp to camp. Not choosing good was *not* the same thing as choosing evil. He *knew* that. Yet . . .

"And partly?" Bernard asked, head cocked, expression determined but patient. At least she meant to hear him out.

He blinked at her. She still smelled of mint and rosemary.

She straightened out of his way. "You said you agreed partly because of the marker. What's the other partly?"

He let his gaze linger on her a moment longer, then shook his head, opened the door, stepped into the rain—and into the call of the evil. Even knowing now that he felt the mingling of many lesser voices, not a single powerful entity, did not diminish its strength over his own bad blood. It beckoned to his father's legacy, louder and stronger and even more distracting for being so close, just beyond the line of trees.

The other partly. He had wanted some peace.

"Yes." He turned on the wet stoop to face Bernard's stubborn persistence. "I will help you. Tomorrow morning. Eight o'clock."

She blinked, taken off guard, then said, "My mother's visiting for brunch. Can we start at noon?"

He nodded. Yes. Fine. Noon. His very decision seemed to push the buzz of the evil farther from his mind, to clear him to an awareness of the cold rain on his hair and face, the patter of it in the yard at his back, the woman who stood before him.

"Wait here a sec!" She vanished from the doorway for perhaps a five-count, then skidded back on her socked feet and pressed something—surely not money!—into his hand. Her energy combined with his own in a way he found almost familiar, rushing through him like a caffeine fix. He rarely drank caffeine.

"So what about the other partly?" she asked again.

"None of your business," he told her, and tried to disengage his hand. Instead of taking offense, she grinned.

"Thank you for helping us, Drake Benedict," she told him, and leaned forward into the rain and kissed his cheek, near the corner of his mouth. The fragrance of her hair and skin mingled with the softness of her lips and the warmth of her energy, the brush of her breath. It took all his will to keep from dipping his head, turning the kiss into something more hungry, more greedy, far less innocent. In only a moment, she had stepped back and released his hand, staring. Had she felt overwhelmed, as well? Served her right.

He saw that she'd given him his mother's seal, clearing their account.

Drawing self-control around him like a cloak, he turned and slogged across her wet lawn toward his car, the smell of the rain fading with each step he took away from her house, his sense of annoyance rising proportionally.

That had been a mistake. All of it. But at least, perhaps, between the two of them, they *could* silence the evil.

Hopefully they wouldn't create other monsters to take its place.

Cypress shut the door, locked it, and closed her eyes for a moment, glad to have acted on impulse. His expensive after-shave had smelled good; his sculpted, clean-shaven cheek had sent a shiver of power into her lips.

And he'd agreed to help them. To help her.

She turned back to the dining room—and to her friends' shocked surprise. "It's going to be fine," she assured them. "I won't be penning the dragons alone. Drake's going to help."

"The two of you alone?" asked Mary.

Cy nodded. "He's okay. I'm really pretty sure of it."

Brigit said, "And we're supposed to find that comforting."

Oh. Cypress guessed she had a point, at that.

CHAPTER FOUR

Cy felt drained, exhausted, as if a psychic vampire had slowly been sucking out every last bit of energy she had.

Her fault. She *knew* she shouldn't let her mother get to her like this. But driving back home from New Orleans, after brunch with her visiting mother, she wondered if she even *cared* if Drake Benedict turned out to be a practitioner of evil arts.

Maybe he would feed her to one of his "dragons" and put her out of her misery.

"Drake," Mama had repeated over *beignets* and strawberries, after wheedling information about Cy's appointment. "That name does *not* sound black." She'd had no idea of the metaphorical irony of her statement. Cy was already beyond appreciating it.

"That's because he's white, Mama. And English."

And Mama had made that face of hers, fretting that Cy was making the same "mistakes" she had. Cy's protests that she wasn't seeing Benedict romantically and that this wasn't the sixties didn't comfort Rose Vega Bernard Washington.

"I'm only telling you this for your own good, honey. As far as society is concerned, you're black."

"Mama, society usually thinks I'm Hispanic, Indian or Middle Eastern." Cy had stabbed an innocent strawberry. "You and Dad had problems, but color wasn't the big one."

Mama thought that she'd get hurt anyway.

Which made Cy crazier than anything else, she decided, pulling into her driveway. It was one thing for someone to care about her, another for that person to try to control her as a form of caring. She loved her mother. Really she did.

But thank goodness Mama lived in the D.C. area, and not around here.

If she heard the words "for your own good" one more time, she was going to puke.

With barely ten minutes before Benedict's arrival, she decided to leave her hair in its beaded braids, but she ditched her mud cloth caftan and changed into clean jeans and a pressed oxford shirt. Then she reconsidered—*was* she trying to dress white now, as surely as she'd dressed black for her mother? She traded the button-down shirt for a khaki pullover.

Compromise—that was her. A living, breathing compromise. Ironic to be working with a mage who could go either way himself.

She heard Benedict's car in the driveway and took a moment to breathe deeply and ground herself, visualizing her feet growing roots into the cold earth, gaining sustenance, like the rest of nature. At least the subject of magic hadn't come up, even when she dropped Mama off at Granny's care home. There was one area where Mama wished Cy *had* ignored her heritage.

Well, social worker Mama can save the world her way, and I'll save it mine.

She opened her front door to reveal a more casual Drake Benedict, in black jeans, a black sweatshirt and boots.

"The traditional robes would likely get tangled in the underbrush," he said pointedly, and she realized she'd been staring at him, there on the front stoop.

"Sorry. I—" She stopped, considered grounding herself again, noted his impatient stance and decided not to. "Do you want me to drive?"

He turned away, and headed back down the drive. "Navigate. You know the town better than I."

Right. Navigate. With an attitude like that, maybe he *was* evil. "I've got to get the map!" she said quickly, and he stopped dead, as if she'd insulted him. Or as if her sheer idiocy had insulted him.

She'd left the map in the oversize pocket of her insulated vest, which she took along for warmth. By the time she got back out to the car, she had control of her temper. She hoped. She wasn't going to transfer her anger at her mother, or at herself, onto Drake Benedict. He was doing her and Stagwater a favor. He'd even changed his schedule to accommodate hers. Hoping he'd be nice about it was probably asking way too much.

And if he didn't stop treating her like peasant scum, she'd spit in his car.

Which would be a shame—she could love this car. Shutting the door closed the rest of the world out, leaving her alone with Benedict in climate-controlled luxury. The shoulder strap glided into place. She leaned her head back and breathed in the scent of leather, relaxing for maybe the first time this morning.

Then she opened her eyes, because the car wasn't moving yet.

Benedict gazed at her, searching her face—but clinically, which disappointed her somehow. "Are you quite certain you're up to this?" he asked, almost in challenge.

"Of course I'm up to it."

His remote expression didn't change.

"I've got to be up to it. It has to be done, right?"

He tipped his head as if to say *whatever,* and, sliding the gearshift into reverse, looked over his shoulder. "I should think your priorities would include surviving the process."

She froze in the middle of fastening her lap belt. "I thought you said it wasn't dangerous."

"I also said it is draining. You're already drained. Left, or right?" Cy pointed. Benedict made the turn.

She liked watching him handle the car, even if she didn't like what he said while he did.

"I'll be fine. I'm just overwhelmed by my mother."

He carefully said nothing; probably so as not to encourage her to unload any more such tidbits about her personal life.

Tough. It was the next best thing to spitting. "She's a social worker. She thinks she has to help everyone, even those of us who don't need it."

The look Benedict tossed her was blatantly incredulous, but all he said was "How soon do I turn?"

"About two miles. Why are you smirking?"

"I've a sudden vision of acorns and trees."

And how far one fell from the other? "I am *not* just like her." After a few minutes more, she said, "Turn right here."

He turned, hands skimming confidently over the wheel and downshifting with ease. He had control of the car as surely as he had control of his other abilities.

And he looked just about as out of place next to her as the Lexus did driving down the shell-and-dirt road.

"Refresh my memory." He sounded almost amused. "Why are we out here?"

"To keep the negative energy from spreading." And to help the town. Mmm-hmm. She got it. "This is different. We're the only ones who *can* do this. That makes it our responsibility."

"Who is to say it must be done?"

"If it isn't, everything will just get worse. There'll be more evil, more fear. Folks could die."

The look he slanted toward her spoke volumes.

He couldn't mean it. "You're not convinced, are you?"

"People," he declared, "will die anyway. The more clever and able townspeople will leave while they can. Those who do not or cannot will suffer the consequences."

"That is truly cold-blooded," she told him, and he stomped on the brakes. Her seat belt kept her from jerking forward, but she grabbed at the dashboard anyway. Maybe he didn't like being called cold-blooded?

Should have thought of that before he put his heart on ice.

He didn't look angry, though. No angrier than usual, anyhow. He merely looked...aware. Sensing.

"That," he returned quietly, distractedly, "is neutrality." And he put the car in reverse, backed up several feet, and stopped again. Killed the engine. He'd found the closest parking spot to the first ley line of the three.

She didn't move to get out. "So what are you doing here?"

He considered that. "Flying in the face of my better judgment." And he got out of the car.

The second Cy opened her door, letting the rest of the world in, she felt it. Something wrong, twisted. She knew these woods—they were her church, her religion—and her usual five senses gave the all clear. Tall, top-heavy pines, maybe wider than the norm, crowded out the light of the overcast sky. The humid chill magnified the smell of dirt and decay and standing water, all as normal. Only the occasional chirp, chitter or cry of an animal or bird seemed out of place against a deeper stillness. But Granny had helped her develop a few extra senses, which warned that she stood on the edge of something dark, powerful—and magic. But not her kind of magic. And not Mother Nature's.

She pointed in the direction of the wrongness. "It's that way, isn't it?"

Drake Benedict stared into the depth of the woods, as if he saw something. Then he blinked, shook off the distraction and met her gaze. "Yes," he agreed, opening the trunk. "That way."

She did truly appreciate him flying in the face of his better judgment and accompanying her. Too bad the man had such lousy personal ethics, she thought, admiring the back pockets of his jeans as he retrieved a practical leather backpack. If she could trust him, she would find him truly attractive.

But he did have lousy ethics—or he sure did pretend to.

And he didn't seem to care much for her, either.

They hiked into the tangled, twisted snarl of nature that made up the so-called forest primeval, Bernard leading the way. Drake told himself that, by helping her and her town, he was merely buying himself some peace.

With the help of her compass and a walking odometer, they located the general location of the first soured ley line, the first of their three "black dragons." He told himself that, left to herself, the earth witch would merely botch this. Then, when he could no longer stand the draw of accumulated evil, he would either have to move or would find himself cleaning up her mess.

He really did have just cause for being here.

He used the pendulum that had belonged to his father and grandfather to sense where the energy beneath this particular tangle of woods changed. They definitely stood atop a ley line; he could feel the not-quite-dormant power flowing deep under his feet, as surely as he could feel the not-quite-dormant abilities of his father thick in his blood. The brass weight swung back and forth, north and south. Watching it, sensing it, he took a careful step forward, then another—

"Poison ivy," warned Bernard, and he stepped more carefully. Perhaps she would not have botched things so badly, after all. She knew her native woods better than he. Anyone with the right connection to the ebb and flow of earth energy could dowse.

But that left him with fewer pretexts for being here.

The pendulum began to swing east and west.

He repeated the process. He controlled his breathing, his heartbeat and, of course, the muscles in his hand, to be sure that nothing moved the pendulum but the magic his father had taught him, used for his mother's purposes. He crouched, hoping any snakes residing in the snarl of brown vines would make way for him, and tried yet again to be certain. Then he breathed the words: "Right *there.*"

As if nonsentient energy would hear a shout.

Bernard placed the iron stake, an old railroad tie, against the needle-covered spot he indicated. With four solid blows, she drove the stake deeply into the ground, murmuring, "By the powers of earth—" *pound* "—air—" *pound* "—fire—" *pound* "—and water—" *pound* "—we contain the progression of this evil and bid it begone."

Mutual power lit the air for a moment, then faded.

He bent closer to the stake—to her—and suspended the pendulum over the affected spot. It swung north-south, indicating positive energy, several inches past the stake, before twitching into an east-west swing. The negative energy had recoiled from the iron, just as it should.

He almost smiled—but to smile would indicate relief, as if failure had been an option. Bernard grinned at him, though, as he straightened. It took surprising effort to ignore that. The distant, wintry daylight, and her presence, muffled the incessant call of evil, even this close to the source. The lure of a more earthly awareness, of the drone and perfume of the chill woods, strengthened in her presence. Even without touching—and he was quite careful not to touch—Cypress Bernard did something to him.

That was *not,* however, the reason he had come. In fact—

He paced past the metal spike, across the invisible line that marked the affected area of the woods. He closed his eyes, tried to sense beneath his feet the evil that had called him.

He could not. He sensed the signature of evil, but no presence. The channel of energy that ran under him felt tainted, nothing more, just as a black dragon should.

"Drake?"

He opened his eyes, and for a moment he thought he saw something move deeper in the woods, toward the nexus. Then he blinked, and the movement had vanished. A snake, perhaps?

"Drake?"

He glanced over his shoulder. "What?" But his annoyance faded at the sight of Bernard, her arms folded and her hips shot. She fit these woods, equal parts light and dark, equal parts wild and tame. He did not find her beautiful . . . but handsome? Yes. Stronger than beautiful. Earthier than merely beautiful.

And not why he had come at all.

"You are *truly* making me nervous, standing over there," she told him. And, though he had seen her truly nervous, fighting off ghosts behind her grandmother's home, he believed her.

He had protected her, that night. It had set an unfortunate precedent. "I told you before, ley lines are not sentient. The ground will not cave in beneath me. Nothing shall slither out and grab me. Depress me, perhaps. Attack me, hardly."

"Fine. You ain't 'fraid of no stinking ley lines. It's still making me nervous."

So he came back to her, stepping clear of the affected ground where the black dragon dwelled—but only because they had work to finish, and because he already felt somewhat drained. If Bernard was smart, she cared about his safety for only that reason. Especially as tired as she looked. Most likely she would not finish on her own.

But the way she grinned at him when she said, "Thanks," intimated that, though she might be competent, determined and, yes, attractive, the witch was not smart at all.

That was not, he reminded himself, his problem.

He extended an arm in the old-fashioned after-you gesture, both because he had been raised to be a gentleman and because she knew the way out better than he. But as she began the trek back toward the dirt road, and the car, he thought he felt something watching....

He spun, peered into the tangled depths of the woods. He saw nothing. That fact conformed with his theory of the ley lines. He ought *not* to see anything, especially in the daylight.

But a heightened awareness deep in his blood, his soul, argued that something remained to be seen, nevertheless. Something powerful. Something dangerous. Something... sentient?

Perhaps one of Stagwater's visiting goblins, attracted by the ley lines' magnetism, just as he was. But perhaps not.

He could not fully trust his soul—or his blood.

* * *

Their second dragon of the afternoon lay a good half mile past Granny's shack.

"I bet this is what killed her garden and made her sick." Cypress stepped on the thickest part of a snarl of black-berry vines to hold them down, so that Drake could cross them without getting ensnared. After all, briars, brambles and bushes like these had helped the Americans win the Battle of New Orleans—against the British. She smiled at that thought.

"A likely possibility." He checked his compass, then continued through the woods. She glanced to their right, where the ley line paralleled their path. She didn't want to accidentally step on the infested ground, despite Drake's assurances of safety.

In fact, she walked a little closer to him. "Did you know that a local girl disappeared earlier this week?"

He glanced back at her. "A child?"

That struck her as odd, considering his Machiavellian survival-of-the-fittest theories. "Does it matter? Isn't your creed that if the baby wildebeest can't keep up with the pack, it deserves to get torn to shreds by the hyenas?"

"Adults have more say in what happens to them," he pointed out. "For example, if I were to reveal my true nature as that of a murderer, and to take your life here in these woods, you would die knowing that, by following me here, you had contributed to your own death. Particularly annoying, do you not agree?"

Talk about working to keep an image! "Like you could take me," she said with a laugh, earning herself a dry stare. "Fat chance. And that wouldn't make the murder any less your fault."

"Nor would my culpability make you any less dead." Okay, so he had a point. "Whether you had come willingly or not, though, might make a difference in how much power I gained through your killing. Was the missing girl a child?"

His meaning sank in, and she stopped dead. He'd finally managed to shock her. "Hold up. You're talking killing for power? Human *sacrifice?*"

He waited calmly for her answer.

What if it really wasn't an image?

Oh, no. She could be friendly with and attracted to a man with borderline ethics, but human sacrifice was way out. "You tell me right here and right now. How do you know what kind of victim would create what kind of power?"

It occurred to her that she *had* followed him out here. And, yes, the thought was hugely annoying.

"How else would I know such things?" He hissed the question, leaning close enough for her to smell his after-shave, and then he glanced at the odometer in her hand. Straightening, he smiled—one of the first honest, teeth-and-all smiles she'd seen on the man—and continued in the direction he'd been walking. "I have heard rumors and read books, of course. Was the missing girl—"

"No, she was an adult." Frowning, she followed him again—more warily this time. She sure *hoped* he couldn't take her. She also hoped he hadn't been lying about always telling the truth. "Friends say she'd been jilted. She might have run off."

"Or one of your local monsters may have dined on her, is that your worry?"

"Mmm-hmm. The thought had occurred to my friends and me."

"If she came unwillingly, she is merely a victim. However, if she was too innocent or stupid to guard herself sufficiently, then she might be deemed a willing sacrifice, and whatever took her is now the stronger for it." And he kept on hiking through the woods. "Were I you, I would hope that she 'ran off.'"

"What if she didn't?"

He didn't respond at first. He toted the iron stakes and mallet without complaint, and he hadn't once griped about the stickers or bugs. And even if he turned out to be evil, he sure wasn't evil to look at—especially in jeans. But she had known better traveling companions, as far as conversation went.

"Drake? What if—?"

When finally he glanced back at her, he looked particularly ornery. "If you shall need strength before we are done, please be forthright and ask. I am hardly susceptible to draining tactics."

"*What?*" Where had *that* come from?

"You are looking for verbal reassurance from me, when you must realize I have no more idea what happened to the missing woman than do you. I can only assume it is comfort and strength that you actually want."

At least she didn't have to appear needy *and* stupid; she knew what he meant. Some folks naturally gravitated to people with stronger personalities, more energy, more love of life... and somehow leeched them dry of it. She had met people like that herself. On a bad day, her mother fit the description.

"First of all, if I wanted comfort, you'd be *last* on my list. And second, don't you *dare* call me a psychic vampire!"

He checked his compass. "Then stop acting like one."

"I'm just asking questions. You're the man who set yourself up as the expert."

"No." He glanced at her odometer. "You came to me expecting an expert. It was only your good fortune that I am particularly well trained."

And he opened his hand, the bronze pendulum dangling from a long cord around his middle finger. Had he been carrying it all the time, or was this a sleight of hand?

Magic really did appear to work differently for him.

He handed her his pack and walked to the right, pacing out the ley line, just as he had earlier this afternoon. She dug out a second stake, and the mallet, and put down the bag. This stake felt heavier; she really was tuckered out.

But not enough to try to suck strength out of Drake Benedict. She was not, and never would be, a needy person.

The pendulum swung back and forth as he walked, then changed direction so suddenly it looked like special effects. He paced that stretch of ground again, with the same results. From what she could tell, ley lines were somewhere between ten and twelve feet across—and extended indefinitely, like an ancient net of energy woven beneath the earth's crust. But from their soured nexus, the arms of the black dragons only appeared to reach anywhere from two to four miles, so far.

She hoped this stopped them.

"Here." He pinpointed the exact spot, and she knelt beside him, placed the iron stake against the ground—and nearly smashed her hand with the mallet when she got to "air" in her litany of elements.

"Tired?" The word held more mockery than concern. Drake slid his hand over hers, just long enough to take the mallet from her; she barely had a chance to enjoy the inevitable tingle before it ended.

But was it the tingle she enjoyed, or that sensation of shared energy? Could she truly want his power, after all?

With three strong strokes—"By the power of the sun, moon, and stars"—he buried the stake, set the sun-filtered air tingling with magic, and contained the stream. As he'd promised he would, he was avoiding his fancier sorcery around her. He wasn't all bad.

"A mite tired," she admitted reluctantly, backing away from the spot where she knew the negative energy still lurked, trapped. They were spending a lot of time near spoiled ley lines today. That, and a morning with Mama, would drain anyone.

She watched him dowse the area again. The pendulum swung one way and then, several inches past the spike, another.

Damn, but the man was competent—and maybe too insightful.

"If I *was* tapping into your energy, I apologize," she said stiffly. "I'll try to stop. I didn't mean to."

"Few people do." Ignoring her annoyed snort, he shoul-dered his pack and gave her that gallant after-you gesture. "It is one of the many reasons I prefer solitude. I must constantly guard against the psychic neediness of others."

Was this guy going for the warm-and-fuzzy award, or what? She trudged ahead. "But you offered to spare some energy for *me*."

"Toward our mutual success, yes," he said behind her.

"So that means you do have the energy to spare."

"If I so wish."

"Just out of curiosity, if these unwashed masses are so needy and you've got energy to spare, why not share some of it?"

"As I am sure you would and do share of yourself." His observation didn't sound flattering.

"At least I try."

"And I do not. It is hardly my place, merely for being the stronger, to protect the weak."

"Sure it is." She wished that, in heading back toward the car, they weren't still paralleling the tainted length of the ley line. Pushing through vines and stickers, past branches of scrub and over rotting, fallen trees, took its toll even on na-ture lovers. "People in cars are supposed to stop for pedes-trians. Men used to say women and children first. Now maybe it's just children first, but—"

His footsteps had stopped. She looked back. He'd lagged behind to stare through the trees toward their left. Toward the ley line.

She trudged back. "Why do you keep doing that?"

"Do you see something?" he returned, hushed.

Maybe he was trying to scare her, like with his "suppos-ing I was a murderer" speech. If so, it was starting to work. She scanned the tangled labyrinth of trees, vines, scrub, shadows. But she didn't see anything, except . . .

She stepped closer, troubled. "Those trees are dead."

"Really." His voice sounded hollow, as if that weren't what he'd meant, but it had *her* attention. She looked at one of the pines beside her, not even over the ley line, and immediately noticed a pitch tube—a small hole, secreting hardened amber resin. Then another. Reddish boring dust sprinkled the crevices of the naturally gray bark—a sign of southern pine beetles.

She looked up, and immediately spotted a swollen gall on the branches. When she turned slowly, examining the other trees around her, she saw more of them. Sure, Benedict kept her distracted, but how could she have missed rust disease?

She wasn't a clairvoyant, but she guessed what she'd see, looking down at the tree's root collar. She looked anyway. Sure enough, when she kicked some of the pine straw away, she recognized the leathery brown conks that indicated root rot.

The trees over the ley line were even worse off, now that she thought to look up high enough to see what was left of the needles—brown, yellow, shortened, sparse, and gone.

"These trees have had everything thrown at them except a rain of frogs and a plague of locusts," she murmured, breaking a chunk of bark off one of the still-living trees.

Definite pine-beetle activity. Poor trees.

How toxic was the energy exuded by the subterranean ley lines, to be destroying not only the trees above it, but a whole pine forest? If she remembered her granny right, root rot shouldn't bother flatwoods at all; only better-drained or overthinned stands. These woods hadn't been harvested during Cy's memory, and she'd lived around here her whole life.

In fact, natural law said hardwoods should be growing in—pushing out the pines—by now. So where were the oaks, the elms?

Welcome warmth shivered down her spine when Drake laid a hand on her shoulder. She glanced up into his sculpted, remote face and wondered if he meant the gesture for unlikely comfort, or to hurry her up? His stony expression didn't give enough away, and his depthless eyes tried to say too much.

He resented helping her and her town, but he helped anyhow. She couldn't trust him. But she surely did need him.

She asked, whispered, "Why *our* woods?"

"Why," he murmured back, "are you asking me?"

But they both knew why. For maybe the first time in her life, she'd run into something she wasn't sure she could fix. "Maybe," she told him steadily, "I just want reassurance."

And, dipping his head in assent, Drake Benedict kissed her.

CHAPTER FIVE

He didn't kiss evil, either.

The distance Drake Benedict had held between them melted away with the touch of his breath, then his lips. As if compelled, she lifted her hand to the softness of his hair. Warmth spilled from him to her, and strength, and need, and—

And magic. Beyond the rich smell of him, and the supple taste of him, flowed the heavy undercurrent of a magic she'd never known, a magic she very much wanted.

She tasted him, tasted his powers—and then he was straightening. He stared at her, his regal face blank, almost forlorn. Then, with a breath and a blink, he became lord of the manor once more. His chin rose, as did his eyebrows, the second in an amused question. "Better?"

Her fingers slid free of his hair, of the last proof that he possessed any softness after all; her hand fell from his shoulder. "Excuse me?"

"More fit, I hope."

She *did* feel stronger, not so shaky. A minute ago, she'd been bone-tired. Now... Was *that* what this had been about? "You gave me *strength?*"

"We have still a third channel to contain," he noted casually, and shouldered the pack, continuing toward the car.

He'd only kissed her to give her strength? She'd thought... Well, she *hadn't* thought, she'd responded. But one of the things she'd responded to was the sudden suspicion that maybe, just maybe, Mr. Powerful Wizard saw something in her that attracted him. Something that maybe *he* needed from *her,* instead of vice versa.

Maybe next time she *should* think. As little as she and Drake Benedict knew one another, they had no business kissing, in the woods or anywhere else. And he had less than no business using his lips to do magic on her...so to speak.

"I don't remember asking!" Yes, she'd asked for reassurance, but that wasn't the same thing. "And if I had, I'm sure you've got other ways of passing along a little juju juice."

He didn't answer, just kept walking. She didn't dismiss so easily. She caught up with him, then passed him and stopped in his path, which stopped him, too—unless he wanted to wade through a briar patch.

His squared, impassive face held her at such a distance, she ought to have chosen a long-distance service just to talk to him. If this was the face he presented to most folks, no wonder he had the social skills of a surly porcupine.

"What game are you playing, anyway, Benedict?"

He didn't deign to look at her. "I prefer not to play games."

Aha—but he didn't say he *didn't* play games. She was learning to read this wizard, whether he wanted her to or not.

"Mmm-hmm. And damned if you haven't found yourself playing one anyway. You know as well as I do that something happens whenever we touch, even by accident. You could have just held my hand, or touched my face like some Vulcan mind-meld. The only reason I can see for you kissing me..."

Was the reason she'd responded to when their lips met.

"First of all, Benedict, if I want your help, I'll ask."

He folded his arms. "I shall endeavor to remember that."

Poor porcupine. Darned if she hadn't stopped thinking again. His hair had fallen boyishly over his high forehead. His jaw seemed clenched, as if he were carefully reestablishing control of himself. Lonely porcupine.

Maybe thinking was overrated. "Second of all, if you want to kiss me, don't hide behind your magic. Just kiss me."

And his gaze dipped to hers, startled.

She stepped closer, spread a hand against his black-fleeced chest. A tingling rush flowed over her at the contact, and her lips parted to savor it.

So did his.

A shame for them to waste parted lips. She leaned closer to him; he met her halfway.

This kiss could have blown fuses and started earthquakes.

Cy would have reminded him not to use magic, but the mingling of their energies felt too good for her to protest. The taste of his mouth, his tongue, intertwined with a sparkling sensation behind her eyes. The rasp of his arms enfolding her, the feeling of his hands sliding, spread across her back, mixed with a shivery, unearthly flare up her spine. They drew back long enough to gasp a breath, to meet one another's clouded, confused gazes, before a second kiss sent energy crackling through every vein, every bone. She breathed him in as if he were nitrous oxide, buried her fingers in his silky hair, her palms cupping his cheeks. It was like holding...

Like holding darkness, light, the secret of life.

Which made her hands feel all the more empty when he wrenched himself away. "No!"

She let him go. Her body ached, despite the residual thrumming of power through her marrow, despite feeling stronger than she had when she left to meet her mother this morning. But no meant no, right?

She watched him clench his own hands, watched his eyes close, his jaw tighten, his whole body shudder once...

Did their embrace affect him the same way?

...and then his eyes opened, carefully devoid of heat, of vulnerability... of interest.

"Do not," he said coldly, "do that again."

And he stepped around her and continued toward the car.

Torn between apologizing and demanding an apology, she followed him. Obviously he wasn't— Well, no, the man *was* interested. But obviously he had a problem with that. It wouldn't be the first time someone had been attracted to her and upset by that attraction.

Was it racial this time? Social? Or maybe magical? Did their otherworldly interests bring her into a whole new category of being objectionable? She'd heard of pagan infighting—some Dianic witches disliked the covens that allowed men; certain Teutonic groups leaned toward white supremacy; and ceremonial magicians had a reputation for dissing simple earth magic. Luckily, with her own circle, none of that had arisen. . . .

But Benedict might be a ceremonial magician.

He pointed his keys as they reached the car, and its locks popped up. Like magic. She climbed in, leaving the door open, while he stowed the stakes and mallet in the trunk. Only when he joined her did she close the door and shut out the woods and the chill and the gray strip of sky—her world.

And, apparently, his silence. He stared out the tinted windshield and said, "I prefer to remain unattached to people."

"As in no commitments?" she asked, fishing for clarification. At least he was explaining. At least he thought she merited that much.

He turned his head, eyes dark and troubled. "As in no connections at all. Or as few as humanly possible. Every interaction develops some bond. I cannot control that. But I *can* control their power, and so maintain my autonomy."

She translated: "You're afraid that if you get involved, you can't stay neutral."

"Fear has nothing to do with it."

Mmm-hmm. "Just how much of your life are you willing to lose for a theory?"

"Hopefully not all of it," he murmured, and the harsh smile that pulled at his mouth didn't make sense at all. Inside joke? Then he said, more distinctly, "It is more than a theory."

She waited.

"You are a good person, Bernard," he told her. "Good to the point of foolishness."

She grinned. "Hush, you—you'll turn my head."

"I do not mean it as a compliment," he snapped, and his vehemence surprised her. "I merely assume that, as a Wiccan, you would prefer being what you would call good, over merely remaining uninvolved . . ."

"Like you," she guessed.

". . . or even antithetically involved, which you call evil."

"Isn't it easier to just say good and evil?"

"I do, but without the moral connotations you assume."

Well, she'd wanted to know, hadn't she? They'd even asked Mary's pendulum, trying to find the truth.

But now she only wanted one particular truth—which made her next statement come out as a question, too weighty for her own comfort. "But you *do* try to avoid doing evil. Right?"

"I also try to avoid doing good, but somehow you have drawn me into it. Were I to pursue this . . . attraction to you, it would only become worse."

"Define *worse.* You afraid you'll end up helping old ladies across the street and giving to the Salvation Army?"

"If I did, the pendulum could then swing just as far in the other direction. I am as apt to do evil as good. It is in my blood, it is part of the balance I live. And so I do neither. You have helped disturb that balance too much already. I mean to stop it right here."

He started the car, and pulled a tight turn between the drainage ditches on either side of the road. A competent driver. A truly competent magic user. A really truly competent kisser, and an eloquent speaker, when he bothered to speak.

But a nutcase, as far as personal philosophies went.

And to think, up until last week, she'd only worried that all the attractive men were married or gay.

She didn't consider herself fanciful. She didn't want to get swept off her feet like Sylvie, or to drown in romance like Mary. But she was earthy and physical, and this particular competent nutcase attracted her as no man had in years. She couldn't just drop it—not with the memory of his mouth covering hers, of his arms encircling her, of that momentary lost look she'd seen in his eyes.

"Pendulum theories aside, don't you think someone as powerful as you has the free will to do what you want?"

"Absolutely," answered Drake Benedict, not looking at her as he drove toward civilization—or at least asphalt. "But you haven't a clue, Bernard, of just what kind of dangerous things I might want out of life—or out of you."

And the only thing more disturbing than the threat beneath his words was her responding tremor of fascination.

She really ought to do more thinking around this man. Otherwise she would be in *big-time* trouble.

If she wasn't already.

He hoped he had frightened her away.

At least, Drake noticed as they hiked to and contained the last of the three dark channels, Bernard gave him plenty of room. She did not impart any more information about her protective mother, her deliriously happy friends or her wise old granny. She'd stopped debating ethics with him.

He told himself this marked an auspicious turn in their relationshi—in their afternoon. Even if he *had* rather enjoyed the way she challenged him, the way her eyes flashed at him, the way her mouth could turn up at a facetious thought during the most serious of conversations. He did not intimidate her. He was unsure why, as he had become quite good over the past few years at carrying himself in such a way as to intimidate most sane individuals. But for whatever reason, his glares did not frighten her, his verbal attacks did not cow her, and his kisses—

No, whether from foolishness or from fortitude, Cypress Bernard did not frighten easily. So he probably had not scared her off, either. But she helped him locate the final subterranean channel of energy. And she joined him in placing the final iron stake to finish their daylong binding. Then she led the way back through the knotted, damp, bug-ridden mess that was the Louisiana woods, back to his car—and she managed to ignore him almost as well as he ignored her. Which was best for both of them.

When he pulled up in front of her home again—a quaint brick house, ranch-style, with a large yard cleared against more woods behind it—he let his engine idle. Otherwise, she might draw out their goodbyes, perhaps even expect some sort of a parting handshake, hug...kiss.

He might feel compelled in that direction, even if she was not.

She rubbed her hands on her thighs. "I'm guessing you don't want to come in?"

Best not to answer that one. "Thank you for the offer."

"Mmm-hmm. So you probably won't want to join my friends for dinner." Surely his expression betrayed nothing; she laughed anyway, an honest, friendly laugh. "No lie! You've done us a big favor. Your mother the magistra would be proud."

He felt the dragon ring on his finger staring at him, taunting. "And my father would be rolling in his grave." Had there been anything left of the man to bury. "Shall we simply call ourselves even?"

As if that would dissolve the bonds that even one after-noon—an afternoon and an evening, and a brief evening before, and a moment in front of his flat—as if whatever bonds they had formed could dissolve so easily.

But ending expectations on either side made a good start.

"Even it is," agreed Cypress. Bernard, rather. "Good luck with your neutrality kick, Drake Benedict."

He almost said, *Good luck with your mother.* He decided against putting even that drop of his energies into her future.

"I bet you're a blast at parties," she muttered, opening the door, but he knew she was merely using sarcasm to mask disappointment. It bothered him that he recognized that.

Unlike in the forest where they had spent their day, he could hear birds from the woods near her house, welcoming the twilight. He could smell the trees, the grass, the humidity—and her. She still smelled of herbs, and of the outdoors. He might miss that.

"Bye, then," she said.

He drew breath to return the goodbye—but she shut the door before she heard him, leaving him in his climate-controlled, separate world.

Just as well.

He pulled away from her quaint house and her forthright ethics and her idealism. He got through the small, endangered town as quickly as seemed moderately legal, slowing down only for children at play—the sort of innocents Bernard remained so determined to protect. Soon he reached the highway, finally done with Stagwater and its good little witches.

He hoped Bernard remembered to cleanse herself thoroughly, lest the negativity to which they had exposed themselves lingered on her. Even an earth witch knew how to cleanse, right? One could not do magic without the ability to visualize. Unbidden, the image of her peeling out of her clothing flirted through his thoughts. She would rub glistening white salt over that rich, tawny skin of hers; perhaps light a stick of incense near her tub and bathe in its smoky fragrance, raising her bare arms, arching her long Nefertiti neck, before finally turning to pure water to work its own magic....

The sound of his wheels hollowed as the car left the wood-shadowed highway for open causeway, bringing him to his senses.

She meant nothing to him. They must keep things that way.

The weather had not cleared enough to allow a sunset. The gray sky was reflected in choppy gray water that stretched so far, he could see only the lake and the bridge ahead of him. Night had not fallen, but day had left, leaving time in a stagnant limbo.

Just like him.

He raised his chin, set his jaw—but thought it anyway. Would he remain alone forever? He could still be with people, with the occasional woman, as long as they did not threaten his impartiality. As long as he did not care.

The concept held little attraction.

And Cypress Bernard does.

But Bernard considered herself one of the good guys, just as his mother had. That implied a certain righteous egotism that he had never wholly accepted. With proper incentive, even the righteous would sell out, or in searching out new quests would leave behind those who truly needed them. And in the meantime—even if she kept her hard-won halo intact—people would start to impose on her. Word would get out, in the pagan underground, where it would bring otherworldly troubles. People with enough imagination to believe in magic, but not enough empowerment to believe in their own, would drain her energy, ask her for love potions, ask her for curses, ask her to investigate their haunted houses and suspicious neighbors....

They would come to her, under attack from less ethical magic users, bringing her into a malevolent cross fire. They would call her in the middle of the night, because someone too addicted to his own power had tried to raise a helper from the bowels of hell, had loosed a creature, fetid and ravenous, on the world. And even if it was neither her doing nor her responsibility, even if she and her friends had no hope of ending such a nightmare, Bernard was the sort of person who would have to try—just as his mother had.

And he would be alone, yet again. He had never been, would never be, anything but alone. Peace was as much a ruse as happiness. Anything would be preferable to this eternal solitude, this aching anonymity. Even nothingness . . .

The blare of a semi's air horn caught him just as his car veered toward the concrete railing and the choppy water beyond. He jerked the wheel back, hard. Metal screamed against concrete and then, after a terrifying moment of friction and sparks, he had cleared the danger. He was back in his own lane, in his own body—the same body that had just steered him toward death.

The truck blasted its horn again, chiding him for idiotic driving. It pulled up beside him, and a passenger leaned out the window, yelled something that looked, in his peripheral vision, like "You coulda killed yourself!"

Not "Are you okay?" Despite idealists like Bernard, the world rarely worked that way.

Still trying to catch his breath, to regain his precious stoicism, Drake did not bother to respond. He most certainly could have killed himself. He suspected that had been the point.

He punched blindly at the CD player in the dash. On the third try, Mozart filled the car. On an afterthought, he opened the electric windows and let fresh, water-scented air blow against his face. He had to make it off this bridge—preferably the conservative way.

As soon as he did, almost fifteen miles later, he pulled off the road and evacuated the car that had nearly become his coffin. He did not have to see the passenger side to know serious bodywork would be needed. *That* hardly worried him. But how he could have slipped into such a funk . . .

But he knew how. He had warned Bernard to cleanse herself, but he had assumed he could live with his extended exposure to the black dragons' negativity until he got home. He was, after all, one of the most powerful wizards in

Louisiana. A mere ley line could not affect him so terribly, right?

And yet he had quite nearly killed himself.

He might not embrace life with both hands, but he was *not* suicidal. Now, after a year of avoiding what felt like an evil summons, only to discover that it was merely a side effect of soured ley lines, he had almost let the negativity of those mere lines destroy him anyway. He was losing his touch. Perhaps he had lost it the moment he listened to Bernard's first request.

Standing beside the Lexus in the early-January evening, barely hearing the zoom of passing traffic or the squawk of gulls overhead, he gathered his energy about him and extended his awareness south, toward Stagwater. He could still sense the psychic beckoning that had tormented him, though twilight, and the cage he and Bernard had laid, muffled it somewhat.

He remembered how he had seen—thought he had seen— something in the woods, like dark tendrils gliding across the ground. Snakes? But he had felt something, too. And now this.

What if this was no mere souring of energy? What if something else had gone terribly wrong beneath the woods of Stagwater? And what if Bernard went after it alone?

He leaned against a satiny black fender. It was hardly his concern, even if he *had* proved his ability to be near the evil without succumbing to it. He would let the witches handle this.

Or at least he would give himself time to recover from exposure before he made any foolish decisions otherwise.

Cypress did as thorough a cleansing as she knew how— salt, incense, candlelight, crystals, and a scented bath—before she met her friends for dinner Sunday night. It didn't keep her from developing a walloping case of the blahs.

The others convinced her to put off exploring the woods for the source of the spoiled ley lines. Sylvie wanted to do more research, Mary wanted to do a tarot reading, and Brigit thought she should recoup lost energy. They didn't know about Drake's particularly enjoyable way of restoring strength.

But she wasn't looking forward to exploring alone, and felt uncomfortable about the others offering their husbands as bodyguards—the men weren't mages, and wouldn't understand. On a more practical note, she had work the next day. Asking for time off to battle the forces of evil might not enhance her managerial potential. So as long as the darkness stayed trapped and nothing else bad happened, she hoped, she could table the black dragons for a few days. Drake, she thought wryly, would approve.

Her job as sales analyst for a local distribution company felt unreal and superficial, after the weekend she'd had. On Monday she reconciled accounts. She also spoke to her mother, safely back in D.C., and her father, who would be in town next weekend for *Grandmère*'s annual costume ball. Mama asked about Dad, and Dad asked about Mama, but neither expressed any interest in contacting the other firsthand. Same ol' same ol'.

Monday evening, she spotted crows in the woods beyond her backyard. She managed not to think of Drake Benedict at all.

On Tuesday, she held meetings with representatives from the company's information systems department to see how she could update the reports from their mainframe computer. She also considered calling one of her old boyfriends, just to get out for a while. Lamarre, or Kevin, or maybe Mario. Not Father Ralph.

Not Benedict, either. He didn't even qualify.

She didn't call any of them, or Sylvie, or Brigit, or Mary. Her circlemates had their own families, even if she didn't.

On Wednesday, however, Brigit called *her*, to cheer the absence of a single paranormal sighting so far. Hopefully Cy and Drake had succeeded in containing the problem. But nobody had heard anything more about the local woman who'd gone missing.

Thursday brought evaluations at work; she dressed her most corporate, only to learn that she'd been passed over for promotion again. She wondered why she even got her hopes up anymore—about her career *or* her love life. The pessimism bothered her. She decided her home needed a good cleansing, too.

She visited the recovery home in New Orleans, and Granny warned her to "watch out for what them woods send." She stopped by Granny's house, too, but as she got there the temperature dropped and the wind picked up. She suddenly felt exposed, right over what she now knew was a channel of sour energy, even if it *was* contained. She'd meant to check out Granny's magic spot, but she changed her mind. It felt dangerous out here, no matter what Benedict said.

She wondered, not for the first time, how much she could trust Benedict, anyway.

Drake Benedict wondered the same thing.

A confusion of slim gray pine trunks created a thicket all around him, no matter how far he walked. They rose up forty feet or more before sprouting branches and needles, their greed for the sun effectively blocking it. Beneath their claustrophobia-inducing canopy, on the ground with him, vines and brush knotted one tree to another in a snarled maze.

Despite his best efforts, something had gone wrong.

He had begun the afternoon with perfect confidence in his abilities and his reasoning. He had no cause *not* to return to Stagwater. Even knowing that no single sentient evil actually beckoned him, he could not ignore its continued draw; if the witches could not silence it, he supposed he had to.

A worrisome telephone call he had received from his uncle Viktor only confirmed that decision—and gave him a deadline.

He had almost contacted Bernard, as this remained more
her mess than his, but then he had questioned his motives.
Managing his inheritance, while time-consuming, left him
with a flexible schedule. But Bernard—like most of society—would be busy at some sort of job. Why should he
disturb the minutiae of her life if he did not have to? Did he
miss her company? Another fix would only postpone withdrawal, not cure it. Did he want the security of her extra
strength? Then he had best overcome that dependence.

Moral qualms aside, using another mage for the odd
"charge" belied his own autonomy, and hardly seemed in
good taste. This way, he need not worry that she would in-
terrupt again, as she had his binding.

In any case, he knew now that Stagwater posed more of
a threat to his rarely sunny disposition than to his ability to
remain neutral. He had breached the forest during the day,
when any unnatural creatures drawn by the ley lines' dark
pheromones—as he himself had been drawn—should remain dormant. Thanks to his time with Bernard, he knew
where to park and how to traverse the woods without un-
due difficulty. And he fully trusted his ability to home in on
the source of his distraction, as surely as a hound responding to a dog whistle.

Which was why getting lost surprised him so.

At first he did not believe his watch—three hours? Even
struggling through the underbrush, he should have managed a minimum of two to three miles an hour. The arms of
the ley lines, according to the map Bernard had carried,
reached barely that far. By now, he should have passed the
center and emerged on the other side...unless he had walked
in circles.

Ridiculous, he thought. He had followed the summons.

A chill wind, above him, made the tall trees sway and
moan, dropping dead pine needles on his head, like a pre-
sentiment of danger. The temperature was falling, and him
without his coat. Not long now until sundown.

Increasingly frustrated, he found his compass and, watching it, continued to follow the incessant pull of evil. He found relief in giving in; an easing of tightness in his shoulders, of resistance in his chest.

That worried him as much as the slow realization that he had not been led in a straight line at all.

The evil could not play games with him—only sentient beings could pull such tricks. He knew this energy was inanimate. He had ventured near it three times with Bernard.

His confusion must stem from negativity poisoning.

He dug his father's pendulum from his jeans pocket and silently invoked its wisdom to point the correct route. It indicated that he should travel northeast. He used the compass to ensure a straight path this time.

The rotting branches of a fallen pine caught at his sleeve, scratched at his face. Toothy blackberry vines bit at the ankles of his boots, no matter how carefully he stepped through their tangle, slowing him considerably. The woods darkened further.

Bernard might have pointed out the sick and lifeless trees, but he now noticed the absence of buzzing insects, of calling birds—as if he were the only living creature in the dragons' dark realm.

The trees above him dipped and moaned in the January wind.

But, despite the chill, there was no wind.

Then he felt the call, as if someone—something—had turned up the volume on the annoying buzz he had dismissed. Like an invisible leash, it tugged at his solar plexus. Stronger than he had ever expected. Nearer than he should have dared venture.

Disturbingly triumphant.

No. This made no sense. Black dragons—ley lines—no matter how sour, were not sentient. They could not disguise their true natures to lure the unwary. They could not cloak whole stretches of the wood to hide their presence.

Which meant he had miscalculated terribly.

Now he saw the dark tendrils that had teased his vision on Sunday. They existed not on the physical but the astral plane, as did auras . . . and magic. And they slithered across the pine straw toward him, headless snakes, animate roots. Evil.

Sentient evil.

Excitement battled fear as he scented the evil, and felt a likeness in himself answering it, succumbing. . . .

Then the ground crumbled beneath his feet—and fear won.

CHAPTER SIX

He could survive this. He could prevail—for a price.

With a kick, Drake rolled away from the shallow pit that suddenly gaped beneath him. Even as he escaped that danger, something unearthly cold—one of the tendrils—bound his wrist and yanked downward. He grasped a pine trunk with his free hand, dug his heels into mud and mustered power around him.

He was Drake Benedict, son of Silas Benedict, last in a long line of powerful sorcerers. Nothing dared threaten him!

The evil—the dragon, he found himself thinking, even yet—seemed unaware of this. Its dark tongue at his wrist burned icily; he gritted his teeth against crying out. Another tendril coiled about his ankle. More slithered near, through the brush, as the trees above him swayed, moaned, and wept dead needles.

And through it all, the summons continued. Like calling like. Evil calling evil.

Belief was half of magic. *He must prevail....*

Drake risked releasing the tree to unsling his pack; immediately the barely visible tendrils tightened, dragging him impossibly fast across the ground, through vines and briars, nearer the nexus—and deeper into mud. When he caught at another rough gray tree trunk, the jolt nearly dislocated his shoulder.

He gasped, but made no other sound. He would survive.

Gulping deep breaths, calling upon the powers he had mastered since his youth, he stared at one of the icy black tongues that still had his wrist. He muttered a single word in an ancient language, older than Latin, older than Hebrew—

The minion sizzled, then recoiled, screeching in an ultrasonic frequency. With the right power, looks could indeed kill.

The ground beneath him, enshrouding his leg up to the knee, trembled in fury. But he had freed his hand.

A backlash of exhaustion shuddered over him—he ignored his abused ankle, his tearing leg muscles. Instead, he dug, one-handed, into his satchel for the one thing that could save him.

His athame.

Folds of silk fell from the antique dagger, revealing its long, double-edged blade, engraved with arcane symbols half worn away by age. Normally he would have unwrapped it with more reverence. The weapon served only ceremonial purposes—for him, at least.

Generations of Benedicts had used this dagger in all manner of wizardry, including magical combat. Even if Drake had less training in such than his ancestors, the athame itself carried wisdom within it, just as it channeled his own powers.

He pointed it toward the ground, toward where he felt icy tendrils dragging mercilessly at his leg, and muttered another series of ancient words. The dagger leaped in his hand with the discharge of energy. His foot pulled free of the dirt and litter, aching but whole.

Again, the ground shook.

A tempest of warring powers tore through the astral plane and leaked into "reality." The wind picked up. A gale force of dark magic rushed by him; he continued to clutch at the tree, to stand against its whirlpoollike draw.

He had gotten on the wrong side of something incredibly powerful. To counter it, he would have to call upon something equally strong and destructive. Perhaps a wind elemental, to blow through these woods and push back the dark tendrils that still crawled toward him. Or a demon to pit against the dragon that still lurked near the nexus of the ley lines that spawned this chaos and tempted him toward it at the same time.

He raised his athame toward the sky, began ancient words of summons. Thunder rumbled around him. The astral wind whipped into a scattering of tornadoes in anticipation of the supernatural battle to come. Again the earth shuddered, perhaps this time in fear, or more likely as a gate somewhere, somehow, began to rumble open, releasing—

No!

He opened his eyes, realizing only then that they had fallen closed, that in his concentration he had leaned his cheek against the amber-dotted tree trunk.

Injured, how could he control whatever he summoned, once it fulfilled its purpose? What would he let loose on the already wounded town? Magic hovered in anticipation of his next words.

With a deep breath and a wince of concentration, he repeated the words he had just spoken—backward. Erased from reality, their power vanished. The thunder quieted. The tornadic activity ceased.

His best hope of survival vanished.

Something cold and black struck at his good leg and pulled him again to the ground. He almost dropped the athame. He did not, could not, even though another tendril captured his wrist.

The more he struggled against captivity, the more his body screamed, suffered. An icy tendril snaked across his throat, and burning agony stopped his breath. Another wrapped his thigh. The ground beneath him seemed to open, to draw him downward, until reddish-brown dirt swallowed his legs completely, sucked his left arm downward, champed hungrily at his shoulders.

He hated to die; more, he hated to die a fool. A fool for coming in the first place. A fool for not recognizing the extent of the evil here. A fool for letting principles cripple him.

Never again, in this life or another.

In a final, desperate move, Drake flipped the athame in his hand. He nearly dropped it, but held on, gripped it even tighter—and sliced viciously downward.

"Begone!"

For the first time since he had owned it, the dagger tasted blood: his own. The steel tip bit into his shoulder and tore downward across his chest, the end of its slice flinging droplets of his blood outward, into the charged air, across scrub and pine straw. His own cry mingled with the blood; this was far deeper than a physical wound. Being self-inflicted increased its cost—and its power.

Teeth gritted, he repeated in an arcane tongue, *"Begone!"*

And suddenly he lay there on his back, half buried in the dirt, staring up at dead pine trees and the watery stars of the night sky. The athame remained in his weak grip, across his abdomen. His pulse pounded through his head as his tortured body tried to assess its multitude of injuries, physical and astral, settling on one overwhelming issue: Could he move?

He could. He had to. Even blood magic and willing sacrifice, the most powerful and deathly dangerous of spells, would not restrain his feeding foe for long.

He struggled from the earth that had tried to entomb him, and rolled to his knees. Panting, he regained his feet—and crumpled. So he hooked his athame into his belt and crawled, the tear of briars child's play against his psychic pain.

After a few desperate minutes, he managed his feet again, and staggered. He could not stand straight. A clutching in his belly would not allow that. But he could lurch, hunched, in the direction that he hoped—

Wait. No! He slumped again, one shoulder catching him against a pine trunk. He had lost the compass in the attack. The top-heavy trees, branches reduced to barren claws, greedily hid all but patches of the sky. Despite his knowledge of astrology, he could not navigate by it. Could he be certain he *was* leaving the danger behind? He had walked in circles all afternoon!

The ground seemed to shift beneath him, the dragon stirring in its magical slumber in the darkened woods. Valuable seconds ticked past. If it caught him again, Drake would not survive. He would die, completely alone, just as he had feared.

He closed his eyes—and thought of Cypress Bernard, held that thought to him. He remembered the comforting scent of herbs on her. He remembered her arguing with him, questioning him, kissing him. He remembered her determination to play hero and, mostly, he remembered the faint bond they had established over the past week. He reached for that—and felt nothing.

Drake slowly slid down the tree that supported him, to the cold, damp ground. The earth shuddered again; the dragon would wake, and win. It would likely take out Bernard and her circle, as well. Cloaking the woods as it did, so that not even he had sensed it, it would wait for the witches to enter its lair....

Cloaking the woods. He caught a deep, painful breath of winter air, and struggled to his feet. The woods were cloaked; Bernard could not likely sense him. That would weaken their bond, make it harder to sense. It might yet be there!

Again he cast his awareness outward, seeking a connection, trying to believe, even if it remained invisible. Be there!

And at a faint tugging in his heart, he knew where to go.

He limped in that direction, ignoring his body's insistence that it could not continue, ignoring the trembling of fury behind him. He focused on Bernard, only Bernard, lest he be turned again.

Lest he die.

He might well die anyway. After he had maintained his feet for some yards, the trunk of a fallen tree in the dark took him down yet again. He dragged himself forward on his knees, then felt, heard, the threat behind him: a dark slithering, an approaching doom. Even someone without magic would have sensed the evil's nearness.

To at least face his murderer, Drake rolled and stared at the shadowy tongues striking at him. Knowing he had not the strength to fight again, he pulled his feet instinctively back—

And nothing happened.

He lay there, watching through the V of his raised knees as the tendrils recoiled, and he did not understand. Whatever he'd just faced was too powerful to just quit. It made no sense.

But when nothing caught at him, nothing hurt him, he accepted the impossible and pulled himself upward again. His hand touched something cold, and he recoiled—

Then reached out, felt and caressed the top of an iron stake. The dragon had not caught him, because he and Cypress had penned the dragon. He'd escaped the war zone—for now.

Drake had no idea how long he lay there, aching, grateful. But whatever sentient being lurked deep in this forest would not be held back indefinitely by spikes of metal in the earth. Finally he struggled to his feet to continue in the one direction that held safety.

Safety for him—if not for the woman providing it.

Who the hell did Drake Benedict think he was, anyway?

By Thursday night, Cypress had started a winter-cleaning binge, turning her frustrated thoughts back onto the sorry man who inspired them. Maybe she and her circle *did* owe him for helping with the ley lines—though even that didn't go down easy with her. But he'd had to be so damned attractive while he did it. And then he'd gone and kissed her....

She dusted, and swept—and took breaks to wander into the backyard and stare at the woods. She felt anxious, as if she should do something and didn't know what. The woods weren't telling. She also felt cold in her cleaning cutoffs, so she would head back into the house, check on her friends by phone, then scrub, polish, and fault Benedict for the whole nonaffair.

He oughtn't to have kissed her. Not that she was Sleeping Beauty or anything, the full responsibility of the prince who'd battled thorns and dragons to reach her. But still, he'd started something he *knew* he had no intention of finishing.

That really burned her.

Well, she had better things to do with her life than moon after a man with no use for her. So she wiped and polished even more, but she couldn't scrub away the deep-down sense that something important was happening, something she should act on, if only she knew what it was. And then she heard a noise at the door.

The noise startled her. It wasn't a knock—more like a dog trying to get in. But she didn't have a dog.

She left her bucket of disinfecting cleanser on the kitchen floor and stood, brushing at her bare knees. She peeled off her green rubber gloves, wiped her forehead on the back of her arm and went to the front door to check the peephole.

Nothing. No surprise this late at night, right?

She stepped back from the door and folded her arms, frowning. Late or not, she *had* heard something—she could even *feel* something wrong. Nothing had breached her protective wards. Yet. But she could almost smell the danger...

Her grandmothers hadn't raised a fool. Cy backed toward the dining room telephone, keeping her eyes on the door. She had friends with big, strong husbands. Time to impose on 'em.

Then she heard another sound at the door, like someone pushing at it. Trying to get in? She'd taken to locking up lately. Something about all the otherworldly threats had made her paranoid.

Now she detoured en route to the phone, to claim a baseball bat from her umbrella stand. She almost dropped it when two sharp knocks sounded at the door.

Real knocks, like a real person, not *Frankenstein Returns*.

She stood there in the entrance to the dining room, clutching her bat, torn. Her visitor knocked again, impatient.

She realized that she was hovering, which she'd always hated—she could take care of late-night drop-ins herself. The light in the foyer wasn't even on. Whoever-it-was wouldn't even be able to see that she'd peeked, right?

But she stepped to the door quietly. With the bat.

The peephole revealed a blurry, distorted Drake Benedict.

Anger replaced fear. Anger that he would make her go through the withdrawal of this past week, just to show up again. Anger that he'd show up this late, without calling— weren't Brits supposed to be polite? Anger that she couldn't fault mere anger for her speeding pulse and adrenaline rush.

And, damn it, she was wearing too-short shorts, a dirty T-shirt and a kerchief around her hair!

Fine. If Mr. Neutrality couldn't make up his own mind, she'd make it up for him, and looking good had nothing to do with it. She threw the deadbolt, yanked open the door—

And stared, bat still in hand. The man looked like hell.

Dirty didn't begin to describe him; smears of mud and grit covered more of him than not, and his jeans looked to be made of silt. Leaves and bits of pine needles tangled in his usually soft hair. Angry welts veined his regal jaw; the shadow under his chin wasn't a shadow but a bruise, like from a noose; and where his long-sleeved shirt was torn in front—

She caught her breath, horrified to realize that his hands weren't coated just with dirt but with drying blood, too.

She searched his usually uncommunicative eyes, and for once they communicated: pain, exhaustion, anger—and need.

"I believe I know," he managed to say weakly, coughing, "what became of your missing person."

And then he collapsed through the doorway and into her arms, to the sound of her bat falling to the wooden floor.

What do you use to get evil out—hot water, or cold?

When he crumpled into her arms, Cypress figured Benedict would smell of the woods, or of his expensive aftershave, or of his car's leather interior. She also figured on feeling their shared tingle. Instead, she felt bone-deep cold, and an exhaustion that she hadn't felt minutes ago. And she smelled evil on him.

Evil stank. She didn't want it in her clean house. More, she didn't want it on Drake Benedict. So she helped him stagger into the bathroom, first thing, and started the shower, and left him crumpled beside the tub to run to the kitchen for salt.

New Age Mary might insist on sea salt, but as far as Cy and Granny were concerned, salt was salt. Incense was incense, too; she swung by her magic cabinet, in the back hallway, and chose sticks of frankincense and sandalwood and, while she was at it, a chunk of protective onyx. No need to look up what worked best for cleansings. She'd just done this, four days ago.

When she got back to the bathroom, a huge knife lay on the counter and Drake was sprawled in the tub, letting the shower run over him, clothes and all. His dark hair clung to his forehead, his cheeks, his neck. His shirt stuck to his sculpted chest, except where it had been torn down the front. A horrible red-brown puddle was running off of him and down the drain. Mud. Blood. Evil.

"What on earth—?" She bit back the question, resolving to deal with his injuries first, *then* with their cause. She set the crystal on the soap dish, near him, and took a moment to light the incense over the sink.

He said nothing. When she glanced back, she suspected from the set of his jaw that he was doing well to avoid collapsing and drowning, right there.

Well, at least she wasn't wearing nice clothes. She stepped into the shower and hunkered over him, and pulled off first one boot, then the other. Mud filled them on the inside, too; had he been wading in the swamp? It oozed over her fingers like insects, like feces, horrible—

"Do not touch it," he managed to warn her.

She tossed the boots to the other side of the bathroom to be dealt with later—so much for having cleaned—and did the same with his mud-slick socks. Then she swished her hands in his runoff before starting to scrape handfuls of the muck off his jeaned legs. If this felt bad on her hands, what would it feel like to *wear* it!

"Do you have salt?" he demanded, each word its own effort.

"Beside the tub. First things first." Having done what she could for his jeans, she straddled his wet hips and started unbuttoning his ruined shirt.

His tortured eyes, level with hers, caught her gaze. Did she imagine the hint of a tingle returning?

This was *not* the time to be getting turned on. Especially when Benedict didn't do involvements. He didn't have the strength to stand up, much less fulfill her fantasies.

She forced her concentration back to his shirt. Whatever had torn it had sliced open a strip of him, too. The cut looked deep, marring what looked to be a decent chest.

Curiosity won out. "What happened to you?" She pushed the wet material back, catching a clean towel off the rack to press against his wound. Bruises blazed his ribs and a shoulder. She could hear how he labored to breathe.

When she glanced back up, he was still watching her face. "I met our dragon."

"You mean one of the ley—? What are you doing!"

But she was too late; he'd already tipped the canister of salt, letting it pour over his neck and, lifting the towel, covering his wounded chest. She winced as he spasmed in pain, and caught his wrist before he could do any more damage to himself.

He refused to release the salt.

"What kind of a masochist are you?"

"One who may—" he paused to catch his breath "—have been poisoned." He tugged on his hand. She held it, trembling as if at his pain. "Help me, or release me."

Fine; she yanked the salt away from him. "Give me that."

Whatever he'd run into, he must have rolled in, too. Cy filled her palm with white crystals, then began to work them into his hair, against his scalp. She'd have him pickled, if that was what it took to help him regain some strength. And not because he wasn't any use to her without his strength. He probably wouldn't be any use to her anyway. Right?

It was hard to remember that, sitting on his hard thighs, soaking-wet, in the shower. If they were both naked and uninjured, this would be an intriguing position. Even clothed . . .

"Talk," she commanded, for distraction.

"I went back into the woods, to find the cause of your spoiled ley lines."

"I was supposed to do that." She used her fingers to comb salt through his hair. She even liked the feel of his hair when it was wet, and filthy. She scowled at him for that.

"I knew I could do it more capably."

She scowled harder. "You talk big, for a man with open wounds to a woman with a handful of salt."

"You asked," he reminded her archly.

"So why didn't you call me?" Her hands moved to his face next. She winced when she inadvertently got salt on the scratches; he didn't. When she started to move her hand away, he caught it beneath his own. Tingles.

He had to feel better; surely tingles were a good sign.

"All of it," he insisted, of the cleansing.

So she made herself rub the salt over the scratches, too. Over his jaw. Over his bruising neck.

"I thought I would be safer than you," he admitted softly, unexpectedly.

It took some effort to stop caressing his neck, but she did. Exasperation made a good motivator. "You thought you were protecting me?"

He said nothing.

"Who asked you to protect me? I sure never did. Sounds more like you were excluding me, and didn't want me to know about it. That isn't protection."

He said nothing.

She began to rub salt onto his chest, carefully avoiding the deep cut, which he'd already "treated." "Besides, I thought you'd rather run out and kick a kitten before you'd let folks call you a good guy."

He let his wet head fall back against the tile wall of her tub; for a fleeting moment, a smile flirted at his mouth.

Hand spread against his wet chest, she felt *major* tingles.

From the way his hips shifted beneath her, she'd have guessed he felt them, too. His gaze dropped to her hand; he raised his own, caught hers—and moved it away from him. "I believe," he told her, his words even quieter than the spray of water, "that I can manage alone from here."

"Like you did in the woods today?" she asked challengingly, disappointed and relieved and tingling, all at the same time.

"Exactly," he agreed. As if he'd shown up at her door in triumph, instead of in pieces.

But she believed in nonmanipulation; if the man felt strong enough to take care of himself, so be it. Suspicious—and frustrated—she stood with a splash, then stepped, dripping, out of the tub. Her sneakers squelched on the bath mat.

Drake put down the bloodstained, salt-encrusted towel, stood unsteadily, then pulled the shower curtain closed.

In a moment, he dropped his filthy shirt out of the tub, onto the tile floor. Then his filthy jeans. Then his briefs.

Cy sank, suddenly very weak and trembly herself, onto the toilet seat. "You were, uh, telling me what happened."

And Drake Benedict related how he had met the dragon.

He told her almost everything—how he had grown disoriented, how he had then found the dragon, how it had attacked him. But, scrubbing himself with salt and then with soap, he left out three important details. He did not tell her how he had found his way out. He did not tell her that, after collapsing through her doorway, he had drunk in her energy as a parched man would water, as a vampire would blood. And he did not tell her that the magic he used to escape had required the letting of his own blood. He would rather she thought the dragon had inflicted his wound; she would feel better about it. About him.

He never lied. But he had to decide how he felt about using blood magic—and so easily—before dealing with her typical witchy reactions to the truth.

"So you're saying we don't have problems with ley lines after all?" she asked from outside the curtain. The water finally ran clear—physically and astrally. He turned it off.

Even without her straddling him, tending him, gazing into his eyes, Drake felt something deep within him respond to her husky voice. So much for not encouraging bonds between them.

"The ley lines are still involved." He accepted the clean towel she handed past the jungle-print curtain. "Otherwise, the spikes we laid would not have stopped the... phenomenon."

"Let's just keep calling it a dragon," she clarified. "It gives me something to picture." Spoken like a true mage.

"The dragon is not a ley line itself," he tried to explain. He finished drying off. Scrubbing his hair hurt his chest, from reaching, and exhausted him so that he had to lean back against the shower wall to catch his breath. Or to try.

"Drake?" She sounded concerned; he felt that from her, too. Deeply. He wished he did not.

"The dragon is not the ley line," he tried again, his words more measured. "It is what moves along them. But it must be more than pure energy. It *is* sentient. It *is* an actual being."

"And it's evil." Her voice dipped in disgust.

"Thoroughly." He draped the towel over the curtain rod, then wondered, blearily, what to do next. He was a guest in her home; he owed her some measure of respect. "I have rather a logistics problem, Bernard. I have no change of clothes."

She was silent for a long moment.

"Cypress?" The name slipped off his lips before he was ready. A pretty name, actually. It fit her.

His easy use of it bothered him, deeply.

"Will a sheet work?" she asked, voice thick.

"I can make do."

After barely a minute, her tawny hand reached in, holding a moss-green sheet. He fashioned a makeshift toga from it, and only then pushed back the shower curtain.

She had cleaned the bathroom while he had cleaned himself; neither a drop of mud nor a scrap of his clothing remained. Now she dragged the bandanna off her hair, which sparkled with unshed moisture. She still wore the T-shirt and indecently high-cut shorts she'd had on when she answered the door, though. He could tell from the wet material that she wore no bra, and wished his powers of observation were not quite so keen.

"Sit down," she told him, gesturing toward the toilet.

He sat, and she used odds and ends from her medicine cabinet to patch up his physical wounds as best she could. She did it matter-of-factly, neither shrinking from the blood nor lingering over him . . . at least, he did not think she lingered. If so, she did not linger long enough for his taste.

Perhaps her house would prove more dangerous than the woods, after all. He closed his eyes, reminded himself that he had soaked up near-deadly doses of negativity in his battle with the dragon. That made him more emotionally vulnerable than usual. He must beware of acting on that, of turning to her innate strength for... anything.

He did not open his eyes until she finished closing his chest wound with several butterfly bandages.

"I don't know what else I can do." She sighed. "No offense, but you still look like something the cat dragged in."

Good. Perhaps they could find a measure of distance in his unattractive appearance. "You can do nothing else for me. The rest of my injuries are more psychic than physical."

She planted her hands on her hips, considered it—oh, dear, he had just issued another challenge, hadn't he?—and then she rang her friend Mary for advice.

Mary insisted on coming over herself. She brought her big young husband with her, and Guy Poitiers—though hardly a Rhodes scholar, to look at him—had the foresight to bring a change of clothes. "I've run into stuff out there too," he explained.

The little blonde—a healer, it turned out—closed her eyes and ran her hands over Drake's aura, several inches from his skin, sensing the extent of his astral injuries. Suddenly her eyes flew open. She stared at Drake, uncertain, accusing.

She knew. He just did not know how much she knew.

"What?" demanded Bernard, returning to the living room with a small basket of stones. "What's wrong?"

He stared at the healer, surprisingly defensive. She knew he had performed blood magic. She knew he had crossed the line.

Would she tell?

Mary stared right back, then resumed sensing his wounded energies. "He's gotten mixed up in some pretty evil stuff," she hedged, keeping his secret for now. He wondered why.

"You haven't seen what I carried out of my bathroom," Bernard—Cypress—agreed.

"Good thing you were able to clean it up, huh?" said Mary significantly, mostly to Drake. Lowering her voice, she murmured, "You get her hurt and you're dead meat, *comprenez?*"

"She may get herself hurt," he returned, in an undertone.

"Make sure she doesn't." As if he could control that!

Cypress had paused in arranging a circle of jade and amber, turquoise and lapis—healing crystals—around them, and now she stared, blatantly curious about the secrecy. So did Guy Poitiers, shifting uncomfortably in a corner.

"Patient confidentiality," explained Mary with a bright smile, which her husband returned warmly. Cypress raised a dry eyebrow, not buying it—but she let them drop the subject. And by the time the Poitiers left, and Cypress leaned against the closed door behind them, Drake did feel considerably better.

More fit, in any case.

Watching the woman who had taken him in, he could not vouch for his emotional well-being. She had seen him more vulnerable than he ever wished to be again. He had accepted her help, taken her strength. Against his best intentions, he now owed her. Even if they never saw each other again, the bond between them had strengthened to the point that it would never vanish. It would persist throughout his life, like a constant ache, reminding him of what could have been—had she only been less the white witch, determined to do pure good. Had he been less the black sorcerer, intent on preserving himself.

Had he not fed blood to the evil that lurked in her woods.

Far behind Cypress's home, deep in the woods, a patch of silty soil beneath dead pine trees shifted, trembled—and the stake between the ley lines' nexus and her warmly lit sanctuary moved. Haltingly, awkwardly, it rose from the earth that rejected it, teetered, then fell, useless, atop the pine straw.

Self-sacrificed blood had given the "dragon" strength. Now it hungered for more.

on the new telephone. It rested, their call, would ring, the phone.

She smiled. Took her eyes from her dragon. She, how it languished for more.

CHAPTER SEVEN

Drake watched Cypress where she leaned against the door in her shadowy foyer. She turned her head and faced his gaze.

He could feel her power from here, and not because she had more than did the usual witch. He felt her magic because he longed for it now, just as he had feared. Like an alcoholic craved drink, a smoker nicotine, so he craved her energies . . . her essence.

By coming to her tonight for help—indebting himself, firmly and finally—he had taken that first drink, fed the waiting addiction. That disturbed him. If he could barely resist *her* simple draw, how could he ever hope to stand firm against the continued call of the waking dragon?

Even now, he felt his attacker beckon him in waves of dark power, like shock waves shuddering over him. Each call seemed to target him, his blood, his heritage. Only Mary Poitiers's skillful healing and the secure wards around Cypress's home offered him protection, strength . . . willpower? Not willpower.

She continued to gaze at him; if she felt fatigue, she refused to show it. In fact, she looked strong. Sure. With her bright eyes, her high cheekbones and her full, inviting mouth, she looked more attractive than any woman in his recent memory.

Unique. And definitely captivating—sensually so. Now dry, her shirt did not trace the topography of her figure as intimately as it had in the bathroom, but it still rode the swell of her breasts to free-fall just past the waist of her shorts. The shorts themselves—cutoff jeans—appeared as comfortable and unpretentious as their model, but they exposed far too much tawny leg for his peace of mind.

"Do you really think the dragon killed Lucille Witt?" From another woman, the words would have seemed needy; from Cypress, they asked only a truthful answer. The mind behind those dark eyes was probably already hatching battle strategies.

He stood up straighter, which pulled at his chest wound. The slash of pain, though bearable, snatched his thoughts back to important matters. "The dragon is very strong, suggesting that it has fed in the past," he admitted. *And more so tonight.* "It is quite capable."

"Why didn't it attack us on Sunday? You stood right over one of the black streams, and nothing happened."

Good question. "Perhaps the entity is most strong where the ley lines meet? It waited until I nearly reached its lair before attacking me."

She continued to hold his gaze a moment longer, her brows furrowed as if in distress at... what? The dragon's attack? "You'll stay here tonight," she decided, voice husky.

Relief and exhaustion nearly undid him, but he managed to say, "No. It may not be safe."

That playful grin lit her face. "You can trust me, Benedict. I've vowed to 'harm none.' "

"I have not."

Instead of flinching from his words, from what he knew to be his coolest expression, she squared her shoulders as if for battle—for a sporting battle, at that. She did not take him seriously. She could not know.

He felt the tingle of her nearness, even without touching her. Temptation.

"Are you threatening my life?" The question was a challenge. "Or just my honor?" He had dared her again, had he? She stepped closer, slid her hands and then her arms over his shoulders, behind his neck. Her essence crashed over him, vibrant and pure. Perhaps her honor, he thought, could withstand even the likes of him.

With an inner wrench of defeat, he met her kiss with his own, hungry for her mouth, hungry to taste her again. Yes . . .

She pulled away from him in a gasping retreat. Had he not warned her? Their mingling powers seemed to arc across the few inches between them; then she surged forward to meet his hunger again. To slake his milder thirst, and to awaken another, deeper one. When he tried to pull her against him, to feel her strong body against every aching centimeter of his own, she braced her elbows against his shoulders to resist. Her continued kisses countered any misunderstandings about her disinterest; she was merely protecting his wounded chest.

Yet another reason for him to regret letting his own blood in the woods.

His blood had other interests now, pulsing through him in a powerful rush, spreading his want of her. He drew her denim-clad hips against him with one hand and ran his other hand beneath the hem of her shirt and up her warm, vibrant back, then around to the side of one of her breasts. He filled himself with her, in more ways than one. Power surged between them, crackled, hummed, and both he and she gasped out of that particular kiss, their heads thrown back as the sensation shuddered through their bodies. He realized, somewhere past the cloud of desire, that their intimacy magnified whatever energy their touch created.

Good.

He took her mouth again while, beneath the cover of her shirt, he explored her softness, drew his fingers over her hardened nipple. He might have groaned his approval, had she not done so for them, the noise muffled by his own lips, his own tongue. The magic of her surged through his ravenous body, renewed his soul. Defended him, protected him—*fed him.*

He stiffened, snatched his hand from beneath her shirt, stumbled back from her as if from the dragon itself.

As if from his own damnation.

"What?" She glanced behind and then around her, as if some danger had prompted his retreat. When she saw nothing, she turned her gaze back to him. "What happened? Did I hurt you?"

Not physically. But she did threaten him. He had not known her two weeks, but *this*—what they had just been doing, sharing—surpassed petting and foreshadowed more than mere sex. Their energies still flared together, just from the weight of *this*.

"I shan't stay here," he managed to say, channeling some of his heightened powers into steadying, cooling, his voice. "Not even for that."

Her eyes, so warm with longing only moments ago, cooled, as well. Her mouth set, and she folded her arms protectively across the breasts that he still longed for, ached for.

"Oh, yes," she told him challengingly. "You will."

He raised his chin, arched an imperious brow.

She did not back down. "You may think you're the best damn magician to come along since Merlin, but I've got a news flash for you, Benedict. You're hurt. You're tired. You left your car who knows how far from here, and I'm sure not loaning you mine. On top of all that, you just told me that I've got some kind of human-eating dragon living in the woods behind my house."

That was not all he had just done. But if she found refuge in denial, who was he to remind her? He said nothing.

"No way," she continued, jaw set, "am I letting you out of here until you at least help me figure out what to do about the dragon. And no way is either one of us up to brainstorming just yet. Our monster's penned up for now, and hopefully no one else is dumb enough to go into the woods tonight, so we can deal with that in the morning. In the meantime, I've got a guest room where your honor will be perfectly safe. You may not want to spend the night with *me,* but you *are* spending the night."

Oh, but he *did* want to spend the night with her. He wanted to learn every tawny inch of her, to bury himself in her, to share himself with her until she screamed from the joy of it...

...and then to lap up the brightest, most high-frequency energy she had to offer him, in shivering, passionate waves, to do with as he pleased. Tantric magic, it was called. Sex magic. Between consenting adults, it had no moral stigma. But without consent, it could be a form of psychic rape.

He did want to spend the night with her—but he did not dare. So, even as he nodded once, in deference to the case she had made, he did not bother to correct her mistaken assumption.

If hurt feelings over his disinterest kept Cypress Bernard from tempting him further, so be it. And more power to them.

Like the princess with a pea under her mattress, Cypress didn't sleep well. She kept waking in the moonlit darkness, staring up at the woven dream-catcher above her bed, trying to reconcile her mixed emotions.

It didn't work.

She should be better at handling rejection, considering how little she'd ever fit into more than the surface of anyone else's world. She had friends—good friends—and she dated. But she would always look different from her companions, white or black. And, except with her circle, she felt different inside, too. Seemed most folks who believed in magic and revered nature as a female deity didn't generally choose business majors.

With Drake Benedict, she felt more unique than different, and inwardly even more normal than him. He dressed and conducted himself much as her colleagues at work did, but he knew a stronger—well, flashier—magic than hers. Though he had a superiority complex the size of Africa, it struck her as such an honest, equal-opportunity arrogance that it rolled off her. Small price to pay for how alive, adventurous, attractive, he made her feel.

Then again, she didn't feel so attractive tonight. He'd unhanded her so fast, she still felt dizzy. Was it for the best? She was too physical, too earthy, to ever be a prude—but she was practical, too. Casual sex could be dangerous, nowadays.

Why hadn't her moments in his arms felt casual?

Maybe, she decided, rolling over, it was because of what lurked in the woods. With the dragon around, the dangers of getting too close too fast with her not-quite-a-magister lessened in contrast. And now he was sleeping in her guest bed, in the very next room . . .

No, she didn't sleep well at all.

Benedict seemed to sleep like a baby, though—the snake. By the time he appeared in her kitchen, dressed in borrowed clothes, she'd already gotten up, showered, called work to let them know she'd likely be late and cooked breakfast. Her inner feminist balked at going domestic so quickly; but her southern-reared inner hostess prevailed.

Besides, there wasn't much difference between whipping up oatmeal for one and making oatmeal for two. Though maybe she should have cooked for one, anyway. When Drake walked into the glass-walled breakfast nook, her appetite dulled beneath a stronger craving. The man looked good. She figured she'd gotten used to that. But he also looked more approachable than she'd ever seen him.

Thanks to Guy Poitiers, Drake wore faded jeans and a long-sleeved work shirt, blue instead of black. Something—perhaps humility, considering the bruises shadowing his neck—gentled his regal posture, his aloof gaze. His hair had dried loose and soft, and in the shafts of morning sunlight that filtered through the ivy growing against the window, she saw for the first time that it wasn't black at all, but a deep, incredibly dark brown.

Maybe she'd just *assumed* he would have black hair, since he was the brooding, mysterious sorcerer. She, of all people, shouldn't be buying into that kind of stereotype. *She* had black hair—and dark skin, too, depending on who did the looking. And she was the least mysterious, least brooding person she knew.

In any case, she told herself as she dished the oatmeal into two green-patterned bowls, just because he looked softer this morning, that didn't mean he was. He'd wanted to appear dangerous and amoral. Considering how callously he'd rejected her last night, maybe she should start listening to him on that front.

"So what exactly is this dragon?" she demanded, putting the bowls on the table and going to the fridge for milk. "Sit down."

He hesitated—rebellious, or taken aback? Then he sat. "I have no earthly idea."

Fat lot of good that did them, but she couldn't fault him. They weren't exactly dealing with something that showed up on *National Geographic* specials. She put the milk bottle on the table, then sat across from him. Normally she didn't get company for breakfast. She reminded herself not to enjoy it. "Okay. You're still the only person I know of who's confronted this thing." The only one alive, in any case. "What *isn't* it?"

"It is not corporeal." He sprinkled sugar on his oatmeal—brown sugar. The way she liked hers. "It inflicted the bulk of its damage through astral means, tentacles of malignancy. The physical damage was merely a manifestation of that power." When she waited for him to clarify, he paused, about to take a bite of his breakfast. "Mind over matter."

The down-and-dirty definition of magic. "Its mind over your matter?" She tried some of the cereal herself.

"Exactly. Whatever it is, were I a gambler, I would give odds that it lies underground. It does not roam freely, but apparently moves via the ley lines, as they are natural conduits for energy. My guess is that it has been slowly expanding its reach outward from the nexus point for some time now."

Like since Sylvie first surprised them by suggesting the town's "serial killer" could be a werewolf? "A year and a half?"

"That would be but a moment to an immortal."

She put down her spoon, her appetite plummeting even further. "It isn't *mortal?*"

"I doubt it."

"Which would make it pretty difficult to kill."

At least one of them was enjoying breakfast. "Rather."

Damn. She took a bite anyway, deciding she might just need her strength. Then she thought: *Damn.* She and her friends had vowed to "harm none." If possible, they should banish this...thing. But she almost wished they *could* do worse.

She wanted to tell herself that her dragonicidal tendencies had nothing to do with how hurt he had been last night. But she didn't buy it. Uncharacteristic or not, she needed to hurt this thing for more than just defensive reasons.

Drake Benedict was *not* a very good influence.

She eyed how he ate his oatmeal; sorcerous battles apparently gave a man quite an appetite. He noticed her attention and stopped eating, waiting for her to say something.

Business. Efficiency. This might be the last chance she had to get his input before she drove him back to his car and he left Stagwater's problems to Stagwater. "Will the spikes over the ley lines keep it contained?"

He didn't meet her eyes, and looked down at his toast instead. "I doubt it. Especially not if it gains power."

"And even if it doesn't get any bigger, it'll go right on attracting other evil, won't it?" Not to mention the likelihood of it swallowing up folks who wandered into the wrong part of the woods. Beware of Dragon signs wouldn't cut it.

He met her gaze again before nodding.

"So," she continued doggedly, "it isn't something we can let solve itself. We have to come up with a plan."

He continued to watch her, his eyes unfathomably deep, a swoop of dark hair ruffling over his high forehead. Probably thinking, *What do you mean 'we,' Kemosabe?*

"My circle, I mean," she explained, before he could switch into cut-and-run mode.

For whatever reason, that managed to stop the conversation. He finished his oatmeal. She gave up on hers, her appetite gone. She'd never doubted her magic before—but then, the dragon didn't seem to use her kind of magic. It used Drake's. Flashy magic. Deadly magic.

Was she jealous? *Things that big probably don't banish very easy.*

"Two members of your circle are pregnant," he pointed out, sounding annoyed. "One is a nursing mother. None of them should be trifling with black streams."

And then there was one, right?

"Well, we aren't relocating," she told him, before he even dared suggest that again. "So something's gonna get done, if I've got to face the thing down myself."

He had fallen into his reserved mode again; now only the bruises and the weariness softened him. So it took her a minute to realize what he was doing when he tugged off his pinkie ring and plunked it down on the breakfast table in front of her, right next to the milk. The ring looked like an emerald-eyed dragon biting its tail. A strange purple tinge colored the gold, as if even now it emanated his warmth, his power.

Her fingers itched to pick it up, to feel that warmth in her palm. But she raised her eyebrows in an unspoken question, and kept her hand fisted until she knew what it signified.

He folded his arms across his chest; remembering his wound, she winced, but he didn't. "Had I not lost my pack in the battle, I would give you the magister's marker. In its stead, accept this."

The ring stared up at her, waiting, like Snow White's apple. He could easily have magicked it. Gifts carried an astral meaning, a bond, even *without* magic. Take it, and she trusted him. Refuse it, and she didn't.

"Please," he added curtly.

Please? She searched his aloof face, with no luck. "Why?"

"For last night, of course."

Oh, of course. If she *had* slept with him, this would be a bad moment. But she hadn't. *But you might have.* She trusted him enough to consider sharing something as intimate as lovemaking...but she didn't trust him enough to take his marker?

She reached out a tentative hand, and claimed the ring and what it meant. It felt heavy, vaguely electric—and, yes, warm. And it meant that he owed her. Her granny-witch and his mother-magistra had nothing to do with it this time. *He* owed *her.*

She could ask him to help her against the dragon. And he knew it. She carefully hid her excitement at that realization; he couldn't change camps that fast, could he? The ring fit around her index finger, like it belonged there. But she wasn't in high school, and he wasn't the football captain. He was the most kick-ass, least principled magic user she'd ever seen.

Bernard, there ain't no such thing as a free lunch.

"Why would you want to stay involved?"

"Why question my motivations, when you need my help?"

"Maybe because someone keeps telling me that you're Dirk Dangerous. You're out for revenge now, aren't you? Those woods ain't big enough for the both of you? Well, they aren't your woods. They're—" She paused. Whose? A technicality to look into. "They're Stagwater's woods, my woods. As long as my town is involved, we're doing what's right, not just what's macho."

"You need me."

She stood up, started clearing the table to disguise her discomfort at his words, and their multifaceted truth. She'd known him barely a week. "Keep telling yourself that."

"My uncle Viktor contacted me."

As she rinsed the bowls, she noticed how the emeralds in the dragon-ring's eyes winked at her. "So what's that got to do with the price of tea in China?"

"Viktor is a powerful mage, as was my father. He has become interested in our—in *your*—local attraction, and spoke of investigating for himself. You do not want this to happen."

She had to fight not to smile, all of a sudden. He thought he knew her, did he? "And why don't I? Maybe he can help."

Now *he* looked amused. "Hardly. You witches would find his methods less than...ethical. He is sure to confront the dragon."

She returned to the table for the milk. "To fight it?"

"To enlist its aid."

She almost dropped the milk. "To *what?*"

"Surely you have heard the legends? Powerful magicians have often pitted themselves against equally powerful creatures, with three possible results. The magician might compel the monster into his own power. If he fails, they do battle. If he then wins, the mage still takes on the creature's power."

"Why would folks want that kind—" She cut herself off before finishing, *that kind of power?* His dry amusement mocked her. Fine, so people would want it for wealth, ego...sex.

"Because it is there?" he suggested archly.

She poured them both some more coffee and sat down, again thankful to know someone with apparent expertise. "Go on."

"If the magician loses the battle, he becomes another sacrifice—a very potent one."

"Like Lucille Witt," she realized softly.

"Except that Ms. Witt was not a first-degree magic user."

So if the dragon killed—absorbed?—his uncle, Stagwater was in even deeper trouble than before. And if Drake's uncle conquered the dragon...

Then they'd have a very powerful sorcerer in their midst. One with "less-than-ethical" methods. Offhand, that didn't sound a heap of a lot different from what they already had in Drake.

"What are your stakes in this? He's your uncle. Don't you want what's best for him?"

"What is best for him," said Drake direly, "is to stay away. His death would give the dragon untold power. His victory would give Viktor the same."

"And you're sure he'd misuse it."

"He may well misuse it against me." When he felt her surprised stare, he added, casually, "We are not close."

Damn. Suddenly it made sense—and she didn't like the results of her analysis. She leaned across the table toward him. "You never lie, right?"

His eyes flickered across her face, as if he were trying to second guess her. "Never. Unless that's its own lie." A dry smile tightened his lips.

She did believe him—maybe too much. "Then tell me something. Tell me if you're going after the dragon for the same reason your uncle is. If it's so that you can get more power, so that you can do unto Viktor before he can do unto you."

He never looked away from her. He could have been a statue, but for the intensity of his eyes. His posture asked how she dared ask that question.

She waited for him to answer it anyway—and tried not to let her own surprisingly personal wishes show.

"I," said Drake finally, "am not the good guy, Bernard. I serve no one but myself. I am not acting in your best interests. But, as much as it is in me to resist, I want nothing to do with the power the dragon offers. Nothing beyond nullifying it."

Relief warred with suspicion. Had he told her the truth, or fed her the biggest load he'd shoveled out yet?

Make up your mind, Bernard.

But she already had, when she took the ring. She already had, last night in her foyer. He hadn't given her any justification for backtracking. So she reached her hand out across the table, toward him. His briar-scraped hand closed over hers with a welcoming tingle of warm, now-familiar energy, and a brief, comforting squeeze. Power ran up her arm, through her shoulder, into her heart, before bursting outward into every bit of her. She wished there wasn't a table between them, wished there weren't even clothes between them. She wished . . .

She pulled her hand free, and her finger slid loose of the ring he still held. He'd agreed to help her, after all. That made it his again.

As if to seal the agreement, he slipped it back onto his little finger. Then he raised his coffee mug in a toast, as if he hadn't felt anything from their touch at all, as if she was nothing more to him than a comrade-in-arms.

When had she gone stupid enough to hope for anything else?

"To dragon slaying," he said softly, intently.

And because that was the business at hand, she made herself lift her mug in a return toast. "To dragon slaying."

And to black knights.

CHAPTER EIGHT

Between them, Drake and Cypress improvised, compromised, and conjured up a plan . . . of sorts.

"I'm not so sure about some of this," hedged Brigit, when Cy phoned her. "You're really starting to trust this guy, huh?"

Don't ask the easy questions, Brie!

"More than I *distrust* him," Cy hedged back. So Brigit agreed to take the baby by her husband's office and to come over later that afternoon. Now, if something went wrong, it would be Cy's fault. Drake might have suggested the core of the plan, but she was the girl inviting her best friends along.

She told herself that it had to be done, that someone had to face what lurked in the shadows of the forest. But so much of what she hoped to do rested on Drake's theories and explanations.

What if he couldn't be trusted, at that?

When Sylvie stopped by on her lunch break to get the news, she whistled, low. "We'd be skirting that ethical edge pretty close," she noted, under her breath so that Drake, in back, wouldn't hear her. "Necessary or not, are you sure you're comfortable dabbling with summonings and magical restraints?"

More tough questions.

"Can you think of anything else we could try?" Cy countered, to cover her own uncertainty. Not a week ago, she'd lit into him for restraining and questioning a ghost. Was it hypocritical for her to now try the same thing? But the ghost might have been the soul of an innocent. They knew the dragon's threat now. And between summoning it to be questioned, and trying to destroy it without even knowing what it was or wanted, the summoning sounded like the lesser of two evils.

"I could do more research," Syl volunteered halfheartedly.

"We may not have time for that." Assuming Drake had been straight with her about Uncle Viktor, too.

So Sylvie agreed to close up her bookstore for the rest of the afternoon, make photocopies of the map, and return in time to go a-hunting dragons.

Cy told herself that they were taking precautions, that her friends would remain out of harm's way. But again, the truth of that rested on how straight Drake was being elsewhere. Could he be using the deadline as motivation, like a salesman saying, "They're going fast?" *What if he really couldn't be trusted?*

After Sylvie left, Cy headed out to the aptly named mud porch where Drake, with a final whispered word of—Latin?—was dropping his muck-encrusted jeans into an aluminum washtub.

Was it her imagination, or did the tepid water truly boil for a moment? Did mere salt and scented oil cause its glow, or did magic? *Double, double, toil and trouble.* She already knew he practiced a less earth-based sorcery than her circle. She didn't trust it, but the special effects sure intrigued her.

Was *that* why she'd agreed to this? Mere curiosity? Worse?

He didn't look up from the tub when she cleared her throat. "I know you are there." But he said it quietly, which gentled the distancing words, whether he'd meant to or not.

Sylvie and Brigit's reservations gave her courage. "Is there a way for you to contact your uncle? I'd feel better knowing what kind of a deadline we're up against."

A tilt of his head turned his gaze to her, his hooded eyes a mystery in contrast to the softness of his borrowed clothing. "Not true. You will feel better only if he has not left yet."

She wished he'd stop second-guessing her. She also wished he'd stop getting it right. "Would you do that for me, please?"

He searched her face for a moment; then he strode into the kitchen and picked up the telephone. See? He was a decent guy.

She lost count of how many numbers he punched in. "Where are you calling, Saturn?"

"England."

"Is that where you grew up?" She really didn't know jack about him. She wished she knew more. She might feel better about this whole unusual alliance, if only she knew more.

"It is where I attended school, yes."

"Where was your home?"

But he held up a hand, listening to the receiver. The pause stretched, taut—and finally he spoke. "Viktor. Hi. I have more information for you. Contact me."

Then he hung up. *More* information?

"Answering machine?" she guessed, disappointed. That told her nothing. Maybe this Viktor person was on a plane for New Orleans, or maybe he'd gone out for a drink.

"Yes."

"That bit about having information for him, that was a ploy so that he'll actually call you, right?"

"Mmm..."

She shouldered in front of him, propping a hip against the black-and-white tiles of her countertop. "Don't just say, 'Mmm...' damn it! Tell me that I can trust you!" Like his pledge would make a difference, if she couldn't.

His eyes widened, mocking. "You did this morning."

True. And last night. "That was before my friends got invited along for the ride. If something happens to them—"

"Then something happens to them! That is their risk."

Her heart plummeted—he really didn't care. He'd told her that, over and over, but proof of it hurt as badly as if she'd been surprised. *But not as badly as if we slept together.*

"Screw you." *Harm none,* she reminded herself, fisting the hand that itched to slap him. Then again, fists made for better punching. She turned away from his cool amusement, her jaw clenched with the effort to control herself.

A warm hand settled on her shoulder, sending delicious tingles down her back. She shrugged it off before she could stretch into the tempting sensation. "Move it or lose it."

"Cypress," he said, low and patient. Almost soft.

She closed her eyes. She didn't want to be seduced...bewitched. No—worse. She *did* want it. But not as much as she wanted her friends' safety. She hadn't sunk *that* far.

He didn't try to touch her again, but she could feel his warmth, the peripheral tingle of him standing right behind her. He said, "Attempt for the moment to imagine a different scenario. Imagine that Brigit was determined to fight the dragon."

Done. Folks who couldn't visualize, couldn't do magic.

"Should she allow you to help defeat it, or would you rather she remain silent, to protect you?"

"I'd want her to ask for my help," she answered. "But she's the one with a family. I'm more expendable."

The hand found her shoulder again, but not in comfort. He spun her around to face him, and for the first time she saw him flat-out angry. His chin lowered, his widened eyes burned into hers. "Nobody," he snarled, "is more or less expendable than anyone else. Ever!"

"Don't you dare manhandle me! You can believe—"

"Know!" he told her. "The luck, or curse, of having family makes a person no less expendable, no more than would wealth, charm, position—or power. You count, too!"

She searched his regal, displeasured face, the weight in her heart easing into curiosity...and into the soothing waves of their mingling magic. Maybe he just meant that she counted to her family, to her circle. But maybe he meant someone else.

Despite his outward coldness, maybe he meant himself.

He still held her shoulder, silent and indignant on her behalf. Who would have thought it?

"I never said I was worthless," she managed finally, feeling less antagonistic. "But I hate to make decisions for other people."

He blinked quickly, as if intrigued. "The only way you could do that would be to not invite them." Like she hadn't invited them to New Orleans with her. Or...

"Like you didn't invite me into the woods with you yesterday?"

"Exactly." Annoyingly enough, he didn't sound the least bit apologetic. His hand slid off her shoulder, for a moment a caress, then gone. "If your friends cannot say no as easily as I can, that is their weakness, not mine. Will that be all?"

She knew a dismissal when she heard it; this man was cutting her off, freezing her out. Maybe she'd gotten too close. Or maybe she really *couldn't* trust him.

She followed him back to the mud porch, and decided against dumping a tub of salt water, oil, mud, clothing and evil over his head. He didn't need any more traces of evil. "Besides helping me save Stagwater from the forces of evil this afternoon? No, that's about it."

So he hunkered down beside the big trash bag where she'd stowed his fouled clothing last night, and he extracted a boot. "Then I would prefer privacy for this, thank you."

To judge by his attitude, he'd prefer privacy for everything. She'd bet good money that if the man had sex at all, it was in one-night stands with women whose last names he wouldn't remember—and at their place, never his, oh, no.

She went inside and left him with his precious privacy, and the last word: "My pleasure."

* * *

By now, Drake knew his way into this stretch of the woods quite well, but he used Cypress's walking odometer and compass anyway. He could sense the lure of evil calling to his blood—stronger for having tasted of it last night. But because of the forest-filtered daylight, and perhaps Cypress's nearness, that lure felt blessedly weaker. This time, the dragon must not confuse or distract him. This time, he would remain in charge of the confrontation, and the dragon's extermination.

The witches hoped to discover an alternative to destroying the dragon, through interrogation. Harm none, and all that. But one way or the other, they would end this today. Before the evil compelled him to make any more uncomfortable sacrifices!

"It's spooky out here," murmured Mary, walking with Cypress behind him. "Like Hansel and Gretel, going too far into the woods, except that *we're* the witches." They smelled of cedar, eucalyptus and pine, as had the other two witches, left to guard the other two arms of the ley lines. Their aromatherapy mixed with a hint of sandalwood smoke from the incense they had burned together before leaving. He might have dismissed their efforts, and the protective amulets they all now carried, as folk superstitions. But the piece of black jet in his pocket, inscribed with a rune for victory, radiated a strong magic indeed. Perhaps another reason for the dragon's call to feel faint?

"Hansel and Gretel," said Cypress, "had it easy. Well, with the witch. They didn't have the compass, though."

"You can still turn back," Mary told her, and he paused to look back at the two friends. Dawn and dusk, one beside the other. Of the two, he found Cypress's mysterious darkness more attractive. She had pulled her hair into an incredibly thick black braid that showed off her neck. She looked more competent, as well—and overly concerned for her younger friend.

"Do you not want us to leave you alone?" she asked.

"Me?" Mary shook her blond head. "Nuh-uh. I'm okay, and Brie and Sylvie will be, too. We're just worried about you."

Drake quirked an eyebrow, wondering if she had meant censure with that. She might not know why he had let his blood to escape these woods last night, but she obviously had suspicions that went beyond mere survival. "Now is hardly the time for second thoughts," he warned.

"Yeah," agreed Cypress dryly. "And later would be even worse. What's got you worried, honey?" She *didn't* mean him.

Mary shrugged, wordlessly, and he tried to hold back his impatience. Or was that guilt? *Blood magic.* But he had warned them that the creature had fed recently—the rest was hardly their business. Telling the truth did not mean telling all the truth. "The dragon is a creature of negativity and darkness. If it senses doubts or uncertainties, it may use them against us. If you cannot do this with confidence, Bernard, perhaps you should stay safely outside the arm of the stream, with Mary."

Cypress turned on him. "No way are you questioning that creature alone." First she had grilled him at breakfast, then she'd demanded he call Viktor, and now this. What kind of pledge did she want from him? Probably more than he could give.

He smiled coolly. "Why, Bernard, do you not trust me?"

She narrowed her eyes, and the overlarge fishing vest she wore suddenly reminded him of armor. "It doesn't matter if I do or not, 'cause I'm going to be with you every minute."

"Not if you endanger me."

"You're the one who got his butt kicked last night!"

"And you have never done this before."

Mary Poitiers pushed between them, like a referee with prizefighters who have not heard the bell. "Enough! Shut up, both of you. This is about the worst pep talk I've ever heard!"

The little blond witch had a point. Were they actually *bickering?* He had never bickered in his life!

Cypress's easygoing nature took root again, her slow smile part chagrin, part wary amusement. She offered her hand, the one not holding the staff. "Truce?"

He hesitated. She obviously *did* have doubts about his ethics, perhaps even his abilities. *Were* they up to this?

She frowned and extended her hand farther. *"Truce?"* It sounded more like a command than a request, this time.

In her determination, he found the one hope he *could* latch on to. If heart counted, she could surely hold her own. Perhaps that was the circle's magic secret: heart.

He took her hand. "Truce."

The magic, the overflow of their magnified energy, rushed through his hand, his wrist, and up his arm. Together, they doubled or even tripled their combined power. Their own secret weapon, their best defense—and perhaps his lifeline against the call of evil that, while they talked, seemed to grow stronger.

She stared at their hands, then at him, and tugged. He belatedly released her, tamping down the bereft sensation of her hand leaving his, of their powers fading back to a normal level. She must not think that he was using her, after all. He was not. He had not explained how their abilities heightened together, but neither had he stolen her energy for his own purposes. Fighting the temptation of Cypress Bernard had become as great a challenge as fighting the temptations of the dragon; had he given in last night, heaven knew how he might have harnessed or used the power their lovemaking would surely have thrown off. But he had *not* given in. He *could* maintain his distance, his neutrality—at least until they had dealt with the dragon. Then he would not have to see her, to face her temptations, anymore. As long as things went smoothly from here on out, he would make it through this.

Then, as if on ironic cue, Mary Poitiers asked, "Isn't this stake supposed to be *in* the ground?"

* * *

Damn damn damn.

Cypress hated movies where the stupid heroine walked into the dark basement despite knowing that an escaped killer is on the loose. And yet here she was, walking into a dying woods to confront a deadly creature, with a man she didn't wholly trust.

Drake had been right last Sunday. If he killed her now, she would be incredibly annoyed.

Dead and dying pine trees swayed above them, as if in a wind, but there was no wind. At one point a branch from a low scrub tree grasped at her hair. She swatted its gnarled fingers away, more alarmed than she would have liked. She *loved* trees.

"They did no damage before," Drake assured her, as if reading her mind. "I believe they are merely a scare tactic."

And a damn good one, she thought, wishing she could be as calm as he. But he paid quite a price for his nonchalance, didn't he? No friends. No real moral code. Maybe calm wasn't so good. It sure seemed less and less practical.

That the stake they'd used to bind in the evil hadn't been in the ground still upset her deeply. After testing the area, they'd learned that the black stream had gained another twenty feet overnight. They'd left Mary back on safer ground, but what about the branches that Sylvie and Brigit guarded, from supposed safety? Mary had insisted that the others were intelligent and capable, that Cy and Drake not worry. But Cy did worry.

"I wonder why the trees would go along with it," she whispered as a distraction, so quietly that when he turned to look at her, he obviously hadn't heard what she'd said.

"If the dragon is incorporeal, it shan't likely have ears. It will know we are coming," he assured her. *Thanks, Drake.*

"I said, I wonder why the trees would help it? Especially pines. Pines should be protective."

As if annoyed at the generalization, a dead branch tumbled from a loblolly pine to land in front of them, its gnarled, gray-scaled claws missing her face by inches.

"Perhaps they are protecting the dragon," he theorized as she moved bravely ahead of him. "Or perhaps they are possessed."

Possessed trees? *Night of the Living Lumber.* She laughed, pleased that he would lighten the mood. He didn't join her.

Oh. He wasn't lightening anything.

The trees seemed to whisper at them—threats? No matter how hard she concentrated, she couldn't make out real words. They bent as if to grab at the trespassers, and they dropped twigs and limbs and dry pinecones, like spiky grenades.

She remembered something from Sunday. "In fact, they shouldn't even be here. This should be old growth—"

"Bernard."

When she realized he hadn't followed her, she managed not to scurry back to him, but walked steadily instead. He was exhuming something from the ground. At first it looked like a root, but then the bulk of it pulled free. Dirt fell from its mucky leather sides. It was a backpack, apparently his, and she had a sickening image of just how his clothing had gotten so muddy. *This* was where he'd been attacked last night.

She turned evenly, looking for signs of struggle, of damage, of the tendrils he'd described. Nothing but the deep Louisiana woods surrounded them, full of swaying trees and stinking evil. The hair on the back of her neck prickled.

"We should almost be there," he advised her, passing her to stoically resume their course, mucky backpack and all.

She followed. "How'll we know—?" But then she saw it.

"Hopefully something will clue us in." Obviously he hadn't. "Something out of place. Perhaps—" When she grasped his arm with both hands, he stopped. "What?"

She pointed. "The oak!"

He followed the point of her finger to the tree. Even dead, the ancient oak's sprawl of low-slung branches was larger than a circus tent, and its trunk was the size of a Volkswagen. She'd seen trees like that in the swamp before, and at antebellum mansions. But she'd never seen one that looked to have been struck by lightning. What remained of it—charred black and shrouded in bits of Spanish moss—looked ancient, desolate, and dead. The pines near it swayed and moaned. The oak did nothing.

"That is the nexus?" he asked quietly.

"Look around, do you see any other hardwoods? This forest should be full of them! Instead, it has old pine trees, and this."

Maybe he understood, maybe not. But he believed her, and his posture tensed. "Cast the circle."

She used the walking stick she'd brought to begin scraping a wide arc in the dirt and pine straw, the start of a circle around them. She moved deasil, or clockwise, envisioning walls of light bursting upward from the line. She pulled a carton of salt from one of the cargo pockets in her insulated vest, pouring it onto the ridge she dug for extra precaution.

Sorry, plant life. But everything here was dead anyway.

Behind her, she heard Drake scraping into the ground, as well, and knew he was drawing the restraining triangle.

The ground moved, awkwardly, under her feet. "Drake!"

"Do not stop!"

And don't remember that the dragon is probably strongest at the nexus point. And don't wonder if that's why it let you get so close. She mentally caught at the magical wall that she'd already raised, and continued. She wanted to hurry, but for something this important, the sphere should be an actual circle—hooray for geometry—and reinforced.

She heard a clink of metal, the spurt and crackle of a match, and then, in a moment, smelled the first waftings of incense.

"Cypress," Drake said, calm and soft, behind her, "hurry."

"I am," she insisted, speeding her pace even more.

"They are getting closer."

She glanced up, saw nothing but tormented pines and the corpse of the gnarled oak. She continued drawing. "What are?"

"Can you not see them?" He came to where she'd started the circle and, with a stick off the ground, began to scratch the arc quickly toward her. He was working counterclockwise—widdershins. Granny said never to do that.

She looked up at the woods again, her heart pounding, and saw no sign of danger, but because he hurried, she tried to speed up more. Her walking stick bounced over several inches of ground. She had to back up and close that—so much for speed.

Then he stood beside her, narrowing the circle's opening from his side while she did the same from hers. He caught her waist with one strong hand, as if ready to sweep her behind him and away from something. She felt the usual tingle—

And, raising her head at a peripheral movement, she saw why Drake rushed. Black, semitranslucent tendrils, like tongues of oily smoke, slithered from the ground, across the forest floor and directly at them. She refused to scream.

Drake finished the circle, widdershins. Not letting go of her, he snatched the salt from her numb hand to reinforce it. "Consecrate it!"

The evil snaked closer. She took a deep breath, drawing on her own energy, and that of the earth beneath her feet, the sky above her—and the sun and the moon and the stars. "We bind this circle with our power, to guard this place beyond place, this time beyond time. As it harms none, so it must—"

The tendrils struck just as he finished with the salt, and they bounced off the invisible protection . . . which wasn't quite invisible anymore. She gaped, overwhelmed.

"So?" he said, and they finished, "... it must be."

For a moment, she let herself lean into the power and protection of him. She'd never felt so glad for a man's arm around her in her life—and not, this time, for either their sizzling connection of energies or their building attraction. Maybe she trusted him, at that. The fact that he stood with her, that she wasn't alone for this, meant everything.

She looked up at him, watched him scan the area around them. *Everything.*

The walls of the magic circle—actually a sphere or bubble, though where it intersected with the ground it made a circle—shimmered, barely visible in this realm. By touching him, she seemed to see their surroundings with his magical perceptions and not just hers. Was that all that made his magic different, just a different level of sensitivity, and not evil at all?

More tendrils joined the first, a coiled ground fog outside the circle. Taking on his perceptions was a mixed blessing.

He gave her a quick squeeze, then took her hand and stepped to the triangle he'd scratched into the ground, well within the safety of the circle. As he edged it with more salt, she fancied that she could see it glow, as well, a three-sided pyramid—but instead of a blue-white light, like the circle, this glow looked darker... more like the tendrils.

What kind of magic *was* he fooling with?

He knelt beside it, in the smoke of the incense he'd lit, and used his wand to trace arcane symbols in the dirt, between the candles. She wished she understood them. What if she was participating in something truly evil, truly wrong?

She tried to tug her hand from his, to give him more freedom. His own grip tightened. When he looked up, his dark gaze held her. "Please," he whispered—and he meant it.

She stopped trying to reclaim her hand, and prayed she wasn't selling her soul on the basis of his plea. She *had* to trust him, at least until they'd defeated the dragon.

She continued holding his hand.

Each symbol he drew sent a different-colored zap of light through the translucent walls of this magical cage, darkening it like smoked glass. The ground beneath them shifted again.

"Will it fit in there?"

"If it is incorporeal, size is irrelevant," he murmured.

"And if it isn't?"

He didn't say anything, so she guessed it: *Then we're screwed.* Wouldn't Mary love *that* pep talk?

The ground shook again, as if from a giant's footstep. The trees above them whipped and bent—one, dead and brittle, snapped. Its full crown, whiskered with dead needles, landed with a crash and a spray of debris, just outside the circle.

An unearthly wind began to pick up, to howl at them, as he stood, his hair blowing back from his regal face, and squeezed her hand. "Are you ready?"

Ready to do a summons? Ready to tamper with powers she didn't fully understand? Ready to risk everything and everyone she cared about? No, she wasn't. Everything around her—the coils of blackness, the trembling earth, the looming oak, the tormented pines, and even being able to see magics that for her entire life had remained invisible—it all felt like a particularly vivid, horrible nightmare.

All except Drake, beside her. *Trust.* He yelled louder, over the devilish wind. "Cypress, are you ready?"

She nodded, and let him raise her hand as he raised his. He began to chant in Latin, pausing every few lines to translate. *By our powers, and all powers at our command, we summon the creature who dares call evil to this place!* Then, more Latin. *We summon the creature who dares attack our people!*

Our people, she thought, not looking at his face, trying to concentrate. *Our* people?

She felt the power that built between them redirect itself into the triangular cage. She felt tricklings of other, blessedly familiar energies—her circlemates, using the natural conduit of the ley lines to send their own strength to Drake and Cypress, to use as they saw fit.

As they saw fit...

He continued his chant. *We summon thee to speak the truth. We summon thee to know thee. Come. Come!*

Power—hers, Brigit's, Sylvie's, Mary's and Drake's—rushed through her, through every vein, every bone, every fiber of her, intoxicating and exhilarating. It filled her ears with a roar, blurred her vision with colors and lights, filled her nose and mouth and lungs. She let her head fall back, savoring the almost orgasmic sensation, and suddenly understood why Viktor—and Drake—would want power.

Her first summons, her first borderline magic—and it felt *good!* He stood beside her, along with her the center of this swirling magic. His head fallen back in similar exaltation, his arms thrown wide, his lips forming words she didn't even understand, he should have frightened her, now more than ever.

When they made it out alive, it probably would.

But for now, she joined him in his magic—*"Veni, veni, veni"*—and in his compromised ethics. But only to defeat the dragon, she thought, to comfort herself. Only to save Stagwater.

"Come! Come! Come!"

Then, in a sickening cold rush, the dragon came.

CHAPTER NINE

Evil really is black?

Hatred and anger lashed outward from their caged adversary like shock waves, and sparks of stray magic from both sides scattered into the ether. Instinctively she ducked her face toward the tall protection of Drake's side, but she immediately felt the resulting ripple in the current of magic that ran through them both. Now was *not* the time to lose focus.

She made herself straighten, made herself look upon the roiling, dark presence that their own magic had called and now held. She shuddered, but the flow of their magic steadied.

"Good girl," whispered Drake, without turning from it. Condescending ass. She squeezed his hand affectionately.

Blackness *did* fill the air over the triangle, but not the color black, not like her hair or Drake's usual I'm-a-wizard clothing. This wasn't the mixture of all colors, but the absence of any. Nothing, color or light, existed where the "dragon" lurked. The being that hovered there, as if on a projection screen, wasn't so much an entity as a nonentity, a void.

A magnified, hungry void, with an attitude. And it wanted them. It stank of sulfur and ozone. Occasionally, as if it were testing its restraints, crackles of something like electricity pulsed out of its darkness. She heard—felt—a forceful call from the darkness, as well, as if it were willing their souls into its depths. *Come...* Like there was any chance of that!

But Drake's gasped ''No!'' sounded strained. More guardedly this time, she glanced toward him. His regal posture trembled. Soft, dark hair stuck to his sweat-dampened forehead and temples, fell over eyes narrowed in challenge. His hand strained to not crush hers. Could the shared power that gave her such a rush be hurting him? Then she realized: No. Not their power.

The dragon's. The dragon was doing something to Drake.

''Stop it!'' she commanded, and let the beast feel a flare of her own power. Drake's grip tightened. ''I said *stop it!*''

And it turned its attention to her.

The urge to lose himself within the drawn triangle lessened as the dragon's focus shifted. Drake took immediate, if shaky, advantage of that. ''As we will it, so shall you answer.''

The darkness before him roiled, twisted, and focused on him again. *Come,* it seemed to purr—and though he knew he only imagined a voice for its telepathic sending, that voice seemed eerily familiar. *Come home...*

It might as well have dug its claws into his heart and tugged. *Home, where you'll be accepted, where you'll be one of us. Come, child. Come home.* He fought to resist the cruel temptation.

His heart shuddered its misery when he succeeded.

''*No!*'' protested Cypress, and pointed shakily at the creature. ''As we will it, so you're going to answer, damn it!''

Her technique left much to be desired. But it worked. Concession struck out at them like a cold, furious blow. *Yes.*

That brought a momentary lull as they reaped the energy of a small victory, and his partner in magic murmured, ''Score one for the home team.''

Knowing that they were not out of the woods yet, so to speak, he locked his arm around her waist. Merely to ground himself, of course. To make it more difficult to obey any summons, should the dragon ensnare him again—because, of course, it was targeting him, not her. She had less for the dragon to appeal to. And it had not tasted her blood.

Their denim-clad hips bumped; her body warmed him against the chill of dark, extreme magic. Strong and real in the heart of the reviving chaos around them, Cypress *did* ground and center him. Their shared energy, tapping her friends' magical contribution, swelled.

"As we will it..." Her words stumbled, perhaps distracted by the forces blowing about them, or by the headachy strain of this sustained battle of wills. Never had he faced anything so strong; that she did not faint spoke well of her.

You ought not have brought her. If you give in, she dies.

He closed his eyes against the thought.

"As we will it," she tried again, more slowly and more powerfully, "so you're going to speak the truth!"

Yes. The dragon weakened with each forced answer.

He opened his eyes, gathered his own authority. "And as we will it, so you shall remain until we dismiss you!"

Together, they stared it down. This time, the creature's defeated *Yesss!* carried images of insects and worms. Was it calling them names?

"Who keeps you here in Stagwater?" demanded Cypress, much as he had behind her granny's shack—his little witch had a good memory, did she not?

Your little witch?

Whatever response the dragon offered came as more emotion—hatred and misery, anger and vicious despair. A dark void.

"Who—?" Cypress began to repeat, but he stilled her by squeezing her hand, which she had let him hold behind her.

"That was its answer," he said quietly. "It serves nobody. It keeps itself here." His headache intensified, pounding, tearing. "Where do you come from?"

Images overwhelmed him. *An ocean, then mud, then foliage growing from the mud. A swamp, then the Louisiana woods. Innumerable suns rise and set, moons rise and set, dizzying. Trees. Animals. Feather-garbed Indians . . .*

The images stopped.

"More!" he commanded, against the dragon's resistance.

Indians. Magic. Oak tree grows. Long imprisonment. Calling to the lightning, again, again. Finally—freedom.

Suddenly the images grew more clear. *A redheaded woman, familiar from the newspaper, hikes unsuspecting into the nighttime woods—until a tendril of darkness strikes at her ankle, captures her, pulls her to the ground.*

Cypress cursed at the truth of Lucille Witt's fate. Drake sensed horrible pride, as if it were saying, *What I shall do to you!*

"Enough!" he commanded, sharply, but his horror at the too-familiar attack weakened the effect.

The woman struggles, screams as tendrils drag her through the pine straw and the dirt. The poor, mundane girl had not stood a chance. He sensed glee: *What I shall do to you both!*

"*Enough!*" This time it would not dispute his demand.

The images stopped. The dragon roiled, venomous, a great beast peering through the small gateway of the triangle.

He braced himself, eyes narrowed against the vortex of conjury that surrounded them, blowing at their hair, tricking their balance—with every passing minute, he and Cypress lost more strength. "What will destroy you?"

Of all their questions, he had expected the dragon to resist answering that, but it offered satisfaction. *Nothing.*

Beside him, Cypress shook her head, unaccepting. "Then what will convince you to leave this world?"

Nothing.

She looked up at him, her face strained, her eyes bright with exhausted frustration. When he offered nothing, her eyes widened, and then she looked quickly away.

You've trained her to count on you. You've let her think you're omnipotent. She'll hate you for deceiving her. Were the thoughts his... or the dragon's? *You want her.* And he did, like an ache, like an addiction. The thoughts could be his. *You want her more than you've ever wanted—and you'll destroy her.*

"Tell us," he tried quickly, belatedly, "what can convince you to stop harming the people of Stagwater?"

Nothing. The dragon felt gleeful, as if it were regaining strength each time it stymied them.

"You're lying!" At Cypress's accusation, the darkness roiled silently. If a featureless, colorless void could look smug, it did. They'd forced it not to lie, after all.

Even evil can tell the truth. You tell the truth. But she'll hate even truthful evil. She could never love such as you. You'll be alone forever, hated forever.... The fears battered his soul, pulling his breath shallow, pressing at his heart. *Alone forever. Hated forever—by her.*

Only Cypress's angry sob dragged him from his self-loathing to realize what was happening, what must be happening. The dragon's main weapon, despair, had struck deep and true.

"It is playing with our minds!"

When she turned to him, he could see she did not fully believe him. Whatever it used against her...

Not you. You could never be important enough.

...was all but drawing blood. But they had summoned this thing. They could control it, *must* control it! Only lunatics or fools lost control of what they summoned. Fools like his father.

Trees thrashed around them. Warring powers battled in a crackling maelstrom of magical currents.

"Drake?" Cypress's weary whisper tore at him; he felt her powers trembling. "I can't do much more of this...."

You will destroy her!

"You," Drake snarled, desperate, "will be silent!"

She blinked and closed her mouth, clearly taken aback—but the punishing images left off, too.

"Get the salt," he commanded into the sudden silence, and thought to glance down at her. "You, this time."

She crouched, grabbed for the salt that one of them had dropped, then looked up at him with the craziest, most inappropriate laugh. Only fools? The sound echoed life into the timeless, placeless boundaries of their circle, and strengthened them as nothing else—almost nothing else—could have.

Their gazes lingered as he drew her back up. Ridiculously, he smiled back at her, and felt their strength grow. He hooked a booted ankle around hers, to maintain contact but free their hands. "Shake it into your clothes," he instructed, his hands fumbling with hers as they upended the carton, grasped handfuls of the white powder, and dropped it down their own and one another's collars, into their waistbands, through their hair. The clutch of despair eased more at the make-do cleansing.

Beside them, the silent dragon pulsed angrily. The pyramid around it flexed and shimmered, catching their attention.

It wanted out.

"Oh, my..." murmured Cypress.

He caught her against him again. "Reinforce the binding."

The walls of restraining energy glowed brighter, and they sagged against one another in its aftermath. *So tired.* Even the energy from the witches had petered out into a small trickle.

If they stayed, they *would* lose control. "We must leave."

She blinked at him, all laughter gone. "But we haven't fixed anything!" *Had* she expected him to be omnipotent?

He had disappointed her. Were his other fears true, too? The darkness that stared back at them shifted, struggled. "If we do not leave now, we will not have the chance!"

She glared, angry—but at least anger built strength. "Are you willing to come back again?"

And do what? He refused to rush a decision, silent.

Her expression hardened. "Fine! So how do we leave?"

Suddenly the darkness before them began to thrash. Pain ripped through his mind as the dragon tore at their magic, at their beings. Cypress cried out, as well, clutched at him for balance, but they willed the beast into momentary complacency.

As soon as he could speak, he clarified himself.

"We make a run for it."

Of course, decided Cypress blearily, her hand still in Drake's, he couldn't keep anything that simple. The trick was to run and to hold back the dragon at the same time.

"Once we have opened the circle," he directed, his usual, crisp diction slurred by his own weariness, "the power we have already accumulated will scatter. The farther we go..."

He didn't have to finish; the increasing hunger that emanated from the trapped entity said it all. The farther they went, the more likely it was that their concentration would waver and the dragon would escape again. Despite their best efforts. Not that she *wanted* to believe him. But she had no choice.

She'd never regretted releasing a magic circle—*ever the circle continues*—as much as this one. Suddenly the haze and shimmer of magic around them vanished, leaving only the darkening, ominously silent Louisiana woods. It felt as if they'd imagined what had just—

Concentrate! She looked back. Despite the deceptive normalcy around her, the void of darkness remained, roiling, over the dirt-drawn triangle and the pine straw. It thrashed again, and her head felt as if it would split under the battle of wills. If loose, it *would* kill them, and others, too. They'd failed....

Drake dragged at her hand. "Now!"

They ran. Neither had the strength to move quickly. They stumbled between now-silent trees, over fallen trunks, through patches of briars and underbrush. If they ended up on separate sides of a tree, one would stop and the other would come back around—he refused to release her hand.

Why? It's not as if he cares, as if he could ever care—

He'd said the dragon was playing with their minds. She made herself concentrate, despite the resurgence of the despair that had shaken her, back in the circle. Her breath rasped in her lungs, in harmony with Drake's. *Harmony? You've never fit into anyone's world. Why would he allow you, want you, in his?*

They had to be nearing safety soon. Mary would be there; Cy wished she could call out.

Concentrate!

A blackberry briar snagged her ankle; too tired, she couldn't catch her balance. Still trying to hold Drake's hand, she fell onto her hip—and their fingers wrenched apart.

Too late to concentrate. All magic stopped.

Then the ground beneath them trembled, as if struck by a god. Had they really thought mere mortals could hold it indefinitely? Had they really thought they could survive?

His hand, at the waistband of her jeans now, wrenched her back to her unsteady feet. "Come *on!*"

"Why bother?" Confusion battled with despair. *Why—?*

He bit back a curse. She'd never seen him so haggard— still bruised from last night, he had new scratches on that regal jaw, his hair was falling over his cold eyes, and there was sweat on his upper lip. As she stood there, watched him blur beneath her own tears—*What's happening to me?*—the lip pressed into a sneer.

"Suit yourself," he hissed, and turned away from her, toward safety. It was just as she'd feared. Despite the hand-holding, the kissing, and her idiotic hopes, he didn't care.

Again the ground trembled. She may not care about surviving—but no way was he surviving without her. "Son of a bitch," she muttered, and stumbled after him.

As soon as she got close, his hand snaked out and caught her own, pulled. He'd *tricked* her? She couldn't fight anymore. Defeated and confused, she let him lead her. Another tremor threw off their balance; so did his sudden burst of speed.

Then Mary stood there, waiting for them. "What's happening? I tried to sense y'all, and I couldn't feel anything!"

"Get back!" snarled Drake. "Where is the stake?"

She saw her younger friend point at a spot behind them. "What happened?" Mary asked again.

Drake released Cy and fell back against a gray pine trunk. Mary immediately reached for her—but when her hands touched Cy's shoulders, the blonde recoiled from her. "Ee-euw!"

Cypress stared at her. Mary the massage therapist didn't want to touch her? Mary stared back, horrified.

"Oh, Cy, I'm sorry, that came out wrong! It's just—you don't feel right. You feel . . . bad. Wrong. Dark."

Well, that could explain her headache and her moods, the way she felt like bursting into either tears or fury at any moment. Unable to explain it herself, any of it, Cy wrapped her arms around her middle and looked expectantly, suspiciously, to Drake.

He stood with his head back against the support of the tree, his eyes closed, his skin so pale that the bruises stood out like dark shadows in contrast. When he felt their stares, his sooty lashes lifted to reveal depthless eyes.

He said, "We must leave these woods. It controls them."

Her stomach lurched. That the ground had shifted again only partially excused that.

"What's happened to Cypress?" demanded Mary. "Why does she suddenly feel like the Wicked Witch of the South?"

"Perhaps because she just spent—" He checked his watch slowly, as if even turning his wrist exhausted him. Maybe it did. "Almost an hour in the presence of something evil."

Cy bit back a humorless laugh. "Perhaps?"

Mary scowled, maybe thinking the same thing Cy was. Had the summoning been more than just borderline magic? Had Cypress stepped over the line, into the so-called "black" arts?

Cy shook her head, then regretted it, as unwilling to face that possibility as she was to leave. "We didn't accomplish a thing! All this, and it's still there! Why's it still there?"

He glared at her. She glared right back. Finally, he pushed away from the tree. "Because I botched it!" And he stalked away from them, toward the road, the car, escape.

The ground continued its otherworldly tremors. Cypress looked at the stake; several inches of it were sticking out of the silty soil. She stepped over to it, viciously stomped the thing deeper into the ground, and followed Drake.

A concerned Mary trailed her. "Look. Guy's brother Ralph is visiting this weekend. Maybe you should meet with him, and—"

"He's a priest." Not to mention an ex-boyfriend. Ralph Poitiers had been a sweet lug, always ready to help out—the complete opposite of Drake. No wonder he'd ended up as clergy.

"That's the point," said Mary.

Was she suggesting a kind of exorcism? "I'm not Catholic!"

"Well, neither am I anymore, but if you've gotten yourself into something over your head, what would it hurt to— Cypress?"

Cy just walked faster.

Mary stopped making suggestions, except to say, "I'll drive," when they reached the road and Cy's car.

Neither Drake nor Cypress argued with her.

* * *

A quick bath in her own home, in water anointed with cleansing lilac oil, helped bolster her strength and her mood. She was alive, wasn't she? Her friends were safe, for now. Yes, the dragon still remained, but surely they could figure out a decent plan B, with or without Drake Benedict's help.

Considering the risks she'd already taken with her soul, she wasn't sure which would be better. With, or without?

She left the steamy bathroom wrapped in her favorite hand-loomed robe and nearly walked right into him. Now that she'd rid herself of the evil's worst residue, she could feel it, smell it, on him. He passed her wordlessly and, disappearing into the steam, locked the door behind him.

Maybe she just felt his anger. Anger at the dragon for outwitting them, at himself for allowing it. And maybe at her?

"Cy, come here!" Brigit waved her into the dining room, where the circle had already set out sandwiches and milk as a "simple feast." After having expended as much energy as they had today, refueling was *not* a bad idea. "Sylvie's got a theory."

Cy sat, and chugged half a glass of milk right there, feeling stronger by the swallow. Mary stepped behind her to rub her shoulders through the robe and said, "You feel clean now. The milk didn't curdle, either."

It took Cy a moment to figure out what they meant; by then, she'd already swallowed a bite of sandwich, too. Food, and a neck rub from Mary; friendship couldn't get much better than this. "Isn't that an old wives' tale about a way to recognize witches?"

"What were most witches—" Sylvie grinned "—but old wives?"

"Apparently it just indicates dark magic," added Brigit. "Never worked on my family, but you should have seen what happened to Drake's glass." She wrinkled her nose.

The bite of sandwich caught in Cy's throat, and she had to gulp more milk to get it down. Then she felt queasy. "Drake?"

Sylvie cocked her head, intrigued. "We figure it's the residual. Probably. You've got some major housecleansing to do, after the stuff you two tracked in."

Yeah. Residual, that was all. "Brigit said you've got yourselves a theory?" She knew they'd come through for her.

Sylvie, the group thinker, nodded. "While you cleaned up, Drake told us what happened."

"Finally," Mary added.

"And we think that the dragon has probably been here all along. For a long time—centuries, maybe—it hasn't caused any trouble, because it's been bound into the oak tree you saw. The one that was—"

Cy followed. "Hit by lightning, which is when the dragon started to get out!" They high-fived each other over the table.

"Since before I met Rand," agreed Sylvie. "It's probably been affecting the town in a couple of ways. Directly, it magnifies illness, depression, feelings of worthlessness, just like the black streams would. Except, being more dangerous than a black stream, it, well . . ."

"Eats the people that get too close," suggested Cy.

"Right. And indirectly," added Brigit quickly, pouring herself some milk, "it attracts other evils, like what we've been running into this past year."

"But the main point," insisted Mary, with an excited bounce, "is if it was trapped once, it can be trapped again!"

Sylvie helped herself to a pickle slice. "Do you have any idea what kind of Indians used to live around here?"

Did she! "Natchez," answered Cy easily, and saw from the glow in Sylvie's eyes that the girl was setting herself up for disappointment, even before Syl's next question.

"Is there some sort of tribal center we could contact, to look for a shaman?"

"'Fraid not. The French killed off most of the tribe in the 1700s, and sold the rest into slavery in the West Indies. Granny says she's one-sixteenth Natchez; she's told me stories. But nothing about their magic, or binding things into trees."

Mary sank back in her chair. "Oh."

Feeling mildly better for having finished her sandwich, Cy leaned forward from hers. "He helped y'all figure this out?"

Mary nodded.

That meant it was only her he wasn't speaking to, only her who inspired his anger. The doubts that had assaulted her in the woods whispered louder. *He doesn't think you're important. He sneers at your craft, at your ethics. He's too rich, too powerful, too self-contained, for you. You embarrass him...*

Did the thoughts' persistence, now that she was clean, fed, safe and surrounded by friends, mean the dragon hadn't been playing with her mind at all? Were they true?

His appearance from the hallway, wearing Guy Poitiers' clothes again, startled her. When his hard gaze touched hers, it immediately moved on. "There is nothing more to be done tonight," he announced to the group at large, as if someone had elected him president. "The sun shall set soon. You had best go home." And, that said, he put his dirty pack down beside the door, as if he included himself among the people about to make an exodus.

Damn. The ache in her chest had nothing to do with today's nightmare...except maybe that they'd gone through it together, and he didn't care. Or he blamed her for its failure. She liked the second idea; it showed him in a poorer light.

"Cypress, why don't you stay with me and Rand tonight?" offered Sylvie, starting to clear the table. When Cy stood to take over, Syl pushed her firmly back down. "With that thing trying to get past the stake between it and your house, you shouldn't stay here alone."

"Or you could stay with Guy and me," added Mary over her shoulder, following Sylvie to the kitchen.

Drake said, very softly, "Or you could stay with me."

The world paused. She stared. "Come again?"

He still looked angry, his jaw tense, his eyes hard. Despite the lighter clothing, despite the dampness of his hair, he looked more regal than ever, and highly displeased about something. But maybe—her pulse sped—not about her. Either that, or he meant to get her alone specifically because she'd displeased him—and he meant to do something about it.

She stood, to silently remind him that she had some height and strength, as well. She was nobody to mess with.

He didn't drop his gaze. "You have done the same for me."

Oh. He was just offering a place to sleep. But something in those hard eyes seemed to offer more than a place to sleep. Something behind that reserved expression, in the eyes that were now drifting toward the opening of her robe, sizzled through her, as surely as did his touch. As surely as did his shady magic.

Maybe her granny had raised a fool after all. It *would* be good to get away from Stagwater, just for a night, wouldn't it?

She nodded, and turned toward the kitchen, where Brigit had apparently filled in the others on this new complication. Her friends' expressions ran from intrigue to disapproval.

"I'll be in New Orleans tonight," she told them firmly.

"But first," returned Brigit, just as firmly, "one for the road." And the woman actually handed Drake a glass of milk.

Like he wouldn't catch on! He looked at the milk, at the witches, then strode into the kitchen with it. Cy's stomach sank; the last thing she needed was more reason not to trust him!

Then, with a cocky raise of the glass, he downed the whole thing. He rinsed the glass, set it in the sink, and folded his arms. Either the milk hadn't curdled, or the man's stomach was as iron as his will. He wouldn't be tricked into revealing the truth, anyhow!

Turning away to go dress and pack an overnight bag before she could change her mind, Cy figured she'd give it even odds.

CHAPTER TEN

They barely spoke during the drive across the lake, into New Orleans. Instead, they listened to opera—Wagner. Drake wondered fleetingly if Cypress caught the irony of that selection, but anger overrode such musings.

Not annoyed, not disturbed, he was feeling the full force of burning anger for the first time in years. How dare the "dragon" insult him with mind games? How dare it try to use Cypress—someone ostensibly under his protection—against him?

He still did not care about good versus evil. But something had changed.

Slumped in the passenger seat, Cypress wore boots, green leggings and an overlong black sweater. Hardly clothes she would don to entice romantic attention—but they did anyway. The leggings hugged her strong, shapely legs like stockings. The wide collar of the sweater threatened to fall off one tawny shoulder or the other, depending on when he glanced at her. The gold ankh around her neck showed one moment, hid the next.

She had brought her overnight bag without question; had she accepted his invitation merely to escape Stagwater for a night—or was there something more? How deep did his unexpected feelings for her run, for that bloody dragon to have so easily used them as weapons?

In pursuit of magical expertise, he had all but trained himself out of emotion, forbidden himself to care. But apparently he truly *had* botched things. He *did* care, *did* feel. And of everything that had happened in the past week, that loss of emotional constraint infuriated him most of all. But perhaps not enough to keep him from testing his limits, from exploring just how much he would risk for a taste…of her.

He found a parking space for the rental car barely a block from his French Quarter flat. She shouldered her overnight bag—did she think he would steal it?—and headed in the correct direction. For better, or for worse, she remembered.

He strode past her, through the veiling mist, to unlock the ironwork gate into his courtyard. He had begun locking the thing two weeks ago, so that nobody else would annoy him with self-righteous requests for assistance. He had been too late.

Together, they climbed the stairs where she had stood when first he saw her—before he had felt anger and attraction. Back when he had been imperceptive, resolute… dead. Wordless, he unlocked the door into the apartment he had refused to invite her into before, despite that day's rain. But she remained on the stoop, mist gathering like silver filigree on her black hair and sweater, even after he entered.

An invitation, in the wrong magical hands, could become a strong weapon. But he knew now that she could not harm him.

Not purposefully.

"Do come in," he said evenly, so that the magical wards that surrounded his home like prison walls would lessen and she might cross more comfortably. "Please."

She stepped across the threshold, and he shut the door behind her while she slowly lowered her bag to the marble floor.

He had two choices now. He could retain the strict focus on which depended his hereditary abilities, and merely show her the guest room. Or he could accept temptation's dare, the threat of addiction—and risk his soul. And hers.

She stood straight and proud, not bothering to examine the room around her, a room full of his ancestors' furniture and egos, a ceremonial sword hanging over the fireplace, pub benches oddly at home beside an Oriental rug. Those things belonged to dead people. With her looking at him, her soft-as-night eyes bright, he felt anything but dead. As always, she magnified his senses, as if her presence cast a stronger light on everything around her. He heard the delicate rasp of her breath, smelled rainwater and lilac and earthy perfume on her, felt the warmth of her from two steps away.

A mere folk magician, she threatened everything he had struggled for—every countless hour studying the kabala, and alchemy, and ancient languages, *dead* languages. He found the sensation heady, dangerously overwhelming.

He did not want to feel dead anymore.

He would never know who moved first; considering their effect on each other's abilities, they might well have teleported. One moment, they simply stared at each other, in awe of the sensations that roiled about them like a powerful spell, like a dark binding. Then, in the moment of a blink, they had somehow surged together, each into the other's hungry embrace. He captured and kissed her, drank in the rich taste and earthy scent and husky purr of her, the intensely vibrant feel of her, the way his personal power spiked as if, with hers, it completed a high-voltage circuit . . . and powered what?

He could not imagine, did not care. She made him feel alive, real, so deliriously physical that magical theories meant naught. Desire—desperate, carnal desire—burst over him, sudden and immediate, like the crash of thunder outside. *Cypress.*

He held her tighter, his fingers digging into her bare shoulder, into her sweatered back, as if he could absorb some needed part of her into himself by sheer force. He kissed her harder, bruising his own lips and surely bruising hers, as if he could drink in her soul with her sweet breath and her low moan.

The woman who had proved herself strong enough to stand against him, and even with him, now swayed weakly into his greedy embrace. Her yielding curves pressed against his hardness; her southern warmth whispered to the protective ice of his soul. She nipped at his lower lip, almost drew blood, as if as desperate to taste him, to devour him, as he was with her.

Wild. She fumbled at the buttons of his borrowed shirt; did he hear one or two clatter to the marble floor beneath them? Even as her palms fed themselves on the bared skin and hair of his injured chest, he displaced them by dragging the huge sweater up and over her head. The sweater he cast outward, toward the pub bench, while she burrowed her fingers again into his chest hair, filled her hands with him, accidentally jarred his wound. He savored the hurt as deeply as the sweetness. *Alive.*

He chewed down her long Nefertiti neck to her now-bare shoulder, then to where her breasts rose full and rich from a bustier-type strapless bra of rich black satin. He kissed her, fed on her, ran his tongue between lace and skin and savored taste and texture. *Overwhelming.* She arched her back with a hoarse cry, clutching at the waistband of his jeans as if to keep from being blasted back from him by the resulting jolt of energy. *Uncontrolled.*

Perhaps they had finally discovered the erotic price they must pay for their mutually heightened powers. It mattered not. He would have her, wholly. Soon, at the rate they were going.

He had not lost his focus. He merely turned the full intensity of his focus onto her, onto them. For whatever reason, they suited. Only she could give his aroused, revitalized body what it so intensely craved, and consequences be damned.

He held her, breathed her, tasted her—and pretended, all too briefly, that in her determination to save mankind, she could save his soul, as well.

* * *

Don't trust him.

Cy considered herself practical and earthy, but "earthy" could mean "carnal." One moment, she'd wondered if Mr. Cool and Collected meant anything more by his invitation than a way to get her, briefly, away from Stagwater's menace. The next moment, they were ravishing each other. Their mingling energies sizzled.

He might still use you, hurt you. But from the frantic way she tugged the blue work shirt off incredibly broad shoulders, too attractive not to sample, she guessed she was as willing to use him as he was her. The gash and bruises that humanized his statuelike body, and the way he caught his breath against her breast when she *did* bite one well-muscled shoulder, proved he risked hurt, too. Could they stop, even if it mattered?

Too soon. If so, why this sense of urgency, of racing him to an unseen end? *Too much.* But no, it couldn't be too much, could it? It wasn't even enough. She wove her fingers through the thick softness of his not-really-black hair, pulled him forcefully back from her breasts—and, when cool air hit her damp, exposed nipple, regretted it. Luckily, her hands remembered her original purpose. She turned his face back to hers so that she could reunite his open mouth with her own. He obliged her, his sure lips and questing tongue already deliciously familiar, but not even close to enough.

While they kissed, she pressed her full length against him, trying to imprint her body on his. Her breasts rasped across his hair-roughened chest, her hips and abdomen teased his straining jeans. Would *that* be enough? It didn't matter. It had to be; *they* had to be together.

Even her practical side couldn't argue that this was only sex. This wasn't *only* anything.

He pulled back from her, leaving her lips tingling from overzealous kisses, as much as from the strange, magical effect they had on each other. "Come," he gasped.

She blinked, surprised at that particular command. Then she grinned wickedly: "Now?" His fingers closed around her wrist; she realized that he meant her to follow him.

As she did, sanity regained a slow foothold, despite the pounding pulse in her ears, behind her eyes. Although a physical person, wasn't she too sensible to jump into something this serious, this fast? She felt as if he'd bespelled her. Even now she let him lead her docilely toward what would surely be his bedroom, the mere act of walking honing her arousal, her sexiest bra—she'd worn it on purpose—hanging half off her bare bosom.

Then they reached the bedroom, and she saw his elegant bed, and the spell momentarily broke. *What was she doing here?*

The huge four-poster, with brocade hangings yet, reminded her of noblemen, of princes. And she wasn't a princess. But while she stared at the bed, blind to the rest of the room, he stepped intimately close behind her and unfastened her bra with sure fingers. Evident even through his jeans and her leggings, his arousal pressed insistently against her rear. Desire pulsed through her with his power, and she swayed unsteadily. Oh, she did want this.

You hardly know the man!

Except, strangely, resoundingly, she felt she *did* know him.

He wrapped his arms around her from behind, and the charged solidity of his forearm under her breasts felt familiar. He kissed her ear, and then her neck, and then her shoulder. She rocked against him, reached back to skim her palms over his denim-covered hips, then to grab hold of his jean-clad behind and pull him and his physical promise more firmly against her. She didn't know his middle name, or what he did for a living. She didn't know his sexual history—good thing she'd come prepared. Were she any other woman, or herself with any other man, this *would* be idiocy. But this was her, and Drake.

Her Drake. She *did* know him.

She knew the press of his lips, the taste of his mouth, as surely as if they'd been lovers forever. He caught his thumbs in the waistband of her leggings and slid the caress of elastic off over her hips, catching her panties en route, deserting the garments somewhere near her knees to run his hands up her bared thighs. She swallowed back an expectant whimper. Even before he touched her *there,* teased the whimper out with surprisingly gentle fingers, she knew how well he would pleasure her.

She melted back against him, letting him do to her, for her, until the ground seemed to shudder blissfully beneath her and she shuddered mindlessly with it. Then, suddenly, he'd deserted her. He gripped her arms, turned her bodily to face him—thinking he could take command again? She craved him too much to protest. His intense, heavy-lidded eyes burned for her.

You've got me, Magister. Holding his gaze, she groped for and found the waistband of his jeans. She used him for support as she stood on one foot and then the other, kicking her leggings and boots loose, then stepping free of their encumbrance. Then she let her gaze drop from his needful eyes to his beautiful, injured chest, then to the last piece of clothing between them.

She unbuttoned the top button of his fly.

He waited, still as a statue. *Hard as one, too.* She wrestled with denim to undo the next metal button, then the next. But when she finished the fourth, and slid her hungry hand into his briefs, he didn't feel like marble. Hard, yes, but hot, too. Vibrant, as if his sexuality came fully to life at her touch.

Lifting her gaze to his again, she watched his expression as she drew her palm up, then down the length of him, exploring, admiring. Damn, but the man had control. Her own rough breath descended into a moan at how her body, how *she,* wanted him. But he only raised his chin, his head back, his lids fallen to half-mast over unreadable eyes. *Composed.*

Maybe she really didn't know him, at that. But she pushed denim and silk off his hips and down his paler thighs anyway. She'd gone too far to turn back. Or, as Granny would say, *You made your bed—now lie in it.*

Gladly.

He kicked off the jeans as surely as she had her leggings, grabbed her around the waist and swept her onto the bed with him. Before she'd caught her breath beneath him, her arms about him again, he began to kiss her—more gently this time, but no less needfully. She felt herself sinking into a luxurious softness that was surely down. His sheltering weight over her felt more protective than ominous.

Magic. Kissing him was nothing less than magic. She'd thought their mingling powers had felt orgasmic during the working—that had been nothing! Anxious to push her limits, hungry for him, she raised her knee, drew her inner thigh up over his hard, hair-roughened leg to his hip, then back down. She'd *definitely* never known magic like this. If he *had* bewitched her, if this *was* evil—well, no wonder evil was so damn popular.

When he broke off the kiss, raised his head to catch his breath, she again searched his sculpted face for something to complement their physical connection. She saw need, dark and desperate, before he ducked to kiss her jaw and her ear, his tongue doing things to her nerve endings that *had* to be sorcery. The air around them practically glittered, tingling into her lungs when she breathed its scent, sensitizing her bare skin, though she'd already passed sensory overload long ago. She couldn't wait much longer. She squirmed beneath him, and slid one hand to his tight, bare backside, to urge things on. And yet, just as he obligingly shifted his weight back, as if in preparation to ease her cravings, sanity reared its ugly head.

She closed her eyes, struggled to manage even a grunt of the protest she had to make. They had to wait a few infinities longer. They weren't . . . They didn't have . . .

Then he ran his hand down her inner arm, and pushed something slippery into her palm. Her eyes flew open as she recognized the feel of a condom.

"Perhaps this once," he hissed into her ear, obviously amused by her relief, "I *will* protect you."

She laughed. "Mmm-hmm. Just me, huh?"

"Of course not. You are not still..." His eyes fell closed, a slip in his effort to control himself while slowly, appreciatively, she rolled the slick rubber down the length of him. "...still—" he gasped "—entertaining notions that..." And he regained control enough to open his eyes, to speak less breathily. "...that I am the good guy?"

She wriggled more intimately against him, not fighting a brazen grin. "Would I be here if I didn't think you'd be good?"

If she didn't know him—think she knew him—so well, the challenge in his gaze might have frightened her. But when he slid into her, buried himself wonderfully in her, her cry had nothing to do with fright. A delicious jolt of fused power sizzled through her, outward from her core, like lightning—like the explosion of a negative and positive current meeting.

She blinked dazedly up at him, shuddering as rippling energy seared through her, and took even more satisfaction from the look of awe that had softened his face. She reared upward then, kissed the Drake who let himself look awed. His return kiss, though passionate, felt...warmer. More human. More like the Drake her soul already thought it knew.

Then he began to move in her, and their coupled energy went wild.

They might have cast a circle, for all that time and place mattered now. Did they spend hours loving, or mere minutes? Did she imagine the unlikely wind that whipped through the bedroom, imagine the pulsing glow that their merging seemed to throw out, or did all that really happen in magical realms? *This* realm, the physical one, yielded miracles enough. The walls he wore seemed to fade, layer by layer, the longer they surged against each other, the more they cried out nonexistent words of ecstasy. His touch surpassed every climax she'd ever known, and still their coupled power built, and built, until she feared that to give herself over to it would kill her.

But what a way to go.

"What—?" He gasped the word against her ear as he chewed on it, straining into her. "What do you most want?"

You. She thought the answer before his question even struck her as unusual. She captured his mouth again.

He returned the kiss, his tongue thrusting deep, mimicking the rest of him. She felt herself teetering at the edge of a high, high precipice—and held him tighter.

Then he dragged his mouth free of hers. "Answer!" Locked in her arms, dark hair falling across his beautifully open, desperate, almost adoring face, he still managed to bark a command! For a moment, she couldn't remember the question. Then it did strike her as weird.

Too weird to answer truthfully. "To defeat the dragon."

He held her gaze, his eyes almost sad with raw yearning, then nodded, surged into her again—

And with the force of a larger explosion, she tumbled over the edge of the emotional, physical, magical precipice. She screamed at the intensity, heard his cry echoing hers. Surely mere mortals weren't supposed to experience such joy or completion at full strength. The world lurched around her; tremors of satisfaction matched their convulsing bodies, on and on, until she thought maybe she really *would* die, and she wouldn't even have minded, since he held her through it.

Neither could she mind—did she have the strength or sanity to mind?—when the tremors slowed, stilled. He held her for that, too, finally shifting his weight beside her, instead of on top of her, resting his head on her shoulder. His hair tickled. She felt safe with him, right or not. Gut instinct said she could.

Heartbeats and rough breathing continued to slow, as did the world around her. She tried to turn her head to see his face again, and realized the extent of her fatigue. Her head seemed to weigh more than all of him. Sleep dragged at her eyelids.

Paranoia made one final, sleepy try: *If he's bewitched you, your gut instinct could be lying.* But, hell, if she couldn't trust her instinct, she was already lost, right?

She managed to look anyway and, through her blurring vision, saw a softness in the graceful sweep of his eyebrows, in his deep-set eyes, a vulnerability to his mouth. She saw something like affection. Maybe admiration. Maybe something like . . . love?

But she could have dreamed that part, because the next thing she knew, she was waking up. And the bed was empty.

It really was a huge mother of a bed, had been even when they were sharing it—with it empty, she felt the way Goldilocks must have in Papa Bear's bed. *Not that you've got the coloring for that particular role, honey.* Oriental brocade closed off the sides, and the bed itself had a roof in the same rich oak as the rest of its massive frame. Apparently Drake wasn't the sort to put mirrors up there. Either that, or they'd all shattered from the intense voltage the last time he'd had sex.

She ignored the idea of him in bed with anyone else and stretched a long, luxurious stretch, then rubbed her eyes. She no longer felt sleepy or made of stone, but she did feel weak, kind of limp. Risking her life and then making the most heart-wrenching, bone-crushing, toe-curling love of her life could probably have that effect, right? The soft comforter that someone—three guesses—had pulled over her, and the equally comfortable bed beneath her, enticed her to go back to sleep.

Without Drake there, the idea lost most of its charm, and her practical side gained ground. *What in the world was that?*

She managed to boost herself up, and in the slice of light coming through the brocade hangings saw a robe draped across the foot of the bed. Touched by the gesture—and from so unlikely a source—she made the effort of putting it on. Raw silk caressed her sensitive skin. Then she drew back one of the bed curtains to reveal an elegant, softly lit room beyond.

The man didn't seem to go in for a lot of furniture, but what he owned was large, old and expensive. Brigit, who restored antiques, would go crazy over this man's furniture.

Cy preferred to go crazy over the man.

Cool January air crept into the sanctuary of the bed, and she realized the practical use of the curtains. As she debated expending strength to shiver, the bedroom's double doors opened.

She had to squint to see details in the black silhouette that filled the lit doorway, but she could recognize Drake even without details. His princely posture, his profile and the breadth of his shoulders gave him away. She smiled.

After a moment's awkward silence, he said, "Hi."

Not exactly a declaration of devotion. "Hi yourself."

Why was he just standing there? Suddenly uncertain—ecstasy aside, this *had* been foolish—she shivered after all.

"You are cold." He stepped into the room, but came no closer. Still, she could see him better. His hair looked damp, his expression carefully aloof. Maybe she'd dreamed the other look, after all. He wore a long black robe with wide sleeves that made him look like a mythical magician. "Are you feeling well?"

Why don't I try feeling you, and we'll find out? She grinned again. "Do you own a laptop computer, or a Minicam?"

He blinked; he plainly hadn't expected that particular question. "I do own a notebook. Why?"

"Then you know how, to refresh the battery, you have to drain all the energy out first, right? That's me. All my energy's been siphoned out, and I need to be recharged."

"An apt analogy," he agreed, his mouth pressing into... If it had been a smile, it left too fast. "We expended quite a bit of energy today, one way or the other." His look dared her to laugh, so of course she did. He ignored it. "I ran a bath for you. Afterward, we will go to dinner."

"Like a *date?*" They'd made the earth move and they'd risked their lives together—but they hadn't gone on a single date yet, had they? She kind of liked the idea.

"You have practiced magic long enough to know food helps to ground you after large expenditures of energy."

Damn, but he sounded serious. And he hadn't come closer. She didn't like that, and she stood up. The floor felt cold beneath her feet, as if the heater she heard hadn't been on for long. Something seemed...wrong. "Which is why we ate at my place."

"But we expended energy since then," he admitted softly.

She folded her arms, the silk sleeves of her own robe trailing to her knees. "Yeah, I was there. But it wasn't—"

Suspicion struck: His distance from her. Her incredible weakness. Sure, she'd been distracted while the power poured off them, swirled around them—ecstasy could make a girl a bit unobservant, couldn't it? "Or *was* it magic?"

He quirked a wry eyebrow at her, the cynic. At least he'd kept his sense of humor. Just in time for her to lose hers.

"That's why we're so tired." She walked barefoot to stand right in front of him, to search his deep-set eyes. That she couldn't read them answered her fears. "That's why you asked what I wanted most, isn't it? We cast a spell together!"

He didn't drop his steady gaze. He just inclined his head, slow accord. He'd used their sex for power—without telling her.

"You son of a bitch!"

"We had raised quite a bit of energy," he noted in defense.

"Yes, both of us! It wasn't just yours to use."

"I asked you what you most wanted."

She stalked away from him, over to the glass-paned doors that looked onto the same courtyard balcony, hugging herself. Thank goodness she hadn't answered, *You.* But she had answered...what? *To defeat the dragon.* She almost relaxed at the assurance that they'd have magical ammunition on their side the next time they went against that...that evil. That relief scared her. She'd known since childhood not to use magic to win fights.

Just how different *were* her ethics from Benedict's? That hurt the most. She longed to trust him, wouldn't have slept with him, surely, if she hadn't at least hoped she could. And now...

"Is that why we had sex?" she asked, her breath fogging a pane of beveled glass. She felt his warmth near her back before she saw his reflection, serious and dark, over her shoulder.

"No," he said. Still she wanted to trust him.

"I would never have knowingly cast a spell like that."

"The energy had to go somewhere," he reminded her softly, not touching. "Surely you felt it, too. It begged for release."

They *had* raised intense power—like enough to run Manhattan for a few weeks. And, yes, if they hadn't directed it somewhere, it might have floated nearby, unseen, waiting to be programmed by a random wish or thought and then doing who-knew-what kind of damage. But that wasn't the point. Respect was.

She turned and glared at him, and the sadness that tipped his eyebrows, that tightened his mouth, surprised her. He looked alone, trapped. Like someone who wanted to apologize, but couldn't.

Or maybe she saw what she wanted to see. She didn't *want* to be angry with him; she didn't *want* to mistrust him.

Foolish, but true. Being angry wouldn't forge any kind of relationship out of this incredible bond between them. If she pushed the issue, then she would have to walk out. And she didn't have the strength to walk out. Not now. More fool her.

Live, on the next "Ricki Lake Show"...

"Other legitimate witches do bindings," he offered. She knew that. A San Francisco coven had once gotten publicity for successfully binding a serial rapist. But...

"That's not the point. You manipulated me. I thought—"

"No." He breathed the word, low, searching her expression. "Manipulation implies intent. I did not intend magic, only..."

She couldn't tell whether he'd fallen into silence because he couldn't explain, or because staring into her eyes rose in priority. Then his attention drifted to her mouth.

The tingling of energies that had sated her earlier this evening began to stir again, with only his gaze touching her. She clutched at her anger with both fists, while her joints seemed to soften, while her knees truly weakened, while a ticklish flip-flopping in her belly stated opposite opinions. She wanted to kiss him again, to touch him again, to make love to him again. She had to be bewitched. She wasn't this stupid.

But the way she sank toward him when he took her shoulders in his strong hands told her that, yes, in fact, she was.

"It was too much energy," he explained. "And I had already abdicated my self-control."

He'd succumbed to her first. Was he implying that she'd robbed him of the ability to do the sensible thing—just as he'd done to her?

"I am..." he whispered stiltedly, and swallowed. His chin rose. "I shall endeavor to see it does not happen again."

The lovemaking, or the tantric magic? That she hoped he meant only the latter convinced her: Foolish or not, she couldn't stay angry. She wanted this too much to challenge the fantasy, wanted him too much not to take the risk.

When she lifted her face to his, the fading sadness in his eyes before he met her kiss made her want to cry. But, oh, the kiss itself! She wilted into the strength of his embrace, not too tired to drink in his passion, to meet it with her own. She let herself sink back into the dream of him, of them.

But she would *not* do a spell toward that, no matter how much she wanted it. It had to happen naturally, between the both of them, or it wouldn't be worth a thing.

His caressing hands found and loosened her belt; her oversize robe fell open. She returned the gesture, learning that he wore nothing under his, either. Mmm...exhaustion be damned. At least they shouldn't be able to raise quite enough energy for more tantric magic. And at least, if he'd had to channel their energies into a spell, she'd chosen one that did not deliberately intend harm.

Though she wondered, just from curiosity, what would have happened if she *had* answered, *You.*

She could pretend, too easily, that it would feel like the electric rush of his scratch-roughened palms on her hips.

CHAPTER ELEVEN

Much later, he took her to dinner. *What* was *he doing?*

But Drake knew exactly what he was doing. He was courting Cypress Bernard. It worried him, when he let it. But he was enjoying himself too much to let it. Just for tonight.

After her bath, she had put on the same outfit she had worn earlier; the one that taunted him with glimpses of her shoulders and showed off her neck. She wore her hair up in a heavy braid, like a crown. She looked beautiful, and not merely because of her strong-boned features and rich skin. Not merely because he knew what she could do to him in bed, either. She looked beautiful because she felt real to him, in a way no woman, no person, had for some time.

Somehow she had gotten through his walls.

Because she felt real to him, he found himself relaxing with her, enjoying their chilly stroll through the Friday-night French Quarter. Because she felt real to him, he took her to his favorite restaurant, hidden away from the more touristy areas.

"Chinese?" Her laugh was delighted, not scornful, so he did not regret not taking her to Brennan's, or to dine on one of the riverboats. "Now I know you're different," she teased, hanging on his arm as they entered the small restaurant. "We eat in the Vieux Carré, and you feed me Chinese."

Surprisingly pleased by her reaction, by her fondness for touching, he said nothing. Mere weeks ago, he could not have imagined liking the way she held his hand, bumped his shoulder, raised a finger to the corner of his mouth to coax a smile from him. But he had changed in mere weeks. Cypress had changed him.

For the better? He doubted it. But for tonight, at least, he savored their intimacy. Once they were seated, her booted feet found his under the table, apparently prepared to stay in contact through dinner, as well. He did not protest.

He enjoyed her reaction when he placed their orders in Cantonese. After he'd summoned a fiend from the bowels of darkness before her—albeit with her assistance—*this* impressed her? It was ludicrous, illogical. And it felt good. Normal.

This *was* what normal people did when attracted to each other, right? That they were not normal people should not matter.

"How many languages do you speak, anyway?" she asked, obviously better at this dating business than he.

"Ancient forms of Latin, Greek and Hebrew." He left out the ones she would not have heard of. "They are of little contemporary value, but quite the thing among ceremonial magicians."

She leaned toward him over her braced arms. "So *that's* what you are, huh? A ceremonial magician?"

He shook his head, tactfully subduing an amused smile. "Hardly. My father and uncle were, until their lodge expelled them, and a few techniques reached me through them. But I have learned from other traditions, as well. My methods are…eclectic. I imagine a ceremonial wizard would find comparisons between us quite insulting. In fact…"

Too much, he thought. But she did look interested. Not telling only confirmed his uncertainty, admitted his weakness.

He pushed on. "In fact, I doubt any legitimate lodge would consider me an acceptable candidate." There.

"But you're really good!" she protested, completely misunderstanding his point. *Deliberately?* "Now, I'm the last person to admit to being closed-minded. But until I met you, I didn't even believe in your kind of magic. Working with nature, the way my granny and my circle do, I can *feel* the magic, but outside of that I can only believe it's working. Your magic—'' she spread her hands, as if to show a pyrotechnic burst ''—it's there! Something I can *see*, while it's happening, no waiting.''

Largely due to her infusion of power—but she was hardly stupid. If she had ignored his previous hint about his legacy, she did not want to know. Why push it at her tonight?

Surely they deserved tonight.

''I speak Cantonese, though very little, because I am originally from Hong Kong,'' he offered instead. The pang he felt at changing the subject—guilt?—surprised him.

''No lie?'' she exclaimed, then grinned teasingly and held up a hand. ''Sorry 'bout that. Forgot who I was talking to there.''

''No lie,'' he agreed softly—and found himself telling her about his childhood as a banker's son in Hong Kong, then his school years in England, until their dinner arrived.

''By the mid-eighties, Hong Kong was somewhat in turmoil, and so was their marriage,'' he was explaining as the waitress arranged different covered dishes in front of them. ''They divorced, and my mother moved back home to New Orleans.''

''And became the local magistra?'' she guessed.

He nodded. ''I declined to go with her, and spent most holidays with Uncle Viktor in England, for the convenience.''

''The one you aren't close to.''

''He *is* a blood relative,'' he admitted. ''And quite a capable mage. And I was more than a little ambitious.'' He watched her calmly spoon rice onto her plate, digesting all that.

''Did you know,'' she said finally, raising her gaze to his, ''that my parents are divorced too? My grandmothers raised me.''

''Did they?'' He found himself surprisingly interested.

So, over dinner, she told her parents' story—how once upon a time, a well-to-do family's only son and their housekeeper's only daughter had fallen in love and eloped. For a moment, her expression softened dreamily, unlike her practical self, but highly attractive. Then she blinked away the distraction.

"I don't even remember them together," she admitted. "They didn't last three years. Mixed marriages were still illegal in a lot of the South back then, and I guess they were just . . . just too young to handle all the hassle folks threw at them. So they split up, and Daddy got custody while Mama went to college. But he travels, so I was more Grandmère Bernard's. And when I never really fit into *her* world, I decided to live with Granny Vega. It was a weird kind of joint custody."

And obviously not the happy ending she would have preferred. "Did you fit into the Vega world?" he asked softly.

She flashed her bright smile at him, as if teasing him about his concern. "I never much fit in anywhere, but Granny was a world of her own. A magic world, you know?"

Oh, yes, he knew. They might be different from the people around them. They might each be lost between two worlds. But the magic made them special. It gave them a sense of worth, of identity, of empowerment—and now, a sense of connection.

Something at the edge of his vision startled him; he snapped his head up and, heart pounding, studied the other patrons. Knowing his penchant for privacy, the host had given them a corner table; the rest of the restaurant lay before him.

He saw nothing to merit the unease that had struck as solidly as today's fear, fury and desire. Backlash, perhaps. *That,* he could imagine his father or uncle telling him, *is the reason you must rule your passions, and not let them rule you.*

Perhaps he'd startled himself, tripped his internal alarms.

"What is it?" she asked, low. "What's going on?"

He shook his head. "Noth—" Damn, how easily had the lie almost left his mouth!

Then again, was this whole evening not a lie? She saw only what she wanted of him, heard only what she wanted, made love to a noble fantasy with his name and face. If he continued to allow it, then he *was* lying, as surely as if he spoke the words.

He could easily ruin himself for her—at least, for the possession of her—were he not careful. But he had seen one mage sacrificed to another's demands. He would not make the same mistake. "I thought I saw something. Perhaps I was mistaken."

That seemed to satisfy her, and she grinned at the man she thought he was. "No dragons, though, right?"

No dragons? Good-natured Chinese dragons surrounded them.

"Not like today's," he made himself assure her. She relaxed, and went back to her food and her story.

Jolted from his own little fairy tale, he had lost his appetite. What the hell *was* he doing here with her? She was a lovely woman, of course, and a competent magic user, and an incredible lover. He had become accustomed, even addicted, to her company. But their bond was illusory.

Yes, they had both found childhood solace in their magic, but there their similarities ended. She had grown up learning to work *with* her world—touching wood for protection, brewing herbal teas, throwing dirt after a departing person to ensure his return. He had grown up learning to distance himself *from* his—meditating himself into altered consciousness, calculating the higher mathematics of astrology, memorizing lost alphabets of ancient symbols and the philosophical ramifications of each. She embraced life and its pleasures. He avoided meat, drugs, sugar, alcohol, caffeine, even sex, except in moderation, in order to cleanse himself, desensitize himself—to create of himself a vessel through which to channel the powers of the universe.

Yes, they inexplicably increased one another's immediate energies. But in the long term, unless she knew to guard herself against distracting him, against allowing him to corrupt her—unless she knew the truth—they would surely destroy each other.

He put down his chopsticks, lest he snap them in his tightening fist. She *must* know—whether she wanted to or not.

"...and she may never be fully accepted by her crème-de-la-crème friends," she was saying, "but she's never once turned her back on me or my father, or even Granny or Mama. A lot of society women would."

It took him a moment to reorient himself with her narrative. "Your *grandmère* Bernard," he supplied cautiously.

She nodded, and then her eyes narrowed with visible suspicion. "Why are you looking at me like that?"

"We must talk," he told her. She grinned, probably because they had already been talking. He did not. "Not here."

The smile slowly wilted. "All right."

So he paid for their food, and they left the restaurant on foot. The January chill would, he hoped, counter the effect of her nearness, of his longing. Perhaps the damp cold would remind him of England, where he had held better mastery over his baser self. England, where he had lost his youth in exchange for a bitter warning. And perhaps the cold would numb his heart.

He managed so much better when he did not care.

Cypress did *not* like this, not one bit. She tried to hold his arm, the way she had on the way to the restaurant, but he pulled stiffly back from her. "No. I think it best that you do not."

So she walked beside him, rejected and cold—and painfully, increasingly, annoyingly, confused. "What's *wrong*, Drake?"

He pressed his lips together, as if choosing his words carefully. "You seem to be softening me, Bernard. I should allow your gullibility to be your own problem. Instead, I find myself feeling guilty for it, compromising myself to it."

What? She frowned. "Mmm-hmm. And how am I being gullible?"

"You are falling in love with me, when you do not even know who I am."

She couldn't have said anything after that, even if she wanted to, because his words packed a double punch. He'd said, "love," as if that was really what was happening, as if she should be ashamed of herself if it was. And he'd just repeated to her what her own conscience had been trying to communicate while she fell into his arms, into his bed. Both times.

She'd argued against her conscience. Drake she merely asked, "So who are you?"

"I am the issue of one of the more notorious wizards of recent times," he told her. "I am a powerful magic user myself. Unless I keep my passions under firm control, I could become a danger to anyone I care about. And..." he went on, while she grasped the words *he cares,* "the person for whom I care makes me a danger to myself, as well."

But he doesn't want *to care.* This again. She took a deep breath of January cold, enjoyed its bite in her lungs, even if it *was* city air. It had to be after midnight, already. They were both tired, and fighting wouldn't help a thing. If he kept coming back to this, it had to mean something to him, right?

"Look, Drake, do you think maybe you've just got cold feet? If you are, relax. I haven't asked for commitments." No matter whether she wanted any, she sure hadn't asked. "You haven't made promises. I can take care of myself."

"You only think you can because you do not know better."

Did he use a crystal ball to determine what would tick her off the fastest? "Oh, I don't, do I?"

"My mother was strong, and a more competent magic user than you. She had to be."

"Because she was a magistra, whatever that means," Cy agreed, waiting for him to connect this back to her ignorance—back to him not caring. *Or not wanting to.*

Their footsteps echoed in the narrow street and off the overhanging balconies, as if someone were following them. Dragons or not, she definitely liked the woods better.

"Magistra, sentinel, guardian, watcher. Different people call them different things; there is no one job title. But, yes, my mother believed her abilities were a gift, one she must return by using it to help others. Rather like a paranormal troubleshooter. So she had to be very good."

His voice remained steady, impersonal. Either he hadn't cared for his mother, or he had raised those shields of his again.

"So I've got a lot of the same values as your mama, but she could outmagic me any day of the week, huh?"

He slanted his gaze back to her. "Perhaps not *any* day of the week," he allowed. "But she had years of intense practice."

She forced a smile. "You flatterer, you."

His mouth pressed into a hard line, and he looked away. He obviously didn't want her to tease him, to make him smile.

Well, I don't want you to freeze me out, so we're even.

"Be that as it may," he continued stiffly, "she *was* quite capable, and yet he *did* destroy her."

"Who did?"

Not a blink. "My father."

And finally things began to fit horribly into place. His father, the notorious wizard. His fear that he'd destroy whoever he cared about, and would destroy himself in the process. What could have happened to make him think like that?

"Tell me," she said quietly.

So he did.

He'd been a university student when his divorced father left Hong Kong for England. The first time Drake visited him after that, he'd known something had changed. His father had crossed the line between magical dedication and obsession.

"When you say obsessed," she asked, "you mean—?"

"With testing himself." He didn't bother to look at her as he spoke. "Like alchemists—also in our ancestry—he tried greater and more dangerous experiments. We had avoided dealing with the darker realms until then, though more from distaste than paltry ethical considerations. The difference between high magic and black magic is much like that between brandy and moonshine, Belgian chocolate and M&M's... sex and sadomasochism."

He did look at her, on that last example, and even from two feet away she felt his intensity.

She cleared her throat. "And that difference is?"

"The latter of each can be crude, sometimes too potent," he explained, the softness of his voice not at all reassuring. "And even more dangerously addictive."

Oh. *Sadomasochism?*

She pushed herself past that thought. "So your father was getting in over his head. What did you do about it?"

His step didn't falter. "Why should I have done anything?"

"Because you're his son!"

"But not his caretaker," he snapped right back. "From the time I could walk, I was trained in autonomy, all of it to make me a more capable magic user. Emotional ties scatter a mage's focus. They make one more susceptible to being drained by those weaker than him, make one more likely to leech energy one—"

His step faltered; he shut his eyes. Poor porcupine. She reached for his arm, felt the familiar rush of contact.

He opened his eyes, his gaze on her hand, and shrugged his arm free. Again. "My father was responsible for his own actions."

He continued to walk, and she followed.

"So you stood by and said nothing while he destroyed himself." He'd tried to clue her in to that part of his personality from day one—it shouldn't surprise her. But it did.

"Of course I said something," he admitted finally, his tone prickly. She could have kissed him from relief, anyway. "I debated with him, argued with him, asked Viktor to try the same. It was Viktor who suggested we call in my mother."

"Because she was a magistra."

"Hardly. There were sentinels in England who could have come sooner. We chose Mother because we believed he still loved her."

And that had led to the woman's destruction—and probably her death. Cy wished she didn't know the end of this story. He had probably placed the call himself, probably met her at the airport. She wondered if his mother had hugged him when they were reunited by the jetway, if she'd smoothed his hair off his high forehead. She wondered how rarely Drake had been hugged since.

She stuffed her itching hands into her pockets. "Look, never mind. You don't have to tell me any more."

"Oh, but I do. You noticed that my magic seems *different* from yours? That, Bernard, is because it is!" His regal profile was angry. "You have no idea what I am capable of! Your friends think simply because you meet by the full moon and achieve nominal success with affirmations, you are adepts. A little empathy here, some clairvoyance there, and poof, you are a witch!"

"Would you stop trying to make me mad?"

"Whereas I," he continued, "have studied the arcane knowledge of the ages. I have memorized alchemical findings, viewed wonders of the cosmos, spoken the secret names of God!"

"Back up. Mr. Neutrality believes in God?"

"Of course I do. I merely doubt God believes in me."

They reached his courtyard, entered into the privacy of his patio, but made no move toward the stairs. She reached out a hand, brushed it across the dull winter leaves of the mimosa tree. The fountain splashed the shadows; the chill wind stroked her cheek. She knew very few people who shared her particular mixed bag of religious beliefs...but his were about as opposite as he could get. Even without specifying a god or goddess, she belonged—to the earth, the wind, the rain, the sun. She belonged to the living. He really was alone, wasn't he?

"So you wanted to tell me you can outmagic me in a fight."

"Easily," he warned her, an edge to his quiet voice.

She considered him, tall and dark and dangerous—and let out a deep breath. "Okay." And she started up the stairs.

"Okay?"

"I can't see myself getting into any wizards' duels with you, Benedict." She wished she could see his face. "As long as we're on the same side, your ability to chart the cosmos, turn lead into gold or be on a first-name basis with the Creator doesn't have much to do with me, does it?"

He stalked up the stairs behind her, seemingly unlocked the door without even using a key and swept inside first, leaving her feeling battered by the sheer force of his presence. If she hadn't stood beside this man against the dragon—if she didn't know the gentleness of his kisses, of his lovemaking—his silence would have intimidated her into an apology, at least, and probably a quick exit, too. As it was, she wished she'd eaten less at dinner. Her stomach suddenly felt touchy.

That *wasn't* all he'd meant to tell her, was it?

He paced across the room, spun and fixed her with his glare. "When we reached the estate, the servants had been massacred."

Rooted to the spot, she understood. "Your father—?"

"He had summoned it specifically for Mother, it seems, perhaps to impress her...." His voice fell off for a moment, but he remembered himself with an angry snap of his head, his gaze piercing hers like a dare. "Perhaps to destroy her. She sent me to fetch Viktor, but as we made our way back, I felt an implosion—" He swallowed, hard, but his face showed nothing. "By the time we returned, nothing remained of either of them, or even most of the house, for that matter. An aura of evil lingered in the air, foul and more powerful than anything I have ever tasted."

His voice had gone hollow, and she tried to imagine the details he'd left out—then shivered, and tried not to.

"Father apparently lost control of whatever he conjured," he continued, more strongly. Dispassionate. Uninvolved. "The only way either of them could have banished or bound something that strong would have been with a sacrifice, preferably willing, but of course we shall never know whether Father sacrificed Mother, Mother sacrificed Father, or perhaps they both gave themselves over toward its banishment. Mages came from across England to cleanse the area, and it was politely but firmly suggested that I not practice further magic in Britain."

"You?"

"He was my father, my teacher. His blood runs in my veins, his ways are mine. I did not argue with the Council, because they were *right*. If you can accept that, and the danger it poses to you, then you may continue to turn those doe eyes on me, to touch me, to tease your way into my bed again, to even have a go at my heart, if you are that foolish. But if you cannot—"

"No." She'd had enough of this. The man stood there in his long black trench coat, his aristocratic face set, his eyes intense, like an offended demon. She felt the power of his presence—if he *couldn't* take her in a fight, he sure could make her work for it. And, yes, he had a bad attitude. But he wouldn't go summoning any monsters he could not control and feeding her to them. She'd bet her life on it.

She already had.

"No," she insisted, closing the distance between them. "First off, don't you *ever* tell me again what I can and can't do. Second, if you think I've got *any* interest in that bed of yours tonight, think again. I don't get turned on by people ordering me around. And third, you're wrong!"

He didn't blink. He didn't move. He merely echoed her last word dangerously. "Wrong."

"As in, you think you're telling the truth, but you're mistaken. Incorrect. *Erroneous.*" That sounded like his kind of word. "Drake, have you even noticed that you haven't done a single evil thing yet?"

He stared at her for a long moment, his depthless eyes unreadable, then turned and walked to the double French doors and stepped onto his balcony, his back to her, while she continued.

"You dowsed, you contained the black streams, you even led my circle against the dragon. You stayed the night at my home, and you were a perfect gentleman. You offered me a place to stay here, and...well, you weren't, but that was good, too."

Did his shoulders stiffen? She took a step closer, but met a wall of cold air and hesitated.

"And," she added, "the whole time, you're doing your damnedest to warn me away from you, supposedly for my own good. That's not someone who's evil, Drake. That's someone who's scared. You don't have to be scared. This..." She decided to avoid as loaded a word as *relationship.* "This whatever-we've-got is like the dragon. If we face it together, we'll be okay."

And now was the point where he was supposed to turn to her, admit he *was* scared, and thank her for being here for him.

Instead of merely turning, he spun and nailed her with his glare. "Do you consider yourself black or caucasian?"

She blinked at him, blindsided by that one—and not just because he hadn't mentioned the race thing until now. He waited, his jaw tight and his eyes demanding, for her answer.

"I'm both," she admitted. "I'm part of each. To label myself either would mean denying who—what—I am."

"Then why do you insist I do just that?" he demanded.

She shook her head, fully annoyed. He still didn't get it.

"I am a mixture of opposites," he insisted. "I reject neither. You cannot actually believe that because I do not drink blood or sacrifice children, my motives have been philanthropic? I have acted for myself!"

"You think you have—"

"Open your eyes! For months that damned beast has beckoned to me, called to me—to the evil in me! I had little choice but to silence it. Choosing evil destroyed my father, and choosing good destroyed my mother. I choose the middle path—neither. And you brought me information, even the assistance with which to do that. I joined with you, used you, for *me,* Bernard. For *me!*"

"I don't believe that!"

"Then believe it when I do not go back!"

The room fell silent then, so silent that she could hear the howl and wail of jazz music from Bourbon Street. Part of her continued the argument—*Oh, you don't mean that. You're just saying that. Give it up, Drake, I can see right through you.*

But she wasn't listening to that part of her anymore, because she knew Drake Benedict didn't lie.

She somehow made it to a large, old-fashioned chair before her knees gave way; she fell into a sit. "You—" The word came out a whisper; surely he couldn't hear her from the balcony. She tried again, with more force. "You would sacrifice my town just to prove you're not like your mother?"

"Your town," he reminded her coldly, "was never my responsibility in the first place."

She stared. She'd been so busy arguing with him, it hadn't fully occurred to her that he really might be right.

He said, "If you cannot accept my right to cut my losses and relocate, then you have not been dealing with me at all. I avoid other peoples' dangers. I perform blood magic! Yet you imagine me as the good guy, despite my warnings."

She shouldn't have come here. She shouldn't have accepted his help. She certainly shouldn't have slept with him!

He stepped inside from the balcony, started for the hallway. "I will turn the covers in the guest room for you."

"You'll call a cab for me," she replied, low.

That stopped him. "You ought not to return home tonight."

Somehow she found the strength to lift her gaze to his. He was scowling down at her. "That's my decision."

"I offered you a place to stay—"

"And I'm turning it down." She called on her inner reserves of strength—with a little help from the energy of the earth beneath her, the moon overhead, the Mississippi River nearby—and she stood up again. "Get me a cab, or I'll just walk to Bourbon Street and hail one there."

And she stalked past him, to the bathroom where she'd left her overnight bag open, her toiletries out on his marble-topped counter. She wasn't going to cry, damn it. She hadn't cried for years, and she wasn't going to start over the loss of Drake Benedict. Certainly not of the real Drake.

The loss of the man she'd *thought* Benedict was, that would take a lot longer to deal with.

By the time she'd stuffed her belongings into the bag and returned to his living room, he was staring at a pair of paintings on the wall. One showed a terrestrial, the other a celestial, globe. Both had been painted as if behind some kind of mist or veil, separate from the viewer. His world. He meant to keep it that way, too—separate from everyone.

Hopefully he'd do a better job from now on.

"Did you call them?" she demanded, heading for the door.

"Yes. There is money in the vase by the—"

"Don't you dare!" She wasn't sure what was worse—that he might be paying her for services rendered, that he thought she couldn't afford it, or that he was once again saying something she could too easily interpret as "nice." He probably wanted to assuage his guilt—assuming he had any.

"You could stay in a hotel—"

She shouldered her way out the door, down the stone stairs. She'd almost reached the bottom when he called out her name.

"Cypress!"

Don't stop. Don't even stop. You've been down this road so often with him it's gonna get named after you.

She stopped anyway, looked back up at him. Why did he have to look so beautiful there, like a solitary, dark angel. "What?"

"Perhaps—perhaps you could come with me." His eyes were bright from the shadows that cloaked him, and his voice was seductive. "Leave the dragon to someone else, and come away with me. We could go somewhere new, somewhere far away. Cairo, or Bali . . ."

His words hurt too much to hear anymore. She all but ran across the courtyard, out through the walled gate and away from the silence that his faltering voice had left. By luck or magic, the cab drove up at that point and she ducked into its shelter. She even managed the right address, after three stumbling tries.

Then she sat, her bag clutched to her like a shield to protect her heart, too damned late. She still didn't cry—even if, by refusing the tears, she gained a sudden, frightening insight into how Drake might have become the hardened shell of a man she'd been fool enough to fall for.

And more of a fool to care, damn it, to care so painfully about losing.

Drake listened to the cab pull away, his feelings still intense. He would rather have missed the sensation of his soul being eviscerated. She truly did not want him. She had only wanted his powers, his ability to help slay their dragon. A few weeks back, he might have appreciated the irony—had he not originally wanted her for the same reasons?

Staring out at the dark cold, he questioned that. Her companionship was hardly unenjoyable. Their lovemaking—rather, their sex—more than satisfied him. She would make an admirable mistress, if only she did not insist on rushing valiantly into doom, and demanding he accompany her. *Watch her*...

No, he should relocate. He would monitor his feelings more sternly. He did not plan to hurt like this ever again.

But gradually, he began to feel something else. He felt the dragon's call, like a pulling at the base of his spine, stronger than ever for its familiarity with his blood and his fears. And he felt a different presence, equally familiar. Not Cypress.

He lowered his gaze to the shadowed courtyard beneath him, resigning himself to the fact that this was not over, after all. "My dear Viktor," he said coolly to the shadows—and what lurked in them. "I trust you had a pleasant flight."

And his last living relative, the uncle who practiced the same dark magic as his father—and who might have heard far too much already—stepped into the light that fell from the doorway.

CHAPTER TWELVE

Never had Cypress been in *less* of a mood for a party.

If she'd been thinking about something more normal than dragons and dark wizards, maybe she would have remembered the ball before the cabbie dropped her off at her grandmother's Garden District home. But considering the past two weeks—the past few hours!—she did well to remember the security code for *Grandmère*'s alarm system when she let herself in.

Then she turned on the foyer light, to leave a note letting *Grandmère* and the staff know she was here, and the glare from the silver and glass decorations almost blinded her. Oh, no. Grandmère Bernard's annual Crystal Ball was tomorrow night!

In fact, she thought, glancing at her watch, midnight had been and gone some time ago. It was tonight.

She left a quick note before she headed upstairs to her usual room. *May miss the party,* she added at the bottom.

But over breakfast, Grandmère Bernard made it clear that that dog wouldn't hunt.

"What," she asked in that genteel yet determined Southern-matriarch way of hers, "could possibly be more important than entertaining New Orleans's finest residents?"

Besides saving my hometown from evil? Cy stalled by taking a sip of chicory-laced coffee from a delicate cup. She'd slept fitfully, lost in dreams and nightmares about Drake. She hadn't wanted to wake up, even from the nightmares. Now the birds in *Grandmère*'s well-groomed courtyard sounded especially shrill, the sunlight of the breakfast room unnecessarily bright. Was there such a thing as a magic hangover?

"You mean New Orleans's richest residents," she said now. "I've met them before."

"Don't be bigoted, dear. It's unattractive." Diamonds sparkled tastefully when *Grandmère* smoothed an imaginary stray hair back into her snow-white coif. "In any case, you did RSVP."

"I rented a costume, too, but something really important has come up." The minute she said that, Cy regretted it. The Crystal Ball *was* important. After her only son married a "colored girl," *Grandmère*'s status in certain circles had plummeted—and *Grandmère* had responded by boldly starting her own pre-Mardi Gras tradition. Nobody who had snubbed her son or daughter-in-law, during that brief marriage, had ever been invited to a Crystal Ball. Instead, she welcomed the nouveau, the open-minded, even the Bohemian.

Assuming they had money, fame or connections, of course. *Grandmère* hadn't lost *all* her societal standards.

Cypress tried again. "I mean, that what I have to do could help a lot of people."

Grandmère blinked. "And must they all be helped tonight?"

Cy wished that wasn't such a good question.

She *really* wasn't in the mood for a party.

She wasn't in the mood to take a phone poll, either, but life caught her in the middle of one by midmorning. First her father called *Grandmère,* who of course handed the phone over to Cypress. As usual, Daddy's job wouldn't let him make the ball. "I love you, Princess," he said, and she suddenly wondered how many people in the world never heard that from their fathers.

She blamed her tight throat on Drake's story.

As she climbed the stairs, her cellular phone rang. It was Sylvie the empath, wondering if everything was okay.

"Everything's so good, you couldn't imagine," insisted Cy.

"So forget the costumes, we've got more important things to deal with?" said Syl, translating.

Costumes? Then she remembered. *Grandmère* had invited her best friends to the party, too.

"We figured as much," Sylvie said soothingly, as if Cy had managed to voice her thoughts. "Y'all have another plan, right?"

But Cy wasn't part of "y'all," and no, she didn't have a plan; and even if she did, she doubted she could implement it right away. She still felt vaguely weak, shaky.

She told Sylvie she'd get back to her.

Then her cellular phone rang again, and it was Brigit. Brie wanted to know why she was at her *Grandmère*'s, instead of Drake's. "Do you need us to come hurt him for you?"

Cy snorted. "You haven't heard? He's some kind of supermage with the powers of the cosmos at his fingertips, and he could beat any one of us in a wizard's duel."

Brigit snorted right back. "Duel shmuel. I'm armed."

Her first smile since last night felt awkward, but healing. She assured Brigit that the situation didn't merit homicide, and that she'd get back to her, too.

Then her cellular phone rang again, so she answered it with "Hello, Mary."

"Obviously, clairvoyance is not your forte." The curt British voice on the other end wasn't Mary's. It caught her like a spell—reminded her of danger, sorcery, ecstasy.

She hit the end button. Then she stared at the phone, annoyed at herself for hanging up. She was an adult, and she could handle herself in a more mature manner than that.

The phone rang again. This time she tried a simple "Hi."

"Playing it safe this time, are you?" asked Drake.

"How'd you get my cellular number?"

"From your business card." Good thing the word *duh* wasn't in his vocabulary—his crisp tone insinuated it anyway. "You'd best meet with me today." A command, or a threat?

"Have you changed your mind about Stagwater?" She tried not to let herself hope, and failed miserably. Her pulse raced, her breath went shallow. If only last night had been a big mistake.

"Hardly," he said. So maybe last night, and leaving, had been her first *non*-mistake where he was concerned.

"Then not even if you said please." And she ended that call, too. But this time, hanging up seemed to be a pretty mature decision, especially in light of how excited she'd gotten at the foolish hope that he'd changed his mind.

She turned the phone off, too, just to be sure. After all, her friends had *Grandmère*'s direct number.

In fact, over the next hour, all three of her circlemates used it. Apparently Drake was trying to find her through them. Not even he could crack her circle. But if she went home today, he'd probably track her there.

Sooner or later, she had to face him again—he was making sure of that. But she didn't want it to be on his terms. And, suddenly, she didn't want it to be tonight, either. She wanted to be here for her *grandmère*. She wanted to see her friends relaxed and out of danger for once. And she *had* given her word.

Magic users who only told the truth should apply that to keeping promises, too.

Too bad Drake Benedict had never made any promises.

The Crystal Ball's name had less to do with fortune-telling than with the season. *Grandmère*'s decorators turned the second-story ballroom into a veritable ice palace, draped with white and silver glitter, glass snowflakes and translucent icicles, beads and frosted streamers. They'd outdone themselves this year; the place looked . . . magical.

And she still wasn't wholly in the mood for a party. But she'd resigned herself to making the best of it by the time Mary arrived with the very last person she'd expected to see.

Tall, black-clad, broad-shouldered—and blue-eyed. Wasn't there a rule against priests looking that good?

"Ralph Poitiers?" she exclaimed, taking her old boyfriend's hands in hers to look him up and down, reconciling memory with reality. "It's okay, I know them," she said to the valet who guarded the door, so that he'd let Mary's husband, Guy, in on the same invitation. Then she looked back at Father Ralph, and despite the past twenty-four hours, she grinned. "Nice costume."

"I should *hope* I make a convincing priest! Yours is very nice, too, Cleopatra."

She spun around to show off her white shift, with its gold lamé collar, belt, cuffs, and headdress, while Guy and Mary, a convincing knight and his lady fair, joined them. "It's an inside joke," she admitted. *Queen of denial, for sure.* "But I'm missing the snake."

Mary snorted, unladylike, and Ralph winced. "Ouch." He showed a dimple when a passing crawfish complimented him on his believable clerical collar. He really did look good, better than in high school—but somehow different.

For one thing, he isn't available. But that wasn't it. Drake wasn't exactly available, either, but if he walked through those doors this very minute, she'd probably have to struggle to keep from running straight to him, angry or not.

Even that brief thought of Drake distracted her from the glittering party. The music surged back when Ralph touched her arm. "Do you mind me stealing some company for a minute?"

"Is it okay for priests to dance?" she asked.

"Ma'am, you've obviously confused us with certain Baptist groups." And Ralph swung her into a relaxed waltz. "Remember when I escorted you to your *grandmère*'s ball my senior year?"

She laughed at the memory. "The angel and the devil!" They'd argued about who got to be the devil, and he'd won.

"No fair blackmailing me to the bishop with pictures," Ralph warned her.

"That would be wicked," she agreed.

"Well, you *are* a witch," he teased back, and surprised her with an experimental spin. She saw Brigit and Steve, disguised as gypsies, standing near Sir Guy and Lady Mary.

"Does that bother you?" she thought to ask. "Witches?"

"Nah. The seminary doesn't brainwash us, and I still remember you and your granny Vega. In fact, that's one reason I wanted to catch you this weekend. Mary said your granny was doing poorly. I'd like to include her in my prayers. That is, if it doesn't go against her beliefs..."

"She'll be thrilled," she assured him, touched by the gesture—and his sensitivity to their differences. He'd definitely joined the side of the angels. If only Drake were more like Ralph, then they...then she...

Then *he* wouldn't hold that delicious, dark, *unhealthy* fascination for her. He wouldn't be Drake. *Whoever that was.*

Sylvie, her antebellum hoopskirt asway, waved at her from Rand's frock-coated embrace.

"You believe in evil, right, Ralph? I mean, Father—"

He smiled. "It's okay. I'm not on duty with you. And, yes, I definitely believe in evil. Why do you ask?"

"Do you think a person can be forced to do evil—even be evil—against their will? Maybe because they were born to it?"

Ralph frowned, a bit like a warrior angel now. "Are you worried about yourself, Cypress? If you're concerned..."

When she shook her head, he looked relieved. It was sweet of him to worry, but Drake posed no threat to her. Did he?

"Well, then, theologians have been arguing that one for centuries," Ralph told her. "Free will versus original sin. But, barring possession, I'd have to say no. People may *do* evil without recognizing it as such, sure. They'll rationalize it away. But against their will, despite recognizing it? I doubt it. There's always choice, room for change and repentance.''

"Oh." As if hearing an argument representing someone else's faith would have helped. But she'd wanted to hear something else, anyway. She'd wanted to hear that, if Drake was really evil, it wasn't of his own doing—even if her own faith wouldn't let her believe that, either.

If he was evil—*if*—it was of his own choice.

"Whatever it is you and Mary have found in the woods," Ralph continued, clueless as to what she really meant, "you be careful, okay? Please? And let me know if you need some help. I've got—" he showed a dimple "—contacts. High up."

She thanked him, tried to smile, but despite the loud music and the boisterous revelers, her heart wasn't in it. His offer only reminded her what good people she'd always known. Until recently, she'd assumed she could expect that kind of support from anyone she cared for, anyone who cared for her.

Why couldn't she expect it from—?

But then, in the middle of another friendly spin, she caught a glimpse of him. Black-clad. Broad-shouldered. Regal and impassive.

She almost tripped herself and Ralph both, trying to look past the priest's arm to be sure—and saw only glittering silver and crystal, harlequins clustered by an ice sculpture, nothing.

"What's wrong?" Ralph asked when they hesitated in the middle of the dancing, while she searched the crowd. *Drake?*

He was here, wasn't he? She hadn't imagined it; he was *here!* Somewhere.

"Nothing I can't handle," she assured Ralph, patting his hand in thanks, then working her way through the crowd, toward where she thought she'd seen the mage. She didn't see anyone else as tall, anyone else wearing that much black whom she could have mistaken for him. When she'd thoroughly scanned the crowd twice, she decided to try the terrace.

The bite of January that kept the other guests from the balcony raised the hair on her arms; most of the light shone through beveled panes in a gallery of French doors. She looked both ways, even over the wrought-iron railing toward the lawn, as if he would pull some daring, Zorro-ish escape. She saw nothing but pools of darkness recoiling from spotlit magnolia trees, azalea bushes, wisteria vines— none in bloom.

She *had* been imagining it. And she was cold. Those ancient Egyptians hadn't exactly dressed for winter weather.

She straightened, and soft, warm material settled over her shoulders. When she spun, the overlarge black cape flared around her.

Drake Benedict, having emerged from whatever shadow had held him, looked like the black prince out of a fairy tale; the sort to kidnap the princess, not the sort to rescue her. He wore a black leather doublet, high boots, even a sword at his hip—a warrior more than a wizard. He looked even better than he had in the sheet toga. He looked too damn good for her own safety.

"Hi," he said softly, somehow making that one word a warning, and her inner resolve wavered. Maybe he *was* part evil. Maybe he wasn't.

But how could she possibly walk away from him again?

Whatever it took to frighten Cypress Bernard was apparently beyond his not-inconsiderable grasp. She did not jump, did not scream, only fixed him with her exotic, kohl-lined eyes. "This is an invitation-only party."

She smelled of herbs, radiated warmth, breathed in time to the orchestra inside. The gold trim of her costume, the gold beads in her braided hair, caught the light from inside, where she belonged. But he was through with worrying about where *she* belonged; her safety and satisfaction were *her* responsibility.

His interests lay in closing his involvement with Stagwater and settling the matters she had left hanging between them, once and for all. That the dragon's call faded docilely from his awareness, simply from the power of her presence, merely freed his attention for the confrontation. He could find peace from the dragon just as easily by catching a first-class flight to Hawaii—and without her righteous demands.

"Quite," he agreed, in answer to her challenge. "But I managed an invitation. My mother was Madeleine *Rousseau* Benedict."

"Your mother was a Rousseau." It seemed Cypress had breeding; she avoided exclaiming, "Of *the* Rousseaus?"

So they both moved in higher circles than either had expected. "It seems we can add blue to the black and white of our bloodlines, does it not?"

"That doesn't change anything."

"Then you do not trade your affection for mere wealth or status. Brava. However, it bought me an audience with you."

"You're that determined to talk to me?"

"If you did not run, I should not have cause to chase you."

She turned away from him, stared across the lawn. Her guarded expression looked as artificial on her as it felt natural on him. *What are you trying so hard to hide, little witch?*

"So what was so important you had to talk to me tonight?"

Your safety. My sanity. Regaining a balance between us.

Stagwater. In the grand scheme of things, the town mattered not at all—to him. But it mattered to her. If she meant to risk her life again, at least she should know the full extent of what she faced. And if she faced reality and gave up, all the better.

"For one thing, my uncle Viktor arrived in town last night." He took petty pleasure in her widened eyes; perhaps she would not turn off her telephone next time. If she lived to have a next time. None of his concern, of course. He must, *must,* remember that. "You might wish to warn your friends."

Still looking across the lawn, she gathered his cape more closely around her—cold? He inwardly braced himself against gathering her to his own warmth. Draped in black, with her golden headdress, she looked ironically like the high priestess of a Hermetic order. She asked, "How much time do we have?"

"I do not know."

"Is he going to go after the dragon?"

"You would have to ask Viktor. I can give you the number where he is staying, if you would like."

She frowned, visibly worried, again taking on far more responsibility than actually belonged to her. His exasperation sharpened to anger. She might not have meant to involve him, to use him—but she had. She cared too much and tried too hard to help others, ignoring her own best interests and those of the people who cared—

No matter. He recognized not just the self-righteousness, but also the danger of her altruism—he had his mother for an example—but she remained quite blind.

"So Viktor's in town," she said, prompting him. "What's the second thing?"

"I want to know exactly why you left last night."

Now she looked back at him, met his eyes too directly. "I left because you weren't who I thought you were when..." When they'd kissed. When they'd made love. When they'd created magic of an intensity to sear realms and realities.

"I suspected that much. And yet I could not have been clearer about myself."

"It was my mistake. I'm sorry if I misled you while I was busy misleading myself."

"Were you really?"

She shook her head, not reading him—or not wanting to.

He pushed it. "Are you truly so innocent as to have misled yourself that wholly? Or are you merely using that as an excuse?"

When she planted her hands on her hips, the cape parted to reveal a floor-length diamond of her white gown. "Come again?"

"We discussed my neutrality at length, Bernard. I repeatedly refused to promise assistance beyond each step. I even warned you that I was dangerous, but still you came with me, still you—" She knew what had happened, what had stirred and blossomed between them. "When I told you of my severely dysfunctional family, you were tolerant. When I warned you of my tainted blood, you were sympathetic."

"You said I was rejecting part of you," she reminded him.

"You were," he shot back. "But at least you had not quit on me. Consider, Bernard, the exact moment at which you decided we had no hope for a future."

Even had she not possessed such a strong jaw, he would have recognized its set. She knew the moment, and it still angered her. She had rejected him when he failed her altruism test. Only champions of her cause deserved her company, her love.

Damn her inflated morality, anyway. "What were you hoping to secure by coming to my home, my bed?"

Her strong jaw dropped. "Are you insinuating that I would prostitute myself for Stagwater?"

He would not have considered the concept so bluntly—now he need not do so. "Stagwater was the deal-breaker, was it not?"

"Get the hell out of my *grandmère*'s house." She shed the cape, went from high priestess to queen of the Nile with one angry shrug. "You don't understand anything."

"Your affection rests solely on whether I help Stagwater!"

"No! My *respect* rests on whether you help Stagwater." She shoved the cape back at him. Their fingers brushed.

Power sizzled through him from her, strong and fulfilling. But, as was the way with addictions, it was no longer enough.

"Then where *do* your affections lie, Bernard?" he demanded, twining his fingers through hers to capture and savor her touch. She did not tug away, only scowled up at him as if caught in his sorcery. "Respect is a quality of the mind. What of your heart?"

She turned her head, to keep from looking at him. As if she could hide anything by profile. "It doesn't matter."

"But it does." It meant, in fact, too much.

"Why?"

"Because..." He leaned closer, the better to feel her unique warmth radiating against his face; to breathe in her scent, her being; to watch her eyelashes sink in defeat. "Because I had a third reason for coming here."

She tried to ask it, but achieved no voice. He lip-read her question. *Why?*

He breathed his answer—"I am bound to you"—against those lips... and then he was tasting her, drinking her, reclaiming her. He caught her to him in a possessive embrace, as if he could keep her from running. With a groan of defeat, she wrapped her arms around his doubleted waist, sank against him, opened her mouth and her soul to him.

She might not respect him, but she wanted him. Perhaps she was addicted, as well. Could she be feeling the kind of high he did from feeding that addiction? The rush of music and chatter from the ballroom harmonized with their gasps of breath; the redolence of the cold garden mingled with the scent of her skin and her hair. Was her vision awash with light, her every fiber suddenly as alive with wanting for him as his was for her?

Such power together. Such might. Such danger. But if she wished to ignore his warnings, who was he to—?

She wrenched away from him—the inches she could manage within his embrace, at least. "No!" She did not wish to ignore his warnings. She had no intention of humoring her heart.

What an untimely moment for her to finally choose distance over involvement!

"Why not?" Unable to let go, he forced the demand against her cheek; she was the one who turned her lips to his, who let her own words become another kiss.

"The others . . ." Kissing superseded talking, until more words spilled from her. "They're probably watching."

As if he cared. But if she did . . . "The lights are on inside, not out. The windows create a mirror for them."

"No, Drake. Stop. Please." She gasped the words against his temple, her breath hot, moist.

He stopped. It took every long year of training, every ounce of his incredible control—but he stopped. When she continued to cling to him, vinelike, he even disentangled her arms and stepped back from her.

He had his pride, if not her ethics.

"If you resolve your position on this," he told her, channeling all his frustration and anger into a cool demeanor, "do look me up. I always check my messages."

He turned away from her to go back inside. He would even have managed to stride through the ballroom, out the doors, and out of her life entirely, were his path not blocked.

Stagwater's other three witches looked up from their concerned huddle near the ice sculpture, set themselves as if for a fight and advanced from one direction. Their male backup could only be their husbands, plus the priest. And on an intersecting course approached a wizard, complete with flowing purple robes and pointed purple hat, both painfully fake, and a pendant inscribed with ancient, arcane symbols, quite real.

He had never seen anything so ridiculous in his life.

Cypress appeared at his elbow to completely hem him in . . . but, oddly, he felt more grounded than trapped by her appearance. The calm energy increased when she touched his arm. "Is that—?"

"Yes," he told her, actually surprised by the man's presence. He ought not be. Why would Viktor not shadow his nephew straight to the magical guardians of the dragon? Neither Drake nor Viktor had strong ethics, but Viktor also lacked the restraint of self-respect. "Unfortunately, it is. I shall take my uncle. You take your circle."

"Oh, no, *I'm* the one who cares about Stagwater. You take the circle. *I'll* take the uncle."

The fool. Had he not explained that Viktor Benedict had been blackballed from the magical community? The only trait that superseded the man's greed for power was his complete lack of compassion—and limits. Even Drake stepped carefully around him.

Her choice, of course. Her responsibility.

However, the witches were women ready to protect their friend against whatever outrages they assumed of him.

"Actually," he murmured under his breath, "I would rather not."

"Too bad," said Cypress from behind a businesslike smile, and dodged in front of him to greet Viktor. "Good evening, Mr. Benedict. Did you know this is an invitation-only party?"

Leaving him to deal with her circle.

apperance. The cuan and eyeincreased when she flinched

And eyes "Phat"?

"Yes," ..he told her, actually, splaed by the man's bace guno. He could not he/ ..Why would Vikor, not shadow his
regime strongly deny? but shifty, unvaf the dictator

langu..the feature of self-respect? Enforcinging in is 1
s .f stake, are not less on man-woneautuefull.

CHAPTER THIRTEEN

Cy felt a bit like Alice in Wonderland now. Instead of worrying about career advancement and mortgage payments, she was worrying about a homicidal heart of darkness in the woods behind her house. Instead of dating a good-natured yuppie, she'd lost her heart to an enigmatic wizard. Somehow, the things she most feared—the dragon, Viktor, Drake's unwillingness to prevent catastrophe— overlapped with the things she most wanted—the dragon contained, Viktor gone, and Drake's willing participation for the good of others . . . her good, if Stagwater's was too much to ask of him. And the right ways and wrong ways of getting what she wanted were blending into more and more gray areas by the moment! She felt uprooted and adrift in a crazy, magical current—dizzy from Drake's kisses, anxious about his near departure, relieved by his timely delay.

If you resolve your position on this, he'd said, *do look me up.* But she doubted she could resolve anything at this point. She was ad-libbing as she went along. Brightly costumed couples swirled past amid the decorations' icy sparkle; music washed over her in a wave. And she wasn't just facing, but facing down, her first evil magic user.

He was evil, right? Drake hadn't actually used the word *evil* to describe him; he'd said *less than ethical.* Viktor was at cross-purposes with them, and would make things worse if he confronted and lost against the already-too-powerful dragon.

"Good evening, Mr. Benedict. Did you know," she asked with forced confidence, "that this is an invitation-only party?"

"You don't say?" He raised an unamused eyebrow beneath his ridiculous purple wizard's cap. Could he have looked less evil? "We've already heard of one another. You must realize that I do not require invitations." And a hematite-colored glint in his eyes, more than just the reflection from any number of silver or glass baubles, warned her not to discount him too quickly. He favored Drake; his eyes were smaller and he stood shorter, but he did have the patrician nose, the carriage, and the luxurious accent.

"You've heard of me?" Had he and Drake talked about her?

If so, he wasn't giving it away. "Of a manner. Shall we dance?" The current of revelers, a brightly colored blur, streamed to either side of their own little eddy. The wizard Viktor offered her his hand, like a dare. Attracting attention probably wasn't the best idea.

She had no idea how to handle this man, but she knew better than to show fear. She placed her hand in his, and thankfully felt nothing. No tingles. No plunging, icy darkness. Just soft fingers, unused to work, closing around her own.

And she'd thought she was playing the extremes when she went from Ralph's arms to *Drake's!* Maybe Drake was middle ground, after all?

With a nod that seemed to say he admired her gutsiness, Viktor stepped her into a clean but uninspired waltz. Even the priest had danced more imaginatively. Then again, the priest was Cajun.

"No one invited you in," she told him. This time she wasn't talking engraved card stock. "Shouldn't you have to hang around outside staring through windows, like a vampire?"

"Only if I meant harm to the inhabitants, and I currently mean none," he assured her. *Currently, huh?* Just because she lacked Mary's psychic perceptions, that didn't mean she lacked powers of observation, too. "In any case, the valet did invite me in."

"Probably not of his own will." Maurice had been with *Grandmère* for years.

"No, but he wasn't difficult to sway." And *he* wasn't talking about threatening to rough the man up, either.

Manipulative magic. Even if he wasn't evil, he sure wasn't a good guy. "That counts?"

It occurred to her that she probably shouldn't look directly into Viktor's eyes, so she looked over his purple shoulder instead. The black prince, arms folded, was arguing with Brigit—and watching Cy. Just his malevolent gaze could make her tingle. Oh, but her heart was in a heap of trouble.

"Lord—" Viktor sighed "—but you are a babe." And he didn't likely mean she looked good. "Of course that counts."

"It's not even the valet's house to invite you into!"

"But, my dear, he was put in charge of it. In any case, it's not yours, either. So if you wish to expel me, you'll cause a scene and risk my bending the minds of more innocents."

"Don't you dare try to blackmail me!"

He blinked, startled. "Blackmail? But, my dear, you misunderstand me! I only meant to forewarn you that I shan't be manhandled out like so much riffraff. Why would I threaten the person to whom I've come for assistance?"

"For assistance?" Darn it, he should be scaring her, not intriguing her. Maybe her recent companionship with Drake had helped her build an immunity. *Not necessarily a good thing.*

"I would like you to lead me to the demon."

She stopped dead on the dance floor. "Demon?" Mary and Guy danced by at that moment—coincidentally close—and Cy saw Mary mouth the word she'd obviously overheard. *Demon?*

"What did my nephew tell you it was?"

"We've been calling it a dragon." She still felt Drake's gaze. She wondered, if she gave him a signal, would he come to help her against his uncle? Assuming the two of them really weren't on the same side. Assuming she needed any-one's help.

Viktor swept her back into the dance. "Dragon," he re-peated, unamused. "I can't imagine why."

"It's a long story. So why not get Drake to play friendly native guide for you?"

Viktor favored her with another of his tight-lipped smiles. "Because I do not trust him. Perhaps you ought not to, ei-ther."

Divide and conquer, Viktor? "Well, I do." She realized she meant that, and closed her eyes in a moment of quali-fied relief. Respect, no. But trust? Oh, yes. "He's never lied to me yet."

"There is such a thing as creative truth, but that's not the point. *I* trust *you*. You are a witch, which indicates a cer-tain strength of ethics, as does your aura. You also feel strongly about ridding your town of this...dragon."

How did he know that? Drake continued to glare at them while Syl joined his tête-à-tête. Cy frowned back. So far, she hadn't mentioned any of the others to Viktor Benedict; she wouldn't endanger them that way. She would have thought Drake would be equally discreet. "He talked to you about this?"

Viktor smiled condescendingly. "Do you think perhaps I lurk outside windows for my information?"

"Doesn't answer my question, whether I think that or not."

"And I am not here to discuss my nephew's indiscre-tions. I am here to help you defeat what threatens your town."

"Real philanthropic of you. What do you get out of it?"

"Your assistance. Surely you've already discovered that two wizards are better than one?"

She recognized that technique, too—the *yes* setup. "De-pends on the wizards."

Viktor scowled. "Obviously I am wasting our time. If you cannot see past your bias against my traditions, I shall simply find a different mage to assist me." And he began to scan the crowd, as if he sensed the nearness of other magic users.

Damn. She leaned into their spin, so that he wouldn't look too long at the other members of her circle. There was a reason the *I'll take my business elsewhere* ploy remained so popular—it worked. He might be bluffing, but if he wasn't, he might pester or even endanger her friends. Or he might find someone she didn't know, another magic user of shady ethics. Maybe someone incompetent, or perhaps a satanist . . .

She was *not* comfortable with that option.

"Why can't you let us take care of it?" she hissed at him.

"Two reasons," he fired back. "Because as you so cleverly noted, I did not fly here from England to gain nothing. And because if I—" His smile looked oily as he smoothly corrected himself. "If *we* do not act by dawn tomorrow, complications could arise."

"What's tomor—" But then she realized what he meant. Tomorrow wasn't anything except the first day of February. But the day *after* tomorrow was a day of power, no matter what your magic tradition—a greater sabbat. "Imbolc?"

"Oimelc," he said, as if correcting her, but he nodded as he did. *A sabbat by any other name.* "The first stirrings of life within the bowels of the earth. Do you wish to wait for that?"

Her tradition celebrated it as a prelude to spring, the awakening of seeds and sap. Similar, but more positive. "You think the dragon can use the power as surely as we can, don't you?"

"I'm thinking that, if it resides in the bowels of the earth, it might well use the power *better* than we."

No way could she dance *and* juggle all her conflicting agendas. They slowed to a stop at the edge of the crowd, near the punch bowl. Viktor smiled, and she hated the triumph in his eyes. "What will it be, Ms. Bernard?"

She glared a warning. "Don't rush me."

"Had we the time, I'd allow you worlds of it. We've only until dawn, and first light, if we're to strike when it is at its weakest."

How did he know that? Maybe the same way he'd read her aura. And, damn him, it made sense! But she wouldn't make a rushed decision—she wouldn't! She wasn't that stupid. "Dawn's at least eight hours away. Give me four."

He quirked an eyebrow, surprised by her offer. "And then?"

"Even if I decide to help you, we'll have to set some rules." She needed time to decide on those. "If you don't hear from me by 2:00 a.m., then do whatever it is you feel you have to—assuming you can find the place—and I'll do the same."

His face darkened. "I would not recommend you interfering in my plans, witch."

"No, I don't guess you would. But there you go."

The moment stretched between them, then Viktor smiled again. He smiled more than Drake, but didn't wear it as well. "Here is where I can be reached. Two o'clock, Ms. Bernard."

She took the offered card warily. "Two o'clock."

"Two o'clock?" The curt tone, deceptively disinterested, shivered down her spine, and she spun to see Drake standing right behind her. He took the card from her hand, lifted an eyebrow as he read it, then turned his formidable gaze to Viktor.

She stepped out of the cross fire, and saw Viktor smile.

"Until later, my dear," the older wizard purred, and lifted her hand to his lips. This time his touch *did* give her the creeps, but not because of its magic. "Drake."

"Viktor," returned Drake with inhuman composure, and they watched the wizard make his way to the front door, wave his fingers in front of Maurice the valet's eyes and exit.

Then Drake turned to her, his expression dark. "Talk. Now."

She plucked the card from his hand, uncaring whether the imperious jerk got a paper cut or not. "Care to dance?"

"No."

She caught a glimpse of *Grandmère* watching her, and smiled reassurance in the elderly woman's direction. "Then I'll go see if Ralph wants to dance again."

Scowling to let her know that he knew manipulation when he heard it, he swept her onto the dance floor. Mmm-hmm, the *I'll take my business elsewhere* ploy really was a good one. Power surged through her from his hand holding hers, his hand on her waist. He danced better than his uncle, better than Ralph. He danced the way he made love. But there was more to life than dancing.

"What did my circle have to say?" she asked casually.

"They were not speaking as your circle, but as your friends. They believe I have made you . . . unhappy."

Go figure. "So did you tell them I walked out on you?"

"I told them it was none of their business, and that no one could make you happy or miserable but yourself. Ever."

"Yeah, but other people can sure tilt the scales."

"You must not trust Viktor," he warned her suddenly. *Not* the smoothest change of subject. Speaking of being made miserable . . .

"Why? Doesn't he tell the truth, too?"

His refusal to answer that answered that.

"So if I made him promise not to hurt me or anyone else with the power he got from the dragon, he really wouldn't."

He snorted, unamused. "One can find loopholes even in the truth. In any case, you consider yourself one of the good guys. The good guys do not help the bad guys."

"Even if the bad guys are helping back? My hands are already dirty, Drake, remember? I allied myself with you."

He spun sharply with her, so that her gown and his cape curled together around them. "I am not my uncle."

"Tell me how you're better than him."

"My neutrality keeps me from disturbing others. I am not so greedy for power as to risk my life and the lives of innocents." And that was their problem in a nutshell, wasn't it?

"Would you risk your life for *anything?*"

His eyes flashed, and they spun to a slow stop near the French doors. He didn't release her hand or her waist as the angry words rasped from his throat. "I believe I already have."

She had the grace to look down. He *had* already gone up against the dragon once for her—and he'd faced it twice. He'd done as much as anyone could have asked. Why did she want more of him?

But it hurt again, still, that he wouldn't *give* more, either. She'd always thought, if ever she finally felt this way about a man, she'd be able to ask him for anything.

Maybe Viktor was right—she really *was* a babe in the woods.

"If I had a seal," she admitted now, "I'd give it to you— I'd owe you—in return for telling me one thing."

His posture didn't relax, but he did incline his head.

"You've seen more of the dark side than me. If you don't help, and Viktor doesn't help, and my friends would endanger themselves and their babies if they help, what choice do I have?"

He shook his head in wonder. "You are that determined?"

She decided not to kick him, and simply nodded.

"Short of attempting a grand coven—and I have not heard of one ever being successfully done in the States— nothing."

"Then Viktor's my only option. He'll go, whether I'm with him or not. At least this way I can impose some rules on the situation." She would also be right there *by* the dragon, if it absorbed Viktor's power in victory. She'd be alone with it. "Do you really think he doesn't stand a chance against it?"

"I really believe you do not stand a chance against him."

"Because of my abilities, because of my ethics, or because I'm a woman?"

"Because I know Viktor." He pressed his lips together, raised his chin, as he took a deep breath, then met her gaze for his next attack. "You owe me a favor now. You did offer."

And suddenly, horribly, she knew what he was going to ask. And she couldn't let him. Stagwater couldn't stand it. *She* couldn't stand it. "Anything but giving up against the dragon."

He continued to stare at her, his eyes searching hers, and then he released her. He took a single step back.

He's writing me off, she realized, wishing it hadn't come to this. But she'd written him off, too, hadn't she? Her head had, even if her heart hadn't. Leaving was his choice, as surely as helping Stagwater was hers.

"Then the consequences are on your head," he hissed, and turned on a booted heel. He strode away from her, away from the dancing, through the glittering wonderland of silver and crystal.

This time, he was leaving her and it hurt worse than she could ever have imagined. She saw her concerned friends watching the drama from a polite distance, saw Mary start toward her, and raised a hand to fend off their concern. Oh, no. The *last* thing she needed right now was sympathy.

Instead, she fled to the French doors, to the cold balcony where Drake had held her, kissed her—and accused her of being interested in him only because of the help he could give her.

She wasn't, was she? Women who manipulated men through their affection—through their bodies—sickened her. She was stronger than that, damn it! Always had been. Her anger over his refusal to help wasn't righteousness, it was common decency, or his lack thereof. It was disappointment.

She could fall in lust with the man's body, with his intelligence, with his lonely-porcupine ways. But if she was ever to really love someone, she'd have to admire his soul.

She clutched the wrought-iron railing and stared toward the brightly lit trees and dark garden, barely noticing the cold. Their separation hurt now. But if she compromised what she knew was right, she wouldn't respect herself, either. She would stop trusting herself. And if she no longer believed in herself, she would lose her magic. Magic took belief—didn't it?

For the first time, she wondered if maybe she *could* give up, leave Stagwater's problems to someone else. She was just one person. A woman shouldn't go meeting strange men— strange sorcerers!—in the woods. Maybe Viktor and whoever he found to help would do fine on their own.

And maybe they'd go off and commit some kind of atrocity with their newfound power. How would she feel then?

Or maybe Viktor would fail. How would she feel, to know that she could have prevented the death of someone, no matter how slimy—the death of a blood relative of the man she'd made love to last night—but had not? The dragon would increase in power and attract more evil manifestations like those her circle had faced for over a year now. Its aura of evil would cause more depression, more illness. How would she feel if Sylvie or Mary miscarried, if there was even the possibility that the dragon was at fault? If her granny Vega could never come home and be healthy? If, for some reason, Drake Benedict *didn't* leave town, and instead finally gave in to the "call of evil" he'd described—and the dragon, more powerful than ever, devoured him?

She would still be safe, still alive. But what kind of life would her conscience allow her?

Damn it, she didn't have to wait until 2:00 a.m. to call Uncle Viktor; she'd already made her decision. As long as she could negotiate an understanding between them—a deal with the devil—that secured the safety of innocents in exchange for her help, she would take the only option available to her. It was the only choice she could live with.

Assuming she lived.

She'd done the best she could, and it wasn't half-bad.

I, Viktor Benedict, do solemnly swear that I shall do nothing—through my magic, words or actions—to cause deliberate or preventable harm to any innocent people or beings, either during my time with Cypress Bernard or with the power I shall receive through our collaboration. By all the powers of the universe, within this and all realms, so I do swear.

Of course, he'd made her take an oath in return.

I, Cypress Bernard, do solemnly swear that I shall not interfere with Viktor Benedict's retrieval of the entity's powers, for only good or neutral use. I revoke any claim I might have on these powers, despite my contribution to their retrieval, and I swear to cause no deliberate or preventable harm to Viktor through our collaboration. By the powers of air, fire, water and earth, so I swear, and so it must be.

Actually, she'd felt a mite silly—they'd stood there like drug dealers on the dirt road in the predawn darkness, illuminated by the headlights of her Honda and his rental, and they'd exchanged oaths with the solemnity of two kids trading a spit swear.

But, hiking into the woods with a different Benedict this time, she felt safer for it. As safe as she could, that is, going to face an immortal repository of homicidal evil.

Thorns tore at her sleeves and jeans. Ferns slapped at her, vines did their best to trip her, and gnarled, leafless branches of scrub trees clutched at her tightly braided hair. She still didn't understand the way the trees were acting. Pines were protective, damn it! They should try to help.

The flashlight she held against the black of the dying night shook in her hand. Maybe, by trying to hold her back, the trees *were* protecting her. Maybe this forest had never gone over to hardwoods because whatever Indian magic had bound the dragon before had also left the pines to help hold its evil in.

And to keep innocents out.

"Somebody's got to do it," she murmured upward, and as if they understood, the trees stopped grasping at her. But they continued to sway, cutting the unnatural breeze into a low wail.

"What did you say?" demanded Viktor, behind her. She would have preferred not to turn her back on him, oath or no oath. But he likely couldn't navigate his way through an open field, much less the dense Louisiana woods, so she went first.

Just doing her friendly-native-guide job right.

"The trees don't want us to go in," she told him now, glancing over her shoulder. He'd been smart enough to wear heavy, durable clothes himself, but he didn't look happy. Neither did he seem to take her tree comment seriously.

"Someone should bulldoze the lot of them," he muttered. As if at a gust of breeze, a cone-spiked branch tumbled from above and barely missed his head, grazing his shoulder as he dodged.

He glared up at the tree, then at her.

She shrugged, aimed her flashlight back at the faint path she and Drake had worn by their recent comings and goings, and started hiking again. If Viktor wanted to pit his abilities against the dragon's, he shouldn't complain about the details.

And if she wanted to police him, she shouldn't sweat the details, either. Right?

Details like not telling the circle what she was up to. Now that she was here, she couldn't help but remember Drake's lecture about considering herself expendable—about manipulating her friends by protecting them.

But she *didn't* consider herself expendable; that was why she'd gotten Viktor to take the oath. That was why she was out here with a wizard even more powerful than the one who had helped her manage at least a stalemate against the creature last time. And as for telling her friends...

Well, she knew them well enough to predict their reactions, clairvoyant or not. They would worry too much. They'd try to talk her out of it. They might insist on coming along, putting not only their lives at stake but their babies', as well, not to mention distracting *her* with worry.

Her life was hers to risk, but theirs weren't.

And nobody's gonna die. More people are killed in car accidents than by subterranean demons, right?

Dead needles trickled from the desiccated canopy of pine branches above her. The suffocating, cold blackness that tried to swallow her weakening flashlight beam reminded her of that old saying about the darkest hour being just before dawn.

She noticed something familiar about a cluster of trees, a tangle of vines, and stopped walking.

"What?" Viktor inquired, too close. When she shone the flashlight around, trying to recognize the source of her unease, she caught a glimpse of metal and suddenly knew where they stood.

The stake that she and Drake had already planted—twice—lay useless above the ground, expelled by the earth. No. Expelled by what lurked beneath the earth's surface, maybe beneath their feet. A sense of vulnerability crawled up her legs to settle, leadlike, in her stomach.

"*What?*" Viktor repeated, more forcefully.

"The dragon's not contained anymore," she told him. "It could attack us at any time."

"Not likely," he noted, and he even yawned. Talk about cool. "I imagine it shall wait until we reach its lair...the nexus?"

Just like that first time—the time she'd gotten so angry at Drake for going without her. And just like the time they came together. She missed having his checked strength beside her, and the support of her friends nearby. It weakened her—badly.

She couldn't save the world alone. She might not even manage with Viktor. Saving the world was a group activity, and she should have told Brigit, Sylvie and Mary. She should have at least given them the chance to be as stupid as her.

That really *was* their decision to make, wasn't it?

But that, and a certain practical edge of caution, was why she'd brought her cellular phone along.

"Now what?" Viktor didn't try to hide his impatience as she pulled the phone from a big pocket of her insulated vest.

"I think we need backup." She opened the phone; its numbers glowed greenly up at her in the dark.

"I did not agree to backup," Viktor protested sharply.

"But you didn't prohibit it, either," she reminded him, dialing Brigit's number from memory.

Viktor's pudgy finger nearly knocked the phone from her hand when he jabbed the end button, interrupting the call. "Now," he warned, "I prohibit it."

He obviously meant it, too. His eyes reflected the beam of the flashlight, cold as a snake's. Now she knew where, in part, Drake had gotten that attitude of his.

How far would *this* Benedict go to get his own way? If Viktor broke his oath and killed her, Drake would have been right again: She would feel really, really stupid.

Mary! she thought, hard. *Sylvie! Brigit! I'm in the woods with Viktor, right now!* She had no idea if any of them would sense her call. They were witches, not psychic radio receivers. But she had to try. She closed her eyes. *Drake?*

But she didn't hear anything—not telepathic reassurances, and not bugs, frogs or owls. Only unnatural wind. If she wasn't so scared, she'd laugh. *The woods were quiet. Too quiet.*

She opened her eyes, ready for battle. "The oaths are already sworn. If you break yours to harm none . . ."

Viktor sneered. "Did that include communication devices?"

". . . then that releases me of my oath, too."

"So I might simply go ahead, face down your demon on my own, and do as I wish with its power." She could tell from his gleaming eyes that what he wished to do with its power did not bode well for her. "You could do nothing to stop me."

"I could do my damnedest to drain your energy to where you wouldn't stand a chance against the dragon."

"Don't make idle threats. You'd never do that, because it would violate your personal code of ethics."

She managed a laugh—*Don't let him see your fear, Bernard.* "If there's one thing these past weeks have taught me, it's the existence of shades of gray. I might justify myself by thinking it's self-defense, and risk the bad karma."

"Try it," he warned, low, "and I shall crush you like a bug. Wholly in self-defense, of course."

"Of course," she agreed, with false amiability. A bug, huh?

He waited, his eyes narrowing, while she slowly lifted her cellular phone to where she could dial again. But the sound of a soft, mocking clap, and then another, interrupted her intentions.

A figure emerged from the black, opaque shadows, continuing his dry applause. "Highly entertaining," said Drake, his breath smoking slightly in the cold air. He looked heroic in his trench coat, a dagger slung on his hip. "If futile. My dear—"

But he didn't get any further, because Cy, at the end of her emotional tether, threw herself into his arms, accidentally whacking him in the back with the forgotten phone. His embrace closed automatically around her—he'd come, after all!—and he accepted her kiss, returned it. The familiarity of his energy rushed through her with his warmth, mingling, strengthening, making her feel truly awake for the first time since she'd woken up in the dark of the morning to head for the woods. He'd come!

But something felt different, too. *He* felt distant, uncertain. He meant to help, right? Surely he'd come to help!

But suddenly, leaning back in his loosening embrace and studying his masked expression, unable to find the slightest hint of concern in his impassive face—

Suddenly, she had a really, really bad feeling about this.

But suddenly, hearing his... in his forearms muffled and studying his masked expression, unable to find the slightest hint of reaction in his impassive face.

Suddenly she had a really, really bad feeling about this.

CHAPTER FOURTEEN

Drake had a bad feeling about this.

Not about Cypress clinging to him, warm and solid in his arms, or even about her rapidly backing out of them, staring at him as if he were a traitor. He *was* a traitor to her values, even if he had never agreed to support them. And by coming here, he'd betrayed his own neutrality, as well. Despite believing that only she was responsible for her actions, he could no longer pretend to deny his involvement in those actions.

Of course we're responsible for her, you jerk, Brigit Peabody had snarled at him last night. *She's part of our lives, and we love her. Anything that hurts her hurts us. That makes her our responsibility.*

Philosophically, he had heard better—but she had reality on her side. After leaving the ball, vowing to stay away, he could not sleep. He knew he was right. He also realized that being right was no longer enough. He had to make one last attempt to save her from herself—not for her own good, but for his weakening sanity.

Considering that he faced both Viktor's greed and Cypress's altruism, he was uncertain he could dissuade either. But at least this way he was...involved?

"As I was saying, my dear Viktor," he repeated coolly now, despite Cypress's appalled retreat, "you might as well let her ring her friends. She shan't reach them."

Viktor eyed him, rightly suspicious—then smiled. His smile showed his canine teeth. "Really?"

Drake nodded, and Viktor turned to give her permission, but she was already dialing, hitting send. She waited, still scowling. "Brigit, Steve, pick up! It's Cy. I'm in the woods."

Her scowl deepened; then she stabbed the disconnect button. Then she tried Sylvie.

Viktor's smile widened as they listened to her second message. "You must tell me how you managed it," he purred.

Do the words fat chance *mean anything to you, Viktor?*

"Someday, perhaps, I shall."

She slapped her phone shut. He imagined that if it was less expensive, she might hurl it at his head. "Where are they?"

"I assure you they are quite safe." He held her gaze, and wished she would not search his for reassurance. He could not allow himself to give it—not in front of Viktor, and not if she meant to see her martyrdom through. "For now, that is."

Even in the faint glow of their flashlights, he saw her eyes narrow. Her voice dropped, dangerous. "What do you mean?"

"Cooperate," said Viktor, "and you needn't ever know."

Her eyes flashed at him now. "You said you wouldn't harm anyone!" Good. At least she had been smart enough to slap some limitations on the old mage.

Viktor's eyes widened. "And I've harmed nobody."

Pine straw crunched beneath her boots. "You son of a—"

Drake stepped between them, glared them both down. "Perhaps the woods are not the best place for this discussion?"

"Then we'll discuss later," decided Viktor, smugly composed. "We must be ready to act by dawn. After you." And, with a dramatic little bow, he extended his arm.

So much for getting them out of this forest.

"I'm not going anywhere." She folded her arms, and he tried not to sigh in relief. Of course she would not be swayed by blackmail. By threatening her friends, his uncle had set her on the path Drake preferred—the one home.

"I would advise you," warned Viktor, "to reconsider. We do have a bargain, you and I." Ah. And if she broke her part of their bargain, Viktor would feel free to break his?

She turned her anger on Drake. "And I thought you didn't want anything to do with the dragon."

"I," purred Viktor, before he could agree, "convinced him otherwise." And the mage had tried, the night he appeared in Drake's courtyard—after listening in on their argument. Apparently Viktor had a high opinion of his powers of persuasion.

"I see," Cypress said tightly, feet planted. "Well, y'all have fun."

Viktor huffed at the delay. "Why, you impertinent little—"

"Let me deal with her, Viktor." Drake interrupted him smoothly, imperiously. "We . . . know each other."

His uncle chuckled, amused by the double entendre. She shuddered. When he stepped behind her and took her shoulders, to reassure her, she tried to shrug away from his touch.

He held on long enough to bend to her ear and inhale her herbal earthiness full force. *Like inhaling magic.* "I do not know what daft bargain you made with Viktor," he breathed into her hair, onto her beautiful and endangered neck, "but I suspect your withdrawal of cooperation may void it, yes?"

She stiffened, neither answering nor shrugging him off.

"I can help you leave, if you wish," he insisted, too aware of the night-black woods around them. "Decide now."

She twisted in his grip to glare at him, but narrowed her eyes when she caught Viktor leaning nearer their conversation.

"I have contacted them." Her palpable anger helped dissuade his whisper from becoming a kiss. "They are safe. Trust me."

She glared at him, jaw set. "Is Viktor right that this is the best time to go after the dragon? Before Imbolc? Dawn?"

Ms. One-Track Mind had to ask that, did she? He had almost gotten her out of here, and then she had to ask that.

Frustrated himself, he spit the answer. "Yes."

"If anything happens to my friends, rot in hell," she told him and, turning, stalked farther down the path they had blazed together. Damn!

Pleased, Viktor repeated his courtly gesture. "After you."

"Age before beauty, Viktor." *That is where you should be, you pompous toad—the front of the line.*

The wizard's eyes narrowed. "But I insist."

Drake should wish them both luck and leave. He had found them. He had done his best. But, assured of her friends' safety, she meant to martyr herself anyway.

Exasperated, he followed her deeper into the woods. Viktor took up the rear, and an unpleasant sense of vulnerability settled between his shoulder blades. It was not the first time.

Even now he could remember Viktor's surprise upon seeing him, that tragic day in England. *You didn't go in with her?* the older man had asked, amazed. And then, in the car, when they both sensed the implosion of great power, great evil, being wrenched from this world, Viktor had looked . . . surprised.

Not confused, as Drake had first felt. Not distraught or dismayed. Surprised and perhaps disappointed. It had taken Drake several years of grief and denial to ask the question: *Did you know what Father meant to do?*

I suspected as much, Viktor had answered, truthfully. They always spoke the truth, when they bothered to speak.

Then why did you not warn me?

But all Viktor would say was *I had my reasons.*

And if they had included Drake's death, then this dragon might be meant to finish what Father's demon had been intended to do ten years previous.

Still well ahead of the dawn, Cypress strode on toward the dark lair; like some foolish, willing sacrifice, he followed. Their feet crunched on the brown pine needles, and their breath misted, pale, against the wet air that shrouded the forest. The flashlights dimmed miserably, until he expended some minor energy on a protection spell. Temporarily freed from the dragon's clammy nearness, the torches brightened. The tree-tangled world around them seemed to vanish into nothing more than this lit tunnel of a wooded path, continuing onward like an endless nightmare.

He really had *not* meant to do this. He resented Cypress's implication that he should, and her foolishness in risking herself. He hated Viktor for manipulating her into it. Mostly, he despised himself for falling prey to useless intercession—

Suffocating in negative thoughts, nearly blinded, he recognized the dragon's signature almost too late. "Cypress!"

He caught her jacketed waist, swept her back against him and away from the chilling black tendrils that barely missed the ankles she kicked into the air. "Viktor, cast a circle!"

"Now?" asked Viktor mildly from behind them. Drake dodged as another streak of power, blacker than the shadows, snaked out and burned past his neck. He guessed, as much as saw, the opalescent glow behind him; a quick glance over his shoulder showed Viktor at the center of a glittering pillar of light, charging and hardening his own aura into a protective personal shield. The dragon might still breach it, should it try, but he and Cypress made good distractions.

Something whipped around Drake's ankle and yanked him to the ground, hard. Cypress grabbed for him, her fingers scrabbling into the leather of his coat, and anchored an arm around him. "Cast the circle, Viktor!"

Drake yelled, "Cast it yourself!" and snatched his athame from the sheath on his hip. It had worked as a weapon before! With an angry slash, it cut him free of one deathly manacle, then parried back another.

Cypress let go of him, the tendril pulled—and at a charge of pure power, the earth shivered beneath him, as if itself shuddering off something vile. Her voice rang out: "I bind this circle with my power, to guard this place beyond place and this time beyond time. By the powers of earth, air, fire and water!''

Suddenly he found himself in a silent patch of safe energy, the eerily calm eye of a black maelstrom. The protective circle—cool, clean white light—even encompassed low, thick limbs of the blackened oak, far nearer than he had suspected, and Viktor.

The wizard's eyes widened as he let his own armor fade and pivoted, an appreciative connoisseur. "Impressive, I must say.''

Standing tall and graceful, her arms outstretched to maintain the instant circle, Cypress still glared at the wizard. Drake found a stick and hastily scratched a line of power into the dirt, just inside where the sphere met the onslaught of darkness. Their magics blended, luminescent, as he finished—*By the powers of the sun, moon and stars, so mote it be.* Then the circle faded to a barely noticeable glint, visible mainly because of the sordid, churning darkness that pressed against its shell. He was trapped in safety. So much for avoiding the dragon.

She lowered her arms and met his surprised stare with her own. "I didn't know I could do that!" Surprised pride—and ill-placed gratitude—lit her expression. Then her eyes touched something beyond his shoulder, and dulled murderously.

Ah, yes. Viktor. Drake turned, met his uncle's dark gaze with his own. "You do know that we could have been killed.''

Viktor admitted nothing of the kind, but neither did he deny it. "A test, if you will. You survived admirably. I now have great faith in your abilities.'' Then he crouched beside his satchel and began to withdraw candles, holders, and a censer.

"No thanks to you!'' She reached his side in three strides—almost the breadth of the circle. "We had a deal!''

Invulnerable to her fury, Viktor withdrew a large obsidian sphere from his satchel. "I don't believe either of us vowed to risk his life for the safety of the other.''

She gaped at him in the protective stillness.

"And was there anything against profiting from the other's destruction?" Drake demanded, eyeing the crystal ball.

Viktor tried to look innocent and hurt; he did neither well. "Are you accusing me of something?"

Cypress turned back toward Drake, brow furrowed. Did she *want* to understand? He was hardly keen on his suspicions, either, but she should know the likely truth. She had courted the danger herself.

"Should either Cypress or I have died in the attack, you could have claimed the sacrifice first and assured your victory—without breaking your oath. Or you could have imprisoned our powers, our *souls,* in the sphere to use at your convenience."

She looked at Viktor again in wide-eyed dismay.

"That," insisted Viktor, giving up his innocent routine for a more characteristic glare, "is a terrible thing to say!"

She looked back at Drake, who folded his arms. "You will notice, Cypress, that he did not deny it."

"I'll not dignify such an accusation with a denial!"

"Stop it!" Now she stepped between uncle and nephew; Drake made a point of toning down his glare, lest it injure her in the cross fire. "The both of you, stop it! It's almost dawn!"

Not that he could tell from ambient light. A sooty gloom pressed against the safe space she had created, more clammy than the chill of the February morning, more vile than even . . . Viktor. This time the dragon was not calling up magics to storm through the forest. This time it seemed to curl around the circle to outwait them, a deathly ground fog, a gaping void. *Come to me, child,* it seemed to whisper, as it had before—but this time they had not contained it. The call surrounded them. *Come home to me.*

He braced himself against its lure, as he had all year, but he was tired. His daily battle for control and neutrality grew wearisome, gained him nothing. Perhaps he *should* give up. . . .

Cypress's hand on his arm, the confusion in her eyes, drew him from the spell—and he immediately noticed Viktor's awed pleasure. She apparently did not feel the creature's call, but Viktor did. "We must not trust him." Drake told her.

"You cannot succeed without my help," Viktor warned.

"But we can't succeed *with* your help, either, can we?" It seemed she had finally caught on. Now that they were under siege by the dragon, and past turning back—*now* she caught on.

"Not if you don't trust me," Viktor agreed pointedly.

"I don't trust you. I trust Drake." When he looked at her in quiet surprise—did she still?—she did not avoid his gaze.

But Viktor ruined the moment by laughing, his droll amusement ricocheting off the darkness that surrounded them. "Do you indeed?" And Drake realized, with a sinking sensation, that Cypress was about to learn more than he had ever intended her to.

"That is rich." Viktor laughed, as if Cypress shouldn't trust Drake. But of course she should. He'd come, hadn't he?

He came to talk you out of this, fool!

But when he couldn't, he didn't leave me.

Torn, she defaulted to being practical, and began to set the candles out at the proper quarters to strengthen the circle—the only thing between them and the tangible nothingness that lurked outside it. "Drake and I may not agree on a lot," she insisted, "but he wouldn't use me just to build his own power!"

Viktor laughed harder. "Oh, but, my dear, he already has!"

She looked up from the candle she'd just placed. Drake met her gaze, his posture stiff, as if daring her to believe it. His vulnerability stabbed at her. It meant Viktor told the truth.

The wizard pushed his advantage. "Just how unobservant *are* you? *I* could see it the moment you two touched! I could even feel the residue of your powers on him, after your sordid little tryst the other night."

"Mind your tongue!" Drake warned him sharply, chin lowered in challenge. "Or I may mind it for you!" But he denied nothing. Maybe refusing to deny things ran in the family.

She'd known, though, hadn't she? *The moment they touched.* Power had surged like electricity through her, and surely through him, too. Near him, she could see things— ghosts, and circles—that she'd never seen before. And when they made love...

He'd been using her only for her power?

"I did try to stay away," he told her stiffly, as if following her thoughts. He'd tried—and failed. And even when they made love, he'd harnessed the power they raised between his dark sheets to cast a spell. But he hadn't cast it for himself. He'd asked what *she* wanted. And she'd lied.

She went to him, touched his cool cheek and caught a breath at the energy that rushed through her at the connection, even as his eyes fell closed, then slowly opened. She'd been responding to him all along, too. Did his awareness of it damn him more than her, or did his proud silence? *Had he needed her that badly?*

Setting her jaw, she faced Viktor. "I hear that it's natural for people with less energy to turn to people with more. I've never begrudged helping anyone, and I surely don't plan to start with him. He hasn't taken a thing I wasn't willing to give, and he's given as much. So I'll still side with him."

Viktor's smile faded. "Fools. You both need me."

"But not your kind of magic. Ours is different. I won't be tainting my powers with yours, and neither will Drake."

Both men looked at her, eyebrows raised. It was Drake who challenged her. "Oh, really?"

She raised her chin, determined. "Yes, really. You plan to do something about that?"

He smiled, smug. "If I did not agree with you, I might."

Viktor's hiss recaptured their attention. "The demon out there," he insisted, low, "is mine, and I will have it. You cannot stand against me, so I advise that you remain with me."

She laughed. "You think we went through this to *join* you?"

Viktor slowly raised his right hand, palm toward them, and warned, "I think you'd be wise to reconsider." His fingertips crackled with visible power—*his* kind of magic.

Considering that, she didn't take comfort in the way Drake murmured a few words she didn't understand and drew a sigil of some sort in the air. The symbol floated like the trailing glow off a sparkler, then melted into a ball of bright power in his palm. "Do not threaten us," he warned.

"Wait a minute," she protested, glancing from them to the coiling darkness that surrounded their small circle and back.

The light that sizzled off Viktor's fingers turned deeply, painfully red. "I know your limits, nephew."

"Correction, uncle. You *knew* my limits." He shifted the pulsing violet glow, as if it were a mud ball, to his left hand.

"And I seem to have guessed correctly about your current weakness." The older man's arrogant gaze glided to... her.

She stared. He couldn't mean... "Me?"

"Why else would I have invited a mere earth witch? Why else might Drake be here? You make admirable bait, my dear—"

But Drake's fist—the one without the fireball—connected, hard against Viktor's jaw, and the wizard slid downward as his eyes slid up. She dived to catch him before he slumped across the perimeter of the circle, and fell to her knees with his weight.

Drake absorbed the glow back into his palm. "Less karmic repercussions this way," he said, slapping his hand clean on his jeans while she wriggled out from under Viktor. She checked the wizard's pulse; as soon as she was sure his heart was beating, she snatched her hand clear of him.

She'd been willing to do a magical working with *this?*

Drake had been right! She'd let her quest against this dragon become an obsession. How else could she explain her truce with Viktor, and how she'd all but blackmailed Drake into helping? In a way, she *had* blackmailed him. It was with her that Viktor had secured his unwilling presence.

When he offered her his hand, she took it, rising straight into the strength and safety of his chest, into a kiss that seemed to surprise him. At least she thought she noticed a flare of surprise in his cool eyes before she buried her face into his leather-caped shoulder, holding on for dear life.

For a moment, she feared he wouldn't reciprocate; then his arms wrapped around her, one hand cupping her neck, fingers stroking her jaw. His touch wasn't angry; it felt concerned.

"I told you that you were one of the good guys," she sighed into his shoulder, turning to kiss his clean-shaven jaw again.

He stiffened; his embrace loosened about her. "Cypress," he murmured, and it sounded like a warning.

She didn't want to know, didn't want to do anything but be held by him, just for a minute. But that wasn't going to happen, was it? They were in a very bad situation. He was already pulling free from her. She met his wary gaze.

He said, "Don't."

She heard a low moan—trees, moving again. "Don't what?"

"Do not glorify me. I *am* his nephew."

You're nothing like him! She had to hold her breath to keep from voicing the protest; he wouldn't want to hear it. He thought she was being fanciful and romantic. Her!

She surely did hope he was wrong, but the trees outside and above the circle were beginning to thrash back and forth again, dropping needles and even bits of branches onto their heads. Though the ground beneath their feet stayed more or less solid, the forest floor outside the circle seemed to be moving, undulating beneath its carpet of pine straw, like the dirt atop a grave that was being evacuated from the inside out.

No, now wasn't the time to argue. The sulfurous stench that pressed like smoke against their circle nearly overwhelmed her; an almost subsonic howling dizzied her. They couldn't maintain this circle forever.

And, according to her watch, the sun was about to rise.

Drake crouched beside Viktor and tied the wizard's hands together with a handkerchief. "Shall we guarantee that he doesn't help?"

"You think we can take out the dragon ourselves?"

He blinked up at her, as if frustrated. Why wouldn't he be? He hadn't meant to be here at all. "I *do not know*."

But he should have a better idea than her. "Guess!"

He opened Viktor's satchel and produced what looked like a small crown. She recognized a crystal-ball stand, supported by three golden dragons. When he glanced back at her, his eyes had softened into something close to an evil smile. "I imagine you stand against sacrificing Viktor to gain extra strength?"

She caught her breath and couldn't let go of it, raised her fists to her temples as if that could stop the way the world seemed to crumble around her. "Tell me you're joking! And if that isn't the truth, then don't say anything—got it?"

Almost instantly he was beside her, gathering her again to his chest, into his arms, in a rush of safety and the scent of leather. "Shh..." he murmured, stroking the worst of the tension from her shoulders. "Shh, Cypress. I *was* joking. Even I have my limits—and no, do not look at me like that." He scowled at her surge of hope. "I said *even I* have my limits. That means they are less strict than your own."

"But more strict than that son of—your grandmother's?" She leaned back from the security of his embrace, just enough to see if she'd insulted him.

"We were not close, either," he assured her, without answering her question. Still stroking her jaw with his thumb, he kissed her on the forehead, then gently on the lips. More needles and twigs rained down on them. It occurred to her that, foolish or not, she was falling in love with this man—which was only a bit less scary than the maelstrom of darkness that was starting to batter at the fragile shell of their circle.

They had to do something, but Viktor had been in charge.

Drake cocked his head. "Hypothetically, Cypress, how are your morals on bindings?"

"I already did one on Friday," she reminded him. "Just don't go after any more innocent ghosts."

He raised a disapproving eyebrow at her bias. "That 'innocent ghost' may have tried to attack you. And those were temporary. I am referring to permanently imprisoning the dragon."

Her dark prince had an idea! "How? Where?"

"In the crystal ball. That may be why Viktor brought it."

Wait a minute. "I thought he meant to use it against us."

"He may have, I do not know. At the moment, it hardly matters! We can force the dragon's essence into the sphere and bind it there, then find someplace safe to keep it, as the Indians did. Shall we try, or does that violate your ethics?"

Put it in the sphere? Enough darkness to fill the woods and to extend its reach throughout Stagwater? "It won't fit!"

"It is incorporeal," he reminded her. "Trust me on this!"

The sky should be lightening to gray, or even blue, but darkness still surrounded them, roared at them like a storm, fighting back the dawn. They had to act now.

"Can we give it an ultimatum?" she asked. She loved that he was trying to preserve her ethics. She loved that he was here—even if it was her fault.

She loved his curt nod. "If you truly must!"

So she nodded back, hopeful again. "Let's go for it!"

Come to me, called the dragon's soul—concentrated evil. The essence of black magic. An arm securely around Cypress's waist, Drake managed to withstand its temptation, barely. *You cannot deny what you are,* it hissed, and the voice he imagined for it seemed familiar. *You shall not find peace until you join me....*

"Let's start!" she urged, unaware of the battle he was waging. Again her simple presence forced the call to mere background noise. Together they lifted the obsidian sphere to their dome of whirling blackness—and he thought he detected a faint graying toward the east. Sunrise! Even the dragon could not resist it forever!

"Listen to me, whatever you are!" Cypress called out. The storm-tossed grove around her seemed to echo her powerful words. "I give you a choice! Leave this world now and return whence you came, or be bound here, powerless, for all eternity!"

She was good. Her eyes widened, as if equally surprised.

Black amusement shivered over them, from above and beneath and around them. Horrible images pressed cruelly into his thoughts, images of Cypress's body lying in bloody pieces atop the pine straw, of his own hand propped lifelessly out of the dirt, recognizable only by his mother's ring.

Like an amateur, he shut his eyes against it, which of course only clarified the detail. Beside him, Cypress gasped.

"I'll take that as a no," she muttered unevenly.

Again, the otherworldly amusement vibrated through the air.

He drew his powers, his heritage, closer to him. "Then we command thee into thy prison!" He started in Latin, then slid into a formal translation instead. "By our powers, and all the powers at our command, we summon to its prison the creature who dares call evil to this place! We summon to its prison the creature who dares attack our people! Our powers are as strong as thine. Our wills are as great! Come, we command thee, come!"

Their combined power peaked gloriously within them and then cast outward from their circle, almost like a magical net. He felt it graze a reprehensible, tantalizing surge of energy—

"Come!"

The power recoiled from their reach, leaving nothingness.

He heard Cypress catch her breath, unbalanced by the
miss. Riding the dizziness of having lost so much energy at
once, and for nothing, he caught her determined gaze, and
they tried again. Power rushed through him, intertwined
with hers, and exploded out from them into the darkness.
"Veni!" he commanded, defaulting to the familiarity of
Latin. *"Veni!"* The net of energy glittered outward, toward the dragon's heart, but somewhere in the roiling
darkness the beast eluded them again.

When she sagged against his side, he was hard-pressed not
to collapse with her; they both gulped in air. The world
dipped and swayed around them, and it was only partially
due to the dragon's special effects. They were exhausting
themselves for nothing.

"Where does it keep going?" Cypress gasped, tears in her
voice.

And suddenly he knew. "The ley lines!"

They stared at one another. As if they were turning down
the volume on a stereo, dimming the brightness of a lamp,
they allowed their mutual power to fade from its fever pitch.
They had not contained the ley lines nearly enough, and in
any case the dragon had been disgorging stakes to counter
their efforts. While they remained trapped in their circle of
safety, it could go where it wished.

Cypress looked as exhausted as he felt, and worried, so
worried. They could manage perhaps one more try; after
that, their only choice would be to claim their own destruction to secure the dragon's binding—a suicide spell. Even as
he considered and rejected that, she asked the one thing he
had not expected from her.

"Think we could manage another draw and get the hell
out of here?"

She wanted to quit? *Now?*

CHAPTER FIFTEEN

Drake stared at Cypress, his anger inflating with each shaky breath. She wanted to quit? She dismissed him as unworthy because he didn't believe in her foolish quest, risked her life—and his—pursuing it anyway, and she wanted to quit? Because of her, he had burned his bridges with Viktor. Because of her, he had just poured the better part of his life force into attempting to capture the essence of evil—despair and fear, jealousy and judgmentalism, fury and apathy—and hold it in his mortal hand. And Cypress wanted to *quit?*

"No!" he snapped, glad he was exhausted, lest his betrayal sear her. Until this moment, he had not realized how much her altruism symbolized something to him, something good and decent in which he had ceased to believe after his parents' death. Slowly, Cypress had begun restoring his faith, even convincing him to act on it, so that now he stood here doing one of the most idiotically noble things in his life—and she was giving up.

"No," he snarled. "We do not have the strength for that!"

She continued to stare up at him, swaying in exhaustion, blinking violently. Cry, would she? As well she should! He retrieved his arm from her waist, yanked the crystal ball from their joint hold and placed it on the ground, more abruptly than was good for it. He stared at the black silhouette of the huge oak, at the faint, sooty glow of an unseen rising sun through the swirling darkness behind it, and he felt lost.

He recognized the feeling, because he had felt that way before Cypress Bernard came into his life. But perhaps he had romanced an illusion as surely as had she.

She laid her hand on his arm; her touch reawakened that extra reserve of their power—what dregs were left of it. He flinched, more from surliness than from fury.

"I'm sorry," she told him. "You shouldn't be here."

"You are rather late in deciding that." What a foolish way to die, carried away by the enthusiasms of a woman he had—had merely slept with. "Obviously neither of us should!"

She frowned. "*I* should be. But I forced you to come."

"I was not forced."

"You were so! I walked out because you wouldn't help me."

He quirked an eyebrow at her, folded his arms. "You value your company highly, to think I bent to some sexual ultimatum."

"That's not what it was!" She no longer looked as if she would cry. She looked as if she would gladly murder him, had she the strength, "harm none" or not. "But I pressured you about something that wasn't your responsibility. And then Viktor used me as bait. And now if you die here it'll be my fault!"

His deepening sense of betrayal stilled. "Is that why you wish to give up? You feel guilty about *me?*"

"I *don't* want to give up, but it's not fair for you to fail here, maybe die here. You didn't have a choice!"

"And you did?" Hope could not restore his strength, but it softened the bitterness of his exhaustion. Perhaps his earth witch had her nobility after all. She just carried with it an annoying martyr complex. "Your overinflated ethics allowed you no other choice. Neither did my..." *Love?*

He dismissed the disturbing thought, the unlikely word. They were tired, rushed. "My own concerns," he said instead. "Do not presume you can manipulate me so easily. You cannot."

Misery hovered on her proud face, diluted by confusion—then a characteristic, if forced, grin. "Oh, I can't, can I?"

He refused to smile back. It took effort. "Once we get out of this bloody forest, you can attempt to manipulate me all you like, but it shan't work. In the meantime..."

She followed his gaze to the lighter patch of whirling, moaning blackness beyond the oak, where the sun rose. Their time had run out. And he had no more ideas—

"I've got an idea!" She grasped his hand, pulled him to his knees with her, then settled the obsidian sphere more securely in its nest of pine straw. Yes. That put it closer to the ley lines from which they meant to draw the dragon, and put them nearer to the ground from which she drew strength. And if they passed out from exhaustion—

But what mattered the distance of their fall, if they would never return to consciousness? He wondered: If he willed his last dying spell toward her safety, rather than toward the dragon's binding, would she despise his memory for it?

She slid her arm around him, underneath the warmth of his coat. He caught her to his side, as well, and they touched the crystal, synchronized their breathing. With each breath, they plumbed the dregs of their power and raised it into the sanctuary around them. Even if they had the strength to trap the dragon again, would they have the strength to contain it? To finish the spell?

But they must try. Another deep breath. More power.

Cy began to speak first. "By the powers of earth, air, fire and water," she called, and an infusion of rich powers—fertile, infinite, hot, deep—wove into their own. "By the powers of the trees and the stones," she added, and his dizziness faded as her words grounded them both. Her hold on him tightened. "By the power of the sun, moon and stars, so we will this! We command you into your prison!"

Drake echoed her words in softly spoken Latin that, for all its ceremonial history, seemed a poor second to Cy's link with the powers of nature. They could make out the glowing disk shape of the rising sun through the storm—nature's powers of light battling against unnatural powers of darkness.

"We summon to its stone prison the creature who brings evil amongst us! We summon to its earth prison the creature who dares attack us and ours! Our powers are as great as yours are, and our wills are stronger! Come to us!"

Higher and higher their power soared, readying for one last attempt. And as it peaked, a new and not-quite-familiar energy infused their own. Was it—?

Cypress laughed her joy at recognizing her friends' contribution flowing through the ley lines. "Come to us!" she called, the stronger for it, and her confidence strengthened his. "Come to us now!"

Then the rising sun vanished.

One moment, the dragon had been recoiling from their attempts to catch it; the next, it returned—and as it reared over their little sanctuary, its blackness blocked out the sky. Though he knew it had no form, Drake could almost imagine a wingspan that dwarfed the clearing, the forest, the whole town. He could almost see a huge, snakelike neck that bowed double as it lowered a horned head to peer and threaten—and beckon with its sonorous, worming call of pure evil to its most likely ally.

Him.

Come, child! It beckoned, and finally he recognized the voice he gave it: his father's. *Feel the longing in your blood, in your heart. Listen. Answer. Come home....*

Had he feared becoming addicted? Too late—he had already succumbed. Over the months, the year, it must have established some sort of bond, of familiarity, with the evil that ran in his veins, because he could feel the draw of it, tighter than ever before. Its leash on him had pulled taut, and he feared he would snap before he could sever it. Drake set his jaw, shut his eyes, fought the dark temptation.

He felt Cy's fingers cinch through the belt loops of his jeans, and he instinctively, desperately, gripped hers in return. He had developed other bonds now, voluntary bonds, and he would not lose them for something as dead as his heritage. The dragon's will tore frantically at him, and abruptly snapped. Its hiss faded to silence under the wail of tree-cut wind, the rumble of disturbed, offended ground. *Come home....*

But, for the moment, at least, Drake *was* home. A sudden burst of erotic power, intimately entwined with hers and several days stronger, burst into the clearing to reinforce that sense of belonging. Their tantric spell meant to fulfill its purpose.

To defeat the dragon.

Like a net woven of magical threads from so many sources, his and Cypress's complementary powers filled the circle around them. Without words, they cast it outward and upward together, and visualized it expanding to fall over the sooty, malformed night of the dragon—catching, pulling secure.

They had the monster. They had it!

For a victorious moment, Cy felt exultant and omnipotent. Her friends were somewhere along the ley lines, their amazing power mixed with other energies she couldn't immediately place. She had Drake beside her, Mother Earth beneath her, and the will, the knowledge, the daring, to capture a modern-day dragon.

Then they caught it, and she nearly crumpled under the pain.

Whatever caused people to kill, she'd just wrapped her thoughts around it. Whatever caused people to hate and hurt others, she was touching it, not merely with her hands, but with her magic—her soul! Drake's thoughts, his will, urged her to hold it even tighter, to compress it and draw it closer, closer, when all she wanted was to recoil in horror.

They shouldn't have visualized it as a dragon; now she couldn't believe the agony in her head was anything besides claws slicing at the bonds she'd thrown over the beast. Her body shuddered with cramping agony, and she pictured powerful jaws snatching her up. Instead of smoke, it

breathed confusion on her, hopelessness, doubt—and hatred.

She didn't want to hold it. But, oh, she wanted to hurt it.
So she drew it to her, and she imagined the net of magic
compacting it in on itself, smaller and smaller. She grew
aware of Drake's soft Latin—he repeated something over
and again, leaving off part with each repetition, as in the
"B-I-N-G-O" song, and the dragon continued to shrink.

This is for Rand and Sylvie and the werewolf! It twisted,
struggled, but it couldn't get free. *This is for Brigit and Steve
and the hell they went through! This is for Mary and Guy
and the creature that almost killed them!* Smaller still. *This
is for Granny, and the Fouchard family, and Lucille Witt!*
Her eyes were squeezed closed, but she thought she felt
sunlight on her chilled face. Good! Maybe together they
could squash it between their fingers. *This is for hurting
Drake, you bastard!*

But something as close to her as her own name—yet not
her at all—wouldn't let her will it into oblivion. Something
would not let her destroy it. *Let you* attempt *to destroy it,*
that something countered sternly, gently. She became aware
of Drake's warm, firm hand pressing hers to the obsidian
sphere, of his will supporting hers. She trusted him, and let
her hate vanish under the gentleness—the love?—she felt
sweeping over her from him. Was that imagined, too?

In her mind's eye, she saw the net of their powers anchored in the sphere, pulling the dragon in, in, as the power
screamed and thrashed and howled. When Drake spoke, she
managed to join him, only a heartbeat behind.

"Into this prison we bind thee, to remain so long as thou
might do injury to others, so mote it be."

She blinked her eyes open, but trees continued to thrash
about them, scattering debris. Churning black clouds continued to obscure the sun. Coils of malignancy pressed fu-
tilely, desperately, at the shell of their circle. They'd forced
the dragon into its prison, but it hadn't reconciled itself to
staying yet. She gasped a breath, fought a wave of ex-

hausted dizziness and concentrated while they repeated it: "Into this prison we bind thee..."

As they finished the third repetition, she felt the spell leaving her, as if draining her life force to coat and seal the sphere. Victory warred with cold emptiness—but she had Drake to lean against as the final dregs of energy faded from her....

And then she heard him speak, crisp and sure, even through his weariness: "And I claim thee and thy powers in my name."

Claim? What was he doing?

"And thou shalt serve no other, throughout eternity."

No, he couldn't! Appalled, she struggled against a spell that had turned into something she abhorred. But by now their energies were too closely woven. Struggling against Drake, she fell weakly to the dirt and pine needles. To stare accusingly at him through the roar of power, through the whirlwinds of energy, took infinite effort, but she did it.

His piercing gaze met hers, defensive and unapologetic, as he cried, "So mote it be!"

With a noise like a thunderclap—like a reverse thunderclap, sucked through a vortex—the spell's closure blasted her backward, sent her skidding across the pine straw. A hard tree trunk to the shoulder stopped her; she hid her face against dervishes of needles and dirt. She didn't notice the pain, couldn't discern the maelstrom that punished the forest from that within her soul. She'd trusted him, even thought she could love him—

And he laid claim to the powers of darkness!

The air pressure dropped around her—cold! The wind roared with a tornado's fury. Would the dragon never admit defeat?

"So we will it!" she screamed into the wind, into the chaos, with all the lung power she had left—and damning her own magic with his. "So it must be!"

And then ... silence.

She opened her bleary eyes immediately, and beneath a sky of new-morning blue the sun shone brightly down on her chilled body. *Where was Drake?* She felt something precious inside her crumble at the realization that, despite what he'd done, her first hope had been for his safety. Maybe, faced with such power, he couldn't help himself. Maybe he'd tried to resist, and failed. Tha she found herself making excuses—that she couldn't will the tenderness out of her heart, even now—betrayed her wounded ethics almost as horribly as he had.

She tried to lift her head, to find him, and barely managed to prop her cheek onto her outstretched shoulder. She didn't hurt anymore, not physically. She just felt more tuckered out than ever in her life. Tired . . . and defeated.

What she *could* see without moving her head was the obsidian sphere, right where they'd left it, at the gnarled roots of the blackened, martyred oak. Somehow it absorbed light instead of reflecting it. It contained evil now, and too much power to fall into the wrong hands. *The wrong hands* . . .

Screw defeat. She had to get to the dragon stone first.

She tried to draw her elbows under her, to brace herself off the ground, but the spell had taken too much out of her. She slumped wearily to the forest floor again—and drew on the strength it offered. Air, fire, water, earth. The morning air filled her lungs with its woodsy sweetness. The sunlight, even filtered through a canopy of dead branches, eased cold from her own stiff limbs. Dampness soaked the knees of her jeans. She dug her fingers eagerly into the dirt beneath her. *Tingles!*

Just as dark power had saturated the forest before, now the grove hummed with energy—a clean, strong, natural force. The ley lines must have turned, their energy healed again. And she lay right on top of one, no more than ten feet from the martyred oak—and the nexus point of power.

With a deep breath, she pushed herself up this time. She reached outward, grasped an exposed root, and dragged herself closer Shifting her knees beneath her, she struggled closer still. If she could get hold of it, she could protect it until her friends came to find her. She crawled a foot closer still.

And then she fell on a jeaned hip, when a slow, mocking clap, and then another, broke her intense concentration and made her twist around. *Drake?*

No. The wizard who stood regally in the middle of the grove, continuing his dry applause, was not the man she had argued with, magicked with, made love to. It was not the man she wanted and feared to see at all. It was Viktor, free of his makeshift bonds, grinning at her with sharp-toothed malice.

"Brava," he said, while she sat up unsteadily. "Quite the show. Useless, of course, but very entertaining."

She couldn't threaten him; she had no powers left to tap. She didn't even have confidence that she'd done the right thing—not with her own magic woven through the spell that had bought Drake the dragon's life force. So she said nothing.

Viktor looked all the more smug at her silence. "I'm sure a good little witch such as yourself won't be needing something as nasty as that dreadful power source," he explained easily. "Consider this my good deed for the year." With a morbidly polite nod, he turned back toward the stone. And he froze.

She followed his surprised gaze to where Drake now stood, dark and impassive, leaning insolently against the charred tree, the dragon stone immediately at his feet. She all but crumpled again under the landslide of mixed emotions that buried her heart. He was alive—still one of the bad guys, but alive. Despite mussed hair and a dirty trench coat, he stood strong. And she knew—prayed—that if she could trust her heart ever again, he would at least keep his uncle from taking the stone.

The lesser of two evils, after all.

His intense gaze flicked to her, ascertained her condition, and flicked back to his uncle. His lordly expression didn't waver—and then the cocky SOB winked at his uncle as if to say, "Let the games begin."

"Hi," he purred, his voice cold and deadly.

And Cy, being no fool, scrambled to the shelter of a fat pine trunk, to have someplace to duck when the fireworks started.

Drake's relief at seeing Cypress mixed with resigned guilt. He knew he had hurt her; their energies joined at the end of the working, he'd felt her horror, her sense of betrayal, drive through him with such force and unbearable pain, that he could not close the spell. She must have closed it herself, disapproving or not.

He hoped he would survive to ask her why.

Toward that goal—survival—he projected amused confidence at Viktor, and he tried not to fall down. His casual posture against the tree trunk must not betray the fact that it was holding him up. With luck, his folded arms implied barely restrained patience, more than an effort to keep them from dangling uselessly at his side. He would regain energy slowly; he needed time.

That Viktor had not come nearer was, he thought, a good sign.

That Viktor had not left was a bad one.

"I want the stone, boy," demanded the wizard, tense. "I came here for that power, and you've no right to rob me of it."

Drake disguised his own weariness as boredom. "I could go to the Tower of London for the crown jewels, but that hardly makes them mine."

He felt tension climb as he faced his uncle in the silent morning grove. Only when Viktor chanced taking a step closer did he muster his strength and command, "Stop!"

Viktor paused at the authority in his tone. So as not to overdo a good thing, Drake softened his voice to cool politeness again. "I would not advise it."

Viktor's eyes glinted knowingly. "You must be exhausted, boy. Nobody can bind a demon almost single-handedly and still walk, much less cast spells. Most people don't even live through the experience." He took another step.

"I did not do it single-handedly. The witch helped."

"The witch?" Viktor laughed, and with a wave of his hand took another step—so much for Cypress. The man could not see that she, too, had pulled herself to her feet and stood propped against a tree trunk, watching the exchange avidly. Drake wanted to frown at her, to warn her to stay back. But Viktor now stood barely two steps from the dragon stone.

Time to move in the big guns. "And in any case," warned Drake, extending one weak hand outward, spread, above the stone, "I have claimed the power." And he tested it, as he might test an animal he believed dead. Just the slightest mental nudge.

The stone glowed. Power, potent and fulfilling, infused him. Dizzied by the rush, he breathed it in like a reformed smoker during a serious lapse. He could do it, could use it too easily. In his peripheral vision he saw Cypress's eyes widen with alarm.

Luckily, Viktor's did the same, and the older wizard took a quick step back.

Drake forced another smile, and drew his hand away, stronger and equally alarmed. But he had made his point.

Still Viktor hesitated. "If you mean to harness the stone's power and destroy me, why haven't you done so yet?" In a moment, his eyes brightened. "It's her! You won't destroy me in front of your white witch!"

A direct hit—to a point. Drake had already destroyed what little of Cypress's trust he had won; he would rather not destroy his uncle in front of her, too. But neither would he sacrifice himself or her, merely to make a moral point. "Do not tempt me."

"But that's my favorite hobby." Viktor oozed a step closer. "Temptation."

Drake reached again, and the urge to fully tap the dragon stone's dark energy shuddered through him. He made a fist; his palm itched to fill itself with power. His chest ached with the need to use that power, to destroy Viktor and anything else, anyone else, in his way. He had to summon all his control to keep from drinking deeply of it, from diving into it and never emerging. To use the power would destroy him. Perhaps not his body, his voice, his existence. But it would blight his soul, rob him forever of his neutrality, his peace.

And yet, if it was his only alternative, he still would do it before he saw Cypress destroyed.

He filed that interesting tidbit of self-revelation away, watched Viktor take another step. The older wizard now stood almost as near the stone as Drake.

And beyond him, Cypress was braced against a pine tree, but no longer, he thought, in order to stand. She looked more like a wood nymph with an arboreal friend, leaning her cheek against its gray bark for comfort because she could find comfort nowhere else in the world. Though her chin remained high, her handsome face lacked the vibrancy he had grown to love. Her eyes glistened, as if with tears and rage. But she said nothing to stop him. He could see that she was no longer managing Drake Benedict's morality. What he did next was his own responsibility.

His own decision.

Drake lowered his hand to his side, and Viktor smiled.

"I knew you were bluffing." His uncle, gloating, fell to his knees before the dragon stone, like a vassal before a king. "Few men can give themselves up to this kind of power. Like father..." He reached reverently for the crystal. "Like son."

Drake stepped on the sphere, letting shoe leather protect him from the worst of the dragon stone's vibrations. "Pardon?"

Viktor's greedy hands hovered as he looked up, annoyed by the distraction. "What?"

"You mentioned my father." He saw Cypress's shocked expression reflect the horror he could not show. *Father*...

Viktor nodded, relishing his triumph. "Yes, I did. Now, if you'll be so kind..." And he reached for the stone again.

"Not. Quite. Yet." Drake smiled, deadly. "Humor me, Viktor. Tell me about my father *before* you claim the stone."

He could see the wheels turning in his uncle's fetid little mind. The older wizard glanced from Drake to the stone to Drake again. At first, he looked amused that a man in so presumably weak a position would make demands. Then amusement faded before confusion—*would* a man in Drake's position make demands? Finally suspicion dawned, and Viktor leaped back from the obsidian as if from a bomb. "What have you done to the stone?"

Drake waited, his own impatience making him dangerous. "You have a story for me, uncle?"

All the false civility fled from Viktor's face. "The stone!"

And Drake shouted back at him, *"My father!"*

And the grove fell silent.

Drake took a deep breath, fought to regain his composure. He wished he could take comfort from a tree, as Cypress did, or from the earth, or the sky. He had isolated himself too thoroughly from the world to access it so easily now, though.

The older man's gaze returned to the stone. His dilemma—had Drake trapped it, or had he not?—played across his face.

Drake recalled his attention. "How did you know what my father meant to do that day?"

"Because we planned it together. What of the stone?"

"Describe the plan."

"Surely you suspected. He would offer your mother to the demon and reap the rewards of the sacrifice."

"I do not believe you," snapped Drake. It was a mistake.

Viktor's chin came up. "You think I lied?"

Of course not—which might be why Drake had never yet demanded the whole truth. Perhaps, like Cypress, he preferred illusory good to the reality of evil in those he loved. But, unlike Cypress, he must risk disappointment for the truth. This might well be his last chance to hear it.

He glanced over Viktor's shoulder and stiffened against another blow. Cypress had left. That would be intelligent of her. That knowledge did not make him feel any less alone.

Then, suddenly, she stood at his elbow, still here. Surprised, relieved, and disapproving—this was *not* intelligent of her—he glared down at her. She hooked her arm through his anyway, and turned to glare at Viktor.

The energy that filtered through him, from her, felt . . . different. Restrained. Now that she knew what their touch did—and now that she knew his kind of magic—the days of them sharing high-voltage bursts of power were likely as much past as their lovemaking. The loss saddened him . . . and yet the fact that she had come to stand beside him anyway, foolish or not, meant more than all the powers of the universe.

"So, what about Drake?" she demanded, with that forthright manner he so admired in her. "Was your brother going to sacrifice Drake, too?"

Viktor's gaze dropped to the sphere again, and he answered angrily, "No. He thought Drake would share his powers. He did it, partially, for Drake's own good."

"Mmm-hmm. But he was wrong, now wasn't he?"

Drake looked from her to Viktor. "Was he?"

"It was hardly difficult to turn him against his ex-wife, you know," snapped the older wizard, getting impatient. "When he began down the left-hand path and perhaps needed her the most, his little magistra left him for it. Her loss. My gain."

Perhaps he would kill Viktor after all. "And?"

"And he soon believed you resented her as he did. By raising one simple demon, sacrificing one fickle woman, he would rid the world of Madeleine Rousseau and harness incredible power for himself and his son. And, of course, his loving brother."

He bowed slightly, as if he were being presented in high society.

Drake had rediscovered emotions just in time for this? Little good it did him to know that his father had planned not his, but his mother's, murder. Planned, and executed. *Evil* . . .

"What was *really* supposed to go down?" demanded Cypress.

Viktor blinked in feigned innocence. "I beg your pardon?"

She planted a hand on her hip, her entire posture a challenge. "You aren't being straight, Viktor. Did *you* believe that Drake would stand by and watch his mother sacrificed?"

An excellent point. He, of course, would not have. And his uncle had known as much. "Do tell," he insisted, low and dangerous. "You have related Father's plan. What exactly was yours?"

Viktor glowered.

"I'm betting," supplied Cypress, "that he hoped the demon would take you *and* your mother. Wouldn't divided loyalties hamstring you in a situation like that?"

"Very likely," he agreed, keeping his tone severe, but finding her hand with his. She wove her fingers through his. "And if the demon fed on us both, Father might have lost control. It could easily have taken him, too."

"It did," insisted Viktor—too quickly.

Cypress gasped. "You're lying!" And not in that *you-must-be-joking* manner of hers. It was obvious in the shift of the wizard's eyes, in the hunch of his shoulders. Good Lord. For the first time in Drake's memory, Viktor had lied.

No wonder the man needed to find outside sources for his power. He had compromised his own!

"I meant," Viktor quickly put in, "they did both die against it." But this belated truth held a subtle distinction that could make all the difference in the world.

"Yet it did not *take* either of them," said Drake slowly. He knew. From clairvoyance, instinct or common sense, he knew. "They sacrificed themselves, together, in order to banish it. Both of them!"

"So it would seem," his uncle admitted, eyes sullen.

Amid their outwardly unemotional exchange, only Cypress dared look relieved. "Your father must have gotten her there, and then changed his mind about killing her. Maybe he hadn't meant to at all. Viktor just preyed on his weaknesses...."

"Little good it did her," noted Drake sharply.

"I don't know 'bout that," she told him challengingly. "There's a heap of difference between being killed by and killed with a loved one. People can change and ... and repent."

Perhaps he now knew why she had closed the final spell, even though she believed he had betrayed her with it. He breathed deeply of the fresh morning air, suddenly tired of the waste. The waste of his parents' marriage and lives. The waste of his and Cypress's uncanny affinity and complementary abilities, pitted against divergent ethics. And the hideous waste of Viktor's own addiction to power.

He moved his foot off the stone. "You want it? Take it."

Cypress stiffened beside him, her hand squeezing sharply around his, and he looked down, intrigued. Of course she did not want Viktor to have the crystal. But would she prefer that he harness the evil himself, after all?

Viktor smiled triumphantly, knelt to the dragon stone... and paused. Perhaps his obsession had its limits after all. When he slowly looked up again, his narrowed eyes demanded answers of his own. "Why did you give in so easily?"

Drake blinked, as if surprised, and said nothing.

"You're up to something."

He almost smiled—unamused. "Am I?"

"What?" asked Cypress, looking from one man to the other.

Apparently Viktor believed *her* innocence, and he explained. "He may have put a spell on it, something to destroy any other mage who tries to use its powers."

Drake considered sending Cypress back a few paces, but decided that would be a bit much. Instead, he finished his smile, confident that it would not touch his eyes. "Did I?"

Viktor looked back at the dragon stone, one last time. He extended an unsteady hand. And then he stopped.

"Faint heart," Drake said softly, "never won foul dragon."

The moment stretched—and then his uncle stood, expression crumpling from hope through hopelessness to sheer rage. Now Drake *did* try to edge Cypress farther back from him.

She did not go. Not even when Viktor raised a hand, eyes narrowed and fingers crackling. Drake felt more of her energy weaving tentatively into his own, empowering them both for the fight, despite her distrust. Altruistic idiot.

With an annoyed glare, he untwined his fingers and his powers from hers—as much as possible, considering the bond they'd recently woven. While she stared, uncertain, he pulled a leather glove from his coat pocket, put it on; and retrieved the dragon stone himself. As Drake straightened, Viktor let his magical pyrotechnics fade. Surely he was not such a fool as to hope?

Drake removed no curses. "You will agree to leave this place and not return, and to no longer interfere with anyone involved. Is that understood?"

His uncle's face hovered between several expressions. "Or what?" he demanded finally.

"Or we play a one-sided game of catch."

At his side, Cypress caught back a surprised laugh. Bloodthirsty little witch. Must be the strain.

Viktor hesitated, going pale, but when Drake hefted the sphere experimentally, he gave in. Fast. "I do so swear!"

"Good." Drake watched him skulk over to his satchel and collect it with an angry snatch. "Leave the stand, plea—"

He had to dodge it. Luckily, he did not drop the dragon stone. With one last glare, Viktor turned to stalk away from the grove—and stopped, face-to-face with a blond couple emerging from the trees. Guy Poitiers, looking for all the world like a handsome bouncer, stood with his hands on his wife Mary's shoulders. Neither Poitiers looked very friendly toward Viktor.

His uncle changed direction, from west to south—and backed away again, this time from the redheaded Brigit

Peabody and her clean-cut husband, Steve. Brigit also appeared willing to shelve that pesky *harm none* vow, just for once.

Viktor tried again—and faced the Garners. The ponytailed Rand stood behind Sylvie, his arms protectively around her and their unborn children. He growled.

Viktor swerved around them, and all but ran from the clearing, past the priest from last night's ball, who blessed him as he vanished, defeated, into the trees.

Drake looked at the circle of witches, their husbands and the priest, from one to another. So the cavalry had arrived. Then he said, "It took you long enough," and knelt to put down the dragon stone. This time he placed it carefully on the golden stand Viktor had thrown at him. He did not intend to touch it again.

"You knew they were coming all along?" Cypress asked him challengingly, as if they were not being descended upon by her concerned friends.

He took off his glove, finger by finger, as he looked up at her. "I told you that I contacted—" But he got no more out, because, surprisingly, she hurled herself against him, knocking him back several unsteady steps to kiss his mouth, his cheek, his jaw, his eyes. When next she hit his mouth, he returned the kiss—he had used enough control today—and she lingered there. Her magic, rich and fertile and strong, like her, rushed through him like a healing drug. But he did not fear this particular addiction anymore. He only feared—

Exactly what happened when her kisses hesitated, when her shared energy trickled away, when she pulled back and stared at him, remembering beyond their victory. Oh, he *would* miss her.

But he was not one of the good guys.

"We did it," she whispered, but she sounded more stricken than enthusiastic. Because of what it had cost them, Drake thought. Not because she hated to see him go. Not the real him.

He stepped back, belatedly regaining his dignity, and she did the same, leaving him cold. "Yes," he agreed pointedly. It suddenly seemed important to have it on record that, good guy or not, he had indeed helped. "We did."

By then, the others had surrounded them.

"Here, drink this," insisted Mary, pushing cans of juice into their hands. "It'll help you get your strength back."

"Are you okay?" demanded Sylvie, feeling Cy's cheek and then Drake's. "What's wrong?"

Brigit crouched nearer the dragon stone and said, "Don't touch this, right?"

"Not unless you have defected to the dark side and hunger for power." Drake pulled the sticky silver tab from his juice, and drank it in five gulps. "Otherwise, do use gloves."

Cypress's expression brightened. "You *were* bluffing! I knew it! Otherwise you'd have threatened him straight off, right?"

Drake went to collect his own pack, glaring when Guy Poitiers stepped forward to assist. He was weak, but not helpless—and he meant to go home and let them celebrate. They were the ones whose town was safe from otherworldly evil. They could raise families in relative safety. And now their friend had no more cause to run about with a wizard of borderline ethics.

"Right?" Cypress said again, not lowering her gaze when he glanced sharply back. Even now, she wanted him to be something he was not. He almost wished he could be. But he could not lie, even to himself. She had changed him, and he owed her for that. But people could change only so much, and only so fast.

"I am neither a gambler nor a fool. Of course I did not bluff. Had Viktor tried to use the stone's power, it would have entrapped him with the dragon forever."

Rand Garner shook his head in surprise, but not disapproval. "Wow! And you didn't warn him, because—?"

"Because I had a singularly bad morning. Now, if you will excuse me . . ."

Cypress came to his elbow. "Now what happens?"

"With what?" he demanded, irritated by the delay. He could not bear her nearness much longer. He needed solitude, a chance to reassemble his battered personal armor through meditation and study. He must focus on what he *could* have.

"The stone!" Of course she would think he wanted it. Anyone not in line to save the world might as well be Viktor.

"Bury the thing. Throw it in the Gulf of Mexico. Display it on your mantelpiece. Just do not let the stone break. Not while I am in the area." And he turned to go, but three women and four men—he still did not understand the priest—blocked his path. He had an inkling of how Viktor had felt, except that this time they looked more concerned than angry. "You are in my way," he told them anyway. He had not wanted their concern. "Get out of it."

"What's wrong?" demanded Mary, her hazel eyes hurt. He could not imagine why. He had not bound *her* energies into a spell she abhorred. But it had been the only way to make sure Viktor could not easily take the dragon stone.

He did not know how to answer her.

Then Cypress had his arm again, looking tired—but not hurt. In fact, when she noticed the informal barricade of friends, she smiled wearily. "You forgot the magic word."

He realized that her energies were charging his again— more warily than before, more controlled, but by no means cut off. *Why not?* "What else do you want?"

"You've asked that before," she told him gently, tugging at his arm. Then she glanced at the others. "Would y'all excuse us for a minute?"

Since it was either follow or do battle with the cavalry, Drake followed her around the wide martyred oak. Even split, the trunk provided them with more than adequate privacy as she turned to him and answered, "You."

He did not understand. Then he remembered the question he had asked as they made love, and frowned away a glimmer of hope, because he still did not understand. He had enjoyed tempting his uncle toward total destruction. He had used—abused—her magic when he claimed the dragon's power. Considering how it had turned out, he would do so again...though perhaps he would discuss it with her first.

She was either more forgetful or more forgiving than he had ever imagined, because she draped her arms over his shoulders and leaned closer against him. Warmth tingled through him, softness, surprising affection—and energy, his for the taking. And then she lifted her lips to his, and he could no longer resist kissing her again. As he had with the dragon's energy, he drank her in. *Cypress*...

Unlike with the dragon power, he stopped fighting it.

Tingles. The grove still hummed with its strong undercurrent of positive energy, but that wasn't what made Cy shiver. Not the morning chill, either. Not their recent danger. Only Drake Benedict had this effect on her.

After fully recharging together, she drew away to kiss the corner of his unsmiling mouth—so serious!—and the line of his rigid jaw, and only then leaned back against the wall of the tree trunk. She couldn't get much dirtier, and wouldn't mind if she did. She just wanted to look at him. Silent, he let her.

He still had an attitude that could choke a cat, but one she'd learned was more protective than merely rude. As obnoxious as he was acting now, he was surely upset about something. He still stood regal and sculpted, like a statue, but she knew she could melt him now and then. Maybe that was the real secret behind the rush of power, the tingle of commingling energies, when they'd touched, kissed, made love. The other witches' magic had felt amazingly stronger this morning, when they were in the company of their husbands. Maybe her and Drake's souls had known they were connected, meant to be together, from the moment they met. The rest of them had just taken a few more weeks to catch on.

Assuming they *had* caught on, at that.

"So will you be around after this?"

He blinked, startled by her directness. He would learn. "Would you like me to be?" he asked, stiff. *Suuure* he didn't lie. Either he couldn't care less, or he couldn't care more.

She took a chance on her instincts. "Yes, as a matter of fact, I would."

"Your friends do not seem particularly fond of me," he cautioned, searching her eyes as if to be sure she was serious. He cared. If he didn't, he'd just say no and stalk off.

"Once they realize you're rude and boorish to everyone, and not just them, they'll warm up to you."

He quirked an insulted eyebrow at her, allowing her to lighten the mood. "Rude and boorish?"

"That they haven't killed you already is a good omen." But her grin faded—this wasn't just a joke. "Besides, if I can warm up to you, I guess anyone can."

He wouldn't accept her soft admission, and he warned, "I am not one of the good guys." And finally she believed he spoke the truth—what he thought was the truth, anyway. Maybe it was the power running through the earth beneath her feet, or the power of nature all around her, or maybe it was the way their energies met, mingled, and became something new and wonderful together. But she felt suddenly light-headed from the guarded longing not quite hidden behind his dark eyes. The full force of his gaze seemed hypnotic, like the first time she'd met him. But he didn't scare her anymore. She knew and trusted his ethics, even if they weren't quite like hers. She knew and trusted her judgment and his, his magic and theirs.

"You aren't one of the bad guys, either," she reminded him, so relieved that he didn't argue that she laughed. "You're neutral. I've realized most folks really are in-betweens, just like us."

"You are not all good?" he asked challengingly, arching a brow.

"I've vowed time and again to harm none, but if you hadn't stopped me, I would've tried to squoosh that dragon like a bug."

"Ah." He leaned closer against her, nearly melting her beneath his intensity. "You thought I was referring to your ethics." And his mouth pulled up into a heart-stopping smile, dimples and all.

Cy considered hitting him, or kissing him. She chose a moment of electric kissing—until he leaned back, falling serious again. "You do understand that I may never become a magister?"

She groaned. Had she once considered him the silent type? "I don't know. I've heard that if someone comes to you from a voodoo shop, asking for help, you'll treat them right."

"No longer. I shall send them to you."

"Fine." She and her friends *had* gotten pretty good at this paranormal troubleshooting, anyhow. "Maybe *we* should be magistras."

"Magistrae," he of course corrected, soft and patient. "Perhaps you already are."

Which didn't bode well for them, did it? "Are you going to decide you can't handle it? Assuming you stick around, that is."

"No, I should not do that." He paused, then clarified. "Change my mind, that is."

She narrowed her eyes. He was being awfully agreeable all of a sudden, wasn't he? "And you might even help us if I asked?"

"Were I to deem it necessary? Yes, I imagine I would."

"Why?"

"Because," he said quite seriously, and stepped back from her embrace. Before she could protest, she felt him slipping the warm gold band of his dragon ring onto her index finger. "I owe you rather an enormous favor." Then he swallowed, eyes searching hers. "You have made me—helped me—fall in love with you."

Love? She stared at him, and only realized her mouth had fallen open when he lifted a hand and gently closed it for her again. He wasn't supposed to be capable of love. Was he?

But she had helped him.

"Yes, well," he agreed, almost nervous. "You think *you're* surprised?"

She laughed then, more at the relief—and pure joy—that filled her, than at the joke. Then she added a tight hug so that he couldn't possibly think she was laughing *at* him. "I thought... I mean, I knew I loved you, but I didn't think you would—"

He smiled, dimples and all, as if at a great victory—well, it was a win/win victory if any. "I love you, I love you, I love you," she told him, until he pressed her back against the tree and kissed her, silencing the "I love you's" that filled her laugh, her heart. His mouth explored hers with a longing that matched her own—a longing finally fulfilled. They weren't alone anymore, either one of them.

"Perhaps magistri," he said between kisses, and she laughed again at him for caring about Latin, but not for long. She couldn't laugh and kiss at the same time. And she wanted his kisses something awful. No, something wonderful.

From the other side of the tree, someone cleared an impatient throat. Morning sunlight filtered through the forest canopy of dead needles to warm the February woods around them. And, surprisingly close by, a songbird began to sing.

Being practical magic users, Drake Benedict and Cypress Bernard did not marry—rather, handfast—for another year. By then, little Morgan Peabody was toddling, the Garners' twin boys were sitting up, the Poitiers' son was an infant heartbreaker, and Drake and Cypress were the proud "parents" of a large stretch of local pine woods.

The witches of Stagwater—and their husbands—had cleared most of the deadwood out of the forest they'd purchased, leaving enough to minimize the disturbance to the wildlife that slowly crept back. Then they planted a new growth of pines. They also planted a new sentinel oak, to guard a buried, fireproof lockbox. That lockbox held a lead box, itself filled with protective salt and a single pulsing obsidian stone.

Sometimes evil couldn't be destroyed.

But love could most definitely keep it in check.

* * * * *

Get SPELLBOUND!

July 1996 marks the end of Silhouette Shadows, but it doesn't mean the end of those passionate stories with a twist that you've come to love!

Just look to your favorite Silhouette series for the

 flash!

Look for these wonderful Spellbound tales in 1996:

THE MAN FROM FOREVER
by Vella Munn, IM #695, 2/96
An ancient Indian warrior sweeps a lovely archaeologist off her feet with an age-old proposal....

HIS CHOSEN BRIDE
by Marcia Evanick, IM #717, 6/96
*A witch and a warlock must produce an heir.
Too bad he's marriage-shy....*

...and other tales of love with an unexpected twist:

MARRIAGE IN A BOTTLE
by Carolyn Zane, SR #1170, 8/96
What's a single gal to wish for when a handsome genie appears on her doorstep?

THE WOLF AND THE WOMAN'S TOUCH
by Ingrid Weaver, SE #1056, 9/96
He's a sexy psychic: she's a woman desperate enough to pay his passionate price....

Look us up on-line at: http://www.romance.net

This July, watch for the delivery of...

An exciting new miniseries that appears in a different Silhouette series each month. It's about love, marriage—and Daddy's unexpected need for a baby carriage!

Daddy Knows Last unites five of your favorite authors as they weave five connected stories about baby fever in New Hope, Texas.

- **THE BABY NOTION** by Dixie Browning
  (SD#1011, 7/96)

- **BABY IN A BASKET** by Helen R. Myers
  (SR#1169, 8/96)

- **MARRIED...WITH TWINS!**
  by Jennifer Mikels
  (SSE#1054, 9/96)

- **HOW TO HOOK A HUSBAND (AND A BABY)**
  by Carolyn Zane
  (YT#29, 10/96)

- **DISCOVERED: DADDY** by Marilyn Pappano
  (IM#746, 11/96)

Daddy Knows Last arrives in July...only from

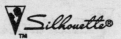

Who can resist a Texan...or a Calloway?

This September, award-winning author
ANNETTE BROADRICK
returns to Texas, with a brand-new
story about the Calloways...

SONS
OF
TEXAS

Rogues and Ranchers

CLINT: The brave leader. Used to keeping secrets.

CADE: The Lone Star Stud. Used to having women
fall at his feet...

MATT: The family guardian. Used to handling
trouble...

They must discover the identity of the mystery
woman with Calloway eyes—and uncover a
conspiracy that threatens their family....

Look for **SONS OF TEXAS:** Rogues and Ranchers
in September 1996!

Only from Silhouette...where passion lives.

Alicia Scott's

Elizabeth, Mitch, Cagney, Garret and Jake:

Four brothers and a sister—though miles separated them, they would always be a family.

Don't miss a single, suspenseful—sexy—tale in Alicia Scott's family-based series, which features four rugged, untamable brothers and their spitfire sister:

THE QUIET ONE...IM #701, March 1996

THE ONE WORTH WAITING FOR...IM #713, May 1996

THE ONE WHO ALMOST GOT AWAY...IM #723, July 1996

"The Guiness Gang," found only in—

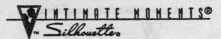

Silhouette's recipe for a sizzling summer:

* Take the best-looking cowboy in South Dakota
* Mix in a brilliant bachelor
* Add a sexy, mysterious sheikh
* Combine their stories into one collection and you've got one sensational super-hot read!

Summer Sizzlers

MEN OF Summer

Three short stories by these favorite authors:

Kathleen Eagle
Joan Hohl
Barbara Faith

Available this July wherever Silhouette books are sold.

Silhouette®

TM

SS96